Life's Big Zoo

Life's Big Zoo

Cover by Saille Tales Book Design

ISBN 978-0982582978

Library of Congress: 2017905916

V-05092017

www.rsgompertz.com

Vía del Prat

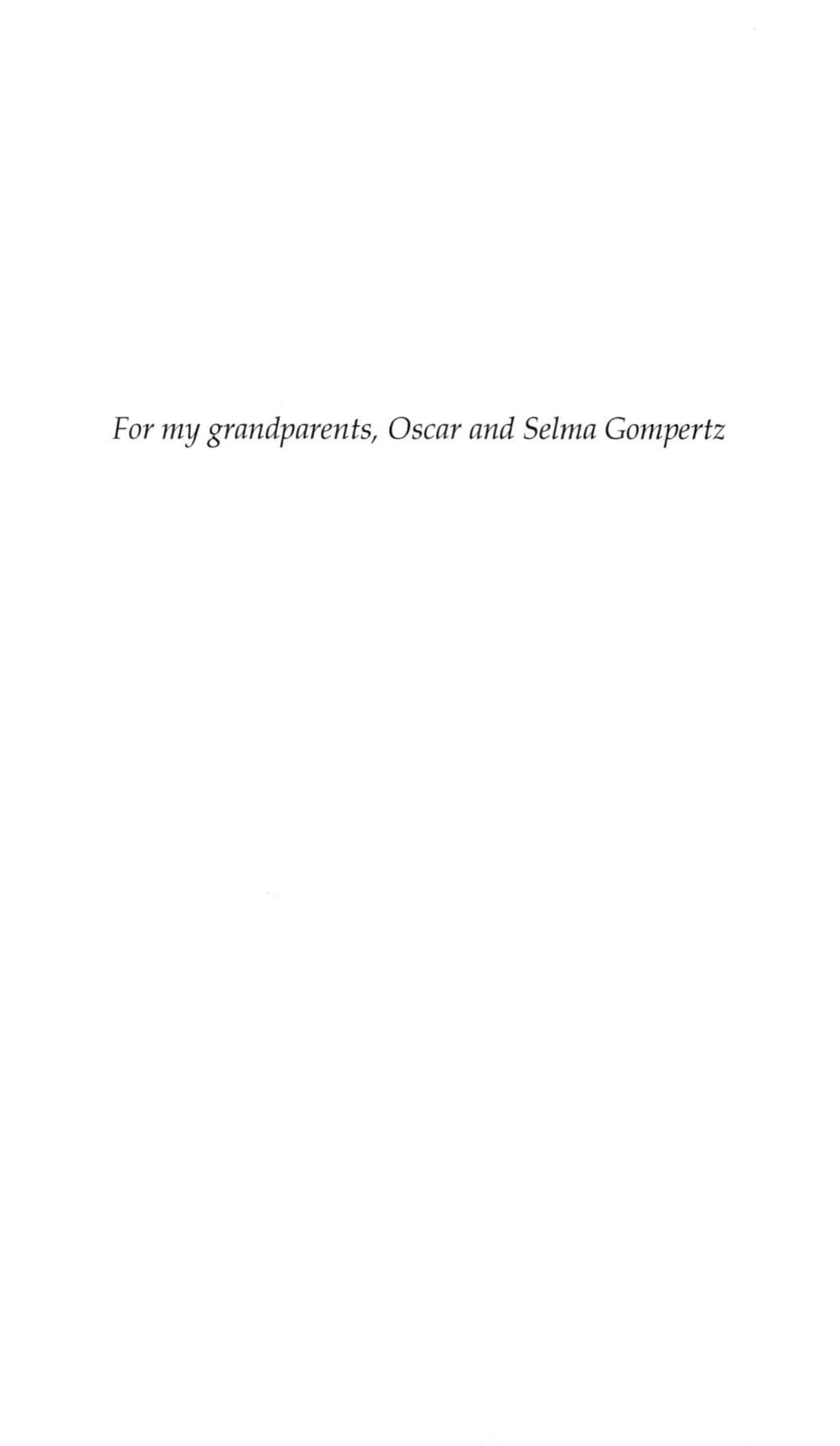

For my grandparents, Oscar and Selma Gompertz

Also by R.S. Gompertz

Historical Fiction
No Roads Lead to Rome
Aqueduct to Nowhere

Memoir
The Expat's Pajamas

Essays
Quirk in Progress

Life's Big Zoo

Among the many wise things my grandmother told me, the one that rings true, time and again, is that God keeps a big zoo. In the summer of 1968 I joined the menagerie.

Duck and Cover

If the future of the free world depends on me, please accept my apology in advance.

It takes me a few seconds to realize that I have missed the cue. My sixth grade teacher, Dr. Blast, shouted at us to drop, and I spaced it. Blast often calls me out for being unfocused though I'm clearly focused elsewhere. I feel The Glare upon me and find myself staring at Blast's chimney-red face. Something about his astronaut haircut and gap-toothed grin makes him look like a jack-o-lantern. When I was younger, back when Bob Hope was funny and the Beatles had short hair, school drop drills scared me so much that I slept with my lights on. Now I barely pay attention. If they drop the bomb, I hope it lands on my head.

"I SAID DROP!"

Doctor Blast, a law-and-order man, instructed our entire class to vote for Nixon in our primary school's mock election today. So much for democracy. He once wished out loud that the Cold War would "heat up already." Blast thinks most of our parents are commies and takes our monthly drop drills so seriously that he conducts them weekly. "Preparedness! Nations have vanished off the face of the earth for not being vigilant," he often tells us.

When the doctor shouts "Drop!" drop we must. Drop our standards. Drop our principles. Drop to our knees and assume a fetal crouch below our tables, fingers interlaced over those precious brain stems that the Russians want to melt. This position will protect us from incoming ICBMs and all manner of fire and brimstone that follows.

I stare back at my so-called teacher for a second and then scramble under my desk. Maybe it's not too late to hide from the H-bomb.

Blast writes my name in the report he will turn in to the front office. "If this had been a real nuclear attack, you would be dead, Strauss!"

"If this had been a real attack, wouldn't we all be dead?" Ben Chang, former genius, asks from underneath his desk.

"Right," says the muffled voice of another child prodigy. "Do you think hiding under school desks would have saved kids in Hiroshima?"

"This insolence will go on your permanent records," Dr. Blast says, as if that's the only thing worse than nuclear annihilation.

This incident is a fresh reminder that I'm the dumbest kid in smart class. Why else would it take me so long to grasp that the drop drill is a farce? I have been taught to fear the falling sky and never questioned how a plywood desk would shield me from a nuclear attack. I'm a bigger Bozo than Ronald McDonald.

The kids under the makeshift fallout shelters start to fidget. Henry Radford makes a loud farting sound to a fifty-percent approval rating. I hold my breath to vaccinate myself against the uncontrollable giggling infecting the room.

The all-clear signal is greeted with the usual chaos. Pencils fly. A desk tips over. Green bubble gum from the underside of Henry Radford's desk finds a path to Agnes Hamlin's hair. She starts crying the way only a redhead can.

Blast boils. "If I ran the country, the draft age would be twelve."

I get up to use the pencil sharpener. Since I'm the only kid behaving, Blast assumes I'm an instigator and orders me to the

2

principal's office. "Three solid swats," he says. "That should set you straight."

I know better than to argue, so I slink off to my unjust rewards while he tries in vain to start a math lesson. As I pass the library I poke my head in to ask the librarian if the Constitution of the United States applies to kids. She says kids are exempt and not even Robert F. Kennedy can change this.

A Day in the Life

Today started out just fine.

The Blue Bomber anticipated our daily descent into the San Fernando Valley by turning over and belching gray smoke. Like me, the old two-door Plymouth Belvedere wakes up only when kicked.

"Breakfast!" Nana Hannah, my feisty grandmother, flies out the front door. Nana's as old as the century but tells people not to be impressed since it took her a long time. She tosses a brown bag with two warm apple muffins through the window that's been stuck open since my brother Tommy tried to fix it. Nana always tells me I'm too skinny, but she's almost too tiny to cast a shadow. They didn't have much to eat back when she was growing up in Germany during the First World War.

Late for school. Late for work. As usual, we're late for everything. The precise German clockwork pulsing through Nana's veins never meshed into my father's loosely wound DNA. She says he'll be late for his own funeral. I suspect the lapse comes from my grandfather's side of the gene pool, but I know not to mention him. The ghost of Otto Strauss still casts a long shadow thirty years after he disappeared.

We back down the driveway so fast a tailpipe sparks against the street. I crane my neck to look back at my grandmother, but she's already bending over to pull weeds from her succulent garden. Thanks to years of yoga she's strong and supple.

Mumu Marie, our weirdest neighbor, is on her knees, extracting microscopic weeds from her perfect front lawn with one hand and working her rosary with the other. When I flash

4

her a peace sign, she points to her crucifix as a reminder that Christ killers like me are going to hell.

Mr. Shreidermayer, aka the Man Who Cuts Legs Off because he's always threatening us with amputation, is walking his little Nazi dog down the hill. He scowls at me with beady little possum eyes and a thin, movie villain moustache. I've given up on trying to make him smile.

The early morning light streams through the giant sycamores that turn Laurel Canyon into a leafy tunnel. Ivy climbs skyward up the trunks, reaching for the sun. I hand my father one of the warm muffins. He swallows it whole and starts in with his daily advice. "Maybe you can intern with the Jet Propulsion Lab this summer," Pater says, forgetting that I'm not yet thirteen.

This idea is almost as crazy as "Trotsky in Love," the novel he's been trying to write since my mother left us for Jesus, an open wound we never talk about. I suck the sticky apple and cinnamon filling from my muffin and try not to listen, but my father, aka Pater Nostrum, is a high school guidance counselor, so he's used to kids ignoring him. His original plan was to become a Rabbi, but that was just to disappoint his Jewish mother.

Using the dashboard as a pulpit, he's preaching about my future, but it's early in the morning and the future still seems far away. "The Space Program," he says. "That's the future."

"You want my *tuchus* should be launched into orbit?" I ask, trying to imitate Groucho Marx but sounding more like a cheek-pinching *alter kocker* at our temple.

"JPL's in Pasadena, not on the moon. Just a few miles away last time I checked."

"You belong in space, Pater. Not me."

Meanwhile, back here on Earth, the Blue Bomber launches past Wonderland Elementary School and wrestles with gravity around the sharp turn to Lookout Mountain Avenue. I notice an old "Kennedy for President" sticker on a parked car and remember that today is Election Day.

"*Aleph, bet, vet, gimel, daled, hay ...*" Pater sings, trying to lure me into reciting the Hebrew alphabet, but I'd rather go to the moon.

The Bomber sputters and chugs uphill as we turn onto Laurel Canyon. A curvaceous old Corvette blasts past us like a Mercury rocket. I reach for the radio hoping to catch KHJ—*Boss Radio for Boss Angeles!*—but Pater slaps my hand away.

"Hey! I want to hear 'Jumping Jack Flash.'"

"And I want to hear Hebrew. I guess we can't always get what we want."

I grunt my dissatisfaction and give him the full-on silent treatment for as long as I can stand it. "Have you ever seen the Monkee-mobile?"

"I'm driving it, Maxie."

The Monkees live in Laurel Canyon along with the rest of us primates. My brother Tommy actually played drums on one of their tunes because he can count to four, keep a beat, and hold sticks with his opposable thumbs.

My rat fink brother is now on his third high school in two years. As a good student and a model citizen, I'm rewarded with a daily *schlep* across the smog-filled valley. Tommy, bad student and drum bum, gets chauffeured door-to-door in Nana's old Studebaker Hawk. I wake up with the roosters; he sleeps late and gets a free ride to Fairfax High on the cool side of the hill.

Tommy managed to get kicked out of Hollywood High, a school with standards so low it should have been built in Death Valley. He was busted for climbing buck naked atop a gym locker and playing a foot-stomping blues on a Marine Band harmonica. In the near-riot that followed, banks of lockers fell like dominoes as half-naked boys spilled out onto the basketball court. Tommy barely had time to wrap a towel around his torso before a gym coach dragged him off to the principal for being a long-haired commie instigator.

Fortunately no freshmen were crushed by falling lockers or stampeding seniors. My brother was exiled to Fairfax High School to soak up the good Jewish influence or, more likely, corrupt his own tribe. The harmonica in question was never found, though Nana's went missing that same day.

Tommy's tomfoolery didn't help Pater's reputation as an upstanding high school guidance counselor. Kind of embarrassing to have Tommy thrown out of a school where Pater once worked. It's hard to earn a living advising "Tomorrow's Leaders, Today!" when your own son is a well-known nutcase. Pater worries that if Tommy doesn't make it through high school, he'll earn a one-way ticket to Vietnam.

Nana Hannah has a simple explanation for what my advanced spelling book might call Tommy's "idiosyncrasies." She says God keeps a big zoo.

"Good kid," Pater says. "Talented boy." Some mornings, before we pick up hitchhiking Sister Hope, when Pater isn't talking about his screenplay, charting my future, or grilling my Hebrew he frets out loud about Tommy. "How can he be so lopsided—good at music, challenged at everything else?"

"Nana says God doesn't hand out gifts in equal measure."

"She's right, as usual."

Tommy may be a musical genius and future rock star, but it's hard to feel sympathy for someone who practices tom-tom rolls on my head. Sure, he's having a hard time, but who isn't? Ever since we lost our mom to Jesus, Tommy's been acting like a looney bird. His face could be on the Cocoa Puff box if he ever stood still long enough to take a picture.

7

I wish I could drive with Nana once in a while, but my school's on the other side of the hill and taking Tommy to Fairfax fits in with her morning ritual. After delivering Tommy, she heads over to Canter's Deli for tea and *hamentashen* with her blue-haired gang of refugees and survivors. They pass the morning reading last week's *Aufbau*, planning Hadassah events, and trying to forget the past. After the daily reunion, Nana spends the afternoon keeping the books and giving voice lessons at a music store on Larchmont. Singing is how she survived Dachau. She probably could have escaped using opera as a weapon because her Tosca can still stop a Panzer tank. She loves Italian opera but has a secret passion for Wagner that she keeps under wraps. Among Jews, especially those who survived the Holocaust, Wagner is less popular than bacon on Passover.

I wasn't a fan of Nana's brand of high-class yodeling until she started coaching some local rock singers. She worries they will all destroy their vocal cords if they don't stop shouting long enough to learn proper technique. I was startled at first, but now I almost expect to come home after school and find Nana teaching scales and breathing to some howling Sasquatch.

I glance over to check the downward progress of my father's sideburns, which are currently winning the race against his receding hairline. I want to suggest adding a moustache, but I'm distracted by an orange Porsche Targa convertible that roars by, radio blaring, top down. A hippie chick rides shotgun with a guitar case between her legs, wind racing through her long black hair. For a second, she looks like one of my old baby sitters.

When we reach the Canyon Store, I crawl into the back seat to make room up front for Hope Springs whose bushy natural touches the top of the car. Sister Hope, as she wants to be called, used to hitchhike, but Pater convinced her it's safer and more interesting for a twenty-year-old student to ride with us. Having Hope in the car makes me feel less sad about leaving the canyon each morning. My lungs will be aching by the end of the day but, for now, her jasmine perfume tickles my nose like a stray feather. A whiff of Hope almost makes the smog bearable.

"Today's Hubert's big day," Pater says. I can't believe my dad likes Vice President Hubert Horatio Humphrey, aka Humperdink. Pater was a JFK delegate in 1960, but for some reason he isn't a big fan of his fallen hero's younger brother.

"All the way with RFK," Hope shoots back. Her passion for Kennedy could melt steel. According to Hope, Bobby will stop the war, end police brutality, and eliminate racism on his first day in office. Hope has registered enough new voters to win a delegate spot at the convention. If Bobby wins today, she's going to Chicago to celebrate her twenty-first birthday.

"Buckle up for safety," I remind Hope for the millionth time. She knows that if I don't hear the seat belt click, I'll sing the "Buckle Up!" jingle until she snaps in.

"I've changed parties," Pater says. "Voting for Nixon today."

"For dog catcher, maybe," Hope says. "Tricky Dicky will never be president."

"Nixon would make a great dog catcher." Pater likes twisting her big statements, wringing out her theories like wet diapers and baiting her with the opposite of what he really thinks. Maybe he likes teasing Hope about her deeply held convictions because he doesn't have any left. "Everyone knows how much Nixon loves his dog."

"Richard Nixon is the American Hitler."

"Hitler? Really, Hope? You can only play the Hitler card once. Trust me, I was there."

"Sorry," Hope says. She knows our family history. "Mussolini, maybe."

"Mussolini bit his weenie, now it doesn't work," I add, in a regretful burst of acting my age. Sheesh. Why do I act like an idiot in front of the people I want to impress most? Almost thirteen, going on seven.

"If Tricky Dicky steals this election, he'll make Mussolini look like a school kid." Hope twists the rear view mirror and smiles at me. "No offense, school kid. We're still solid, right?"

"Right on." I try to maintain eye contact but only catch the reflection of my thick black Encyclopedia Brown glasses before Pater adjusts the rear view mirror back into position. I wish my glasses weren't so dorky. Pater refuses to buy me wire-rimmed granny glasses, the kind John Lennon wears. He also refuses to buy me bell bottoms because Sears Tough Skin Jeans cost less and last longer. I think he's really just worried about me going hippie like my brother.

"Speaking of school kids, did you know that Max is going directly from sixth grade to high school?"

"Far out!" Of course she knows. Pater has been talking about my mental moonshot ever since I tested out of junior high school. "I can help you start an underground paper."

"Neat," I say. "But isn't an underground paper above ground the moment it's printed?"

"You should go straight to college, kid."

"I'd rather go to Pacific Ocean Park. How come we've never been to POP, Dad? I heard they have a roller coaster that goes all the way underwater. Can we go to POP when I graduate?"

"When you graduate high school?"

"I meant when I graduate elementary school."

"We'll see."

That means no. As achievements go, graduating elementary school rates somewhere between Tommy taking out the trash and me remembering to close the refrigerator door, though my graduation is more likely than these other triumphs.

"Born late, kiddo," Hope says. "Hate to break it to you, but POP closed last year."

We approach the bottom of the canyon, and I wonder if anything will be visible or if the suburbs will still be snoring under the brown blanket of progress that Angelenos confuse with air. Amazingly, Ventura Boulevard looks clear and hopeful this morning. For the moment. Once the smog monster warms up it will smother the streets and swallow the nearby hills.

The Valley is where Laurel Canyon goes to die. Thank God we live in the hills and not down below on the desert floor. Instead of wandering the asphalt jungle, I can explore deer trails, ridges and fire roads. I know Laurel Canyon backwards and forwards from the Rain Forest to Lookout Mountain. I even know where to find running water in the heat of August. Someday, when the Hollywood hilltops rise like islands above the rubble and radiation, Hope and I will dress in buckskin and live like the Chumash. Until then, I need to catch the bus by 7:30 or endure another "Tardy" stamp on my permanent record.

Will I ever get to see my permanent record or is it sent directly to God on the night before *Yom Kippur*?

The forest greens and ramshackle canyon homes give way to an ocean of brightly colored billboards that fade into the distance beyond Ventura Boulevard. Tan, don't burn—use Coppertone! TWA to Europe. Plymouth 1968. Zippo Windproof Lighters. When you're out of Schlitz, you're out of beer. Winstons taste good like a cigarette should.

Living in the Valley must be like smoking two packs of Winstons every day.

We stop at a red light and watch the slow parade of chrome and glass. The car ahead of us has a bumper sticker that says, "Beautify America. Get a haircut." The driver looks like President Johnson so I flash him a peace sign before we ease into the gridlock. An angry lady in curlers shouts at two brats wrestling in the back of her station wagon. Her fake wood paneling is peeling from her doors like a sunburn. Someday, after the bombs fall and the asphalt boils, these streets will be the new La Brea Tar Pits. Radioactive Mustangs, Impalas, and Cougars will be trapped here like mastodons for future generations to ponder.

By late afternoon my lungs will be begging for oxygen so for now I inhale every last, fresh word Hope Springs has to say. She is so different from the hippie girls who float around the canyon like wingless fairies.

"All the way with RFK!" Hope leans out her open window and shouts at a lifeless street sign that says "AMERICA NEEDS NIXON." Her big Afro bobs in the wind. She flips a bird at Nixon's creepy chipmunk smile and ski-slope nose. "America needs Nixon like a hot lead enema!"

"What's an enema?" I ask. "Can I have one? Is an enema the same thing as an abortion?"

"Nixon's the One!" Pater shouts. Pretending not to hear my question is proof that both words are worth looking up as soon as I get to school.

Hope waves to a driver with an "R.F.K. in '68" bumper sticker. He smiles as if spotting an old friend. RFK has to win. He has to. Bobby Kennedy is coming to town tonight, and Hope will be in the crowd. To her, Bobby is bigger than The Beatles.

I barely remember the assassination of RFK's brother, JFK. I might have forgotten that sad Friday five years ago if it weren't for my first grade teacher crying and sending us out onto the playground for an early lunch break. Pater says that America's

12

optimism was lost that day. I came home to find Nana fretting that "the whole Nazi business" was starting all over again. Walter Cronkite's black glasses seemed especially foggy as we sat around the dinner table that evening. My mother, still with us though not for long, was teary-eyed for a month. I miss her for a second and then swallow hard to push the memory away. I refuse to feel bad about this. She left us, remember?

Pater pulls over to drop me off at the corner of Laurel and Ventura in front of the Home Savings with the big mosaic about Southern California history. I used to like these images of ranchers, gold prospectors, and movie makers until Hope pointed out the Spanish Padre brandishing a foreign cross above the grateful Indians.

"Don't forget Hebrew school this afternoon, Maxie. I'll pick you up at six."

I wish Pater wouldn't mention Hebrew school in front of Hope Springs. Hope is so groovy and Hebrew school is square beyond square. "Bobby's got my vote," I say to Hope as I slam the door. "At least, he has my vote in the mock election at school today."

"Solid, kid."

I wish she wouldn't call me kid, but I'm glad she thinks I'm solid. Solid's better than liquid, way better than gas. I flash a peace sign and Hope answers with the black power salute.

The Magic Bus

I see my bus, the RTD 90, inching through traffic, so I don't have time to race over to the Thrifty Drug store for a five-cent scoop of Rocky Road. Groaning brakes announce the 90's arrival a minute later at the bus stop in front of the Buster Brown shoe store. The door squeaks like wet shoes on linoleum, and I climb aboard for this morning's magical mystery tour.

"G'morning, Pilgrim," Billy the Bus Driver says in his best John Wayne. Over the years he's taught me to recognize his impressions of old movie stars. Peter Lorre is my current favorite.

"Hey, Billy." I drop my dime in the coin counter like I have every school day since the age of seven.

"Hitch your horse, park your pistols and come sit by the campfire." Billy abandons John Wayne, breaks into his trombone imitation and hums a rendition of "Michelle," the only Beatles song he knows. He used to specialize in Bing Crosby tunes, but even Billy is changing with the times. I've gotten to know him over the years and imagine him as the goofy uncle I never had. Billy's an ex-marine, proud of having survived the war in the Pacific where he lost part of his left foot in an explosion. He drives the happiest bus in L.A., but like everyone in this town, he wants to be in showbiz. At least once a week he tries to convince me that his lip trombone and celebrity imitations will land him in the spotlight on the next King Family Christmas Show.

Some Fridays Nana Hannah wakes up even earlier than normal to bake challah and sends me off with a warm one for

Billy. "Tell her it tastes like cake," he says. "And don't forget to ask your granny if she's ready to marry me yet."

They've never met, but Billy claims he's in love with my grandmother. I always pass on the compliments about the challah, but I never mention his proposal. Technically speaking, Nana's still married.

The bus fills with well-dressed grownups on their way to work. Trombone Billy knows every one of his riders. "Come in, come in. Warm your hands by the pot-bellied stove." Billy salutes Sam, a sales clerk whose thin black ties have recently widened into the wonderful world of color. Sam's feet sport Hush Puppies where Wing Tips once squeaked supreme. Billy flirts with the women whose smart skirts, bullet shaped breasts and flouncy rayon blouses make him very happy. "G'mornin', Doris Day! Where's Rock Hudson?"

"Doris Day? Do I look that old?"

"How's my second wife? Can I buy you coffee and a donut after my shift?" He takes her dollar bill and pumps out a few coins from his four-cylinder money changer. "Let's blow this pop stand and spend the day in Santa Monica!"

"You're one bus stop short of a full route, Billy. Unlike you, some of us have to work." The women laugh, find seats, and double check their makeup in their tiny mirrors.

If Billy notices their hemlines creeping north, he's smart enough not to mention it.

We turn right at Sportsmen's Lodge, Bar Mitzvah capital of America, where my neighbor Grumpy Chuck brings his grandson Danny to fish for trout in the artificial lake. Chuck claims he once saw the Duke drink an entire six-pack without taking a breath. He also claims to hail from Texas, but Mumu Marie, the neighbor who keeps trying to convert me, says he's just another damned Okie.

Pater took me to the Sportsmen's for breakfast a couple of weeks ago. He was scouting locations for a screenplay he'll never write based on the novel he'll never finish. I had buttermilk pancakes from a mix and metallic-tasting orange juice from concentrate, falsely advertised as home-made and fresh-squeezed. Pater asked the waitress if the Vagabond Combo was made with fresh vagabonds. She yawned and asked if he wanted toasted white bread or English muffin. This didn't bode well for "Trotsky in Love," his novel-screenplay combo where every other pun is a double entendre. Neither did the framed posters of old movie cowboys and signed head shots of actors nobody's ever heard of. John Wayne wouldn't be caught dead there, though if the beer is as watered-down as the OJ, he might be inspired to shoot up the joint.

Billy's bus heads down Coldwater, crossing the dry concrete gully some joker named "The L.A. River" and then turns left onto Riverside Drive. Riverside, my foot. More false advertising. "I'm gonna lay down my sword and shield. Down by the riverside," Billy sings for the millionth time. "Down by the riverside."

"Go back to Berkeley, you peacenik!" Salesman Sam shouts. It's the same joke every day but all the grownups laugh. Hope Springs once called Berkeley the center of the universe. That's where I want to go for college.

I used to sing along with Billy back when I was a kid with no concept of cool. Now I just stare out the window and wish I had remembered to put a new 9-volt battery in my transistor radio.

"When Nixon wins the White House, he'll show those college brats a thing or two," Sam growls to general approval. He thinks hippies, radicals and peaceniks are destroying America.

16

A clutch of well-groomed Catholic school boys, the opposite of Berkeley peaceniks, crowds into the bus. The coin counter rattles long after they jostle toward the back in a pungent wake of Right Guard and Brylcreem. More of these fallen angels board at the next stop, all heading to Notre Dame High School, where Jesus dies daily for their sins.

Fascinated with their bonhomie and braggadocio—two of my favorite twelfth-grade vocabulary words—I have been moving steadily toward the back of the bus this year. Jews are invisible to Catholics, so these wayward choirboys haven't noticed me soaking in their steady stream of insults and delinquency. Monsignor O'Brian French kissed a nun! No way, Jose. My dad sold the Monkees matching Eldorados! Big wow, you dick shiner. Jimi Hendrix is playing the homecoming dance! Yeah? Only because your Aunt Lucy promised him a hand job, you pudwhack. Bull puckey! I pissed in your mother, queer bait. So what? Last night, I felt up a girl with three boobs. Fugnay! I rounded third base with your sister. Say it again and I'll kick your ass. Really? Damn straight, you pussy.

I listen in awe as the Notre Dame boys try to outdo the devil. They break wind and blaspheme, hock loogies and flick boogers with absolute confidence that Jesus will forgive any transgression confessed by sundown.

A jock strap shoots through the air like a stray rubber band. The owner is too embarrassed to recover his gym gear. For my money, there is no class of boy more lawless than one forced by parents, priests, and God Almighty to wear straight-legged slacks when everyone else is in bells.

Today Billy decides to make a martyr out of the most brazen delinquent by busting him for smoking a cigarette in the rear stairwell. Billy stops the bus and pretends to be collecting transfers but instead uses his foot to shove the young James Dean out the open back door. As the bus pulls away, the

17

remaining cohort jeer from the windows and flip the bird at their fallen friend. The tallest boy stands up on the rear seat bank and bares his butt out the back window.

When the bus finally stops in front of Notre Dame High School, the naughty apostles clog the aisles, tripping, pushing, and shoving each other out the door. They turn what should be an orderly exodus into a demolition derby. "God bless you, my son!" one boy shouts to Billy as he stumbles out onto the sidewalk. One freshman's regulation blue trousers get yanked down and crumple at his ankles. He falls onto my bus bench so I climb over the seat to avoid him. The other boys seize the moment to spank his forbidden Fruit of the Looms as they pass by.

And then the daily miracle occurs. By the time these hooligans reach the arched entrance of their venerable school, they are buttoned-down angels. Tousled hair is slicked back into place. Shirts are tucked in, belts are tight. Order is restored as they shuffle single-file past the Father, the Son, and the black-frocked priests, none of whom have managed to put the fear of Jesus into these future leaders of the nation.

Once the swamp has been drained and the steam clears, the bus feels ten times bigger. A few upside-down print ads and a trampled gym sock bear lonely witness to the teen tornado. Old RTD 90 rumbles back into traffic with a blast of diesel and collective sigh of relief. One stop later, the business people unload at Lincoln Savings and Loan. At Fashion Square, the ladies who work at Bullock's Department Store scurry away to serve the rich people from south of Ventura Boulevard.

Almost empty now, the bus rolls back up to Ventura and past Casa de Cadillac, Casa de Carwash, and Casa de Petrol; the Holy Trinity of the Coupe de Ville. A convertible red Fleetwood in the showroom window has been waiting all year for Elvis to notice. If I had money to burn, I would buy that creampuff for my grandmother even though Pater says Caddies are impractical and too big for our narrow canyon roads. Pater doesn't understand that owning a Cadillac isn't about being practical. It's about the American Dream.

Dumbest Kid in Smart Class

I have just enough time to stop and pick up provisions at the Kester Street Liquor store, where three of the seven deadly sins are on daily display. My customers depend on me, so I risk the corrupting influence of this den of iniquity. When Nana said liquor stores sell candy to hook kids as later customers for booze and cigarettes, I pointed out that they also sell Playboy. She said I'm lucky that Jews don't believe in hell or I would surely go there.

I buy a pack of individually wrapped Bit-O-Honeys that I can sell piecemeal for three times my cost, a giant jawbreaker, a couple of Wacky Packs, and a green bubblegum cigar for Henry Radford. Henry's the oldest kid in our school, but he hides his advanced age behind a cloak of immaturity. Lacking the gene for willpower, Henry will pay double, stuff the whole thing in his face and be forced to spit it out a few minutes later when he gets to class. I buy two candy necklaces for girls, one to sell, one to give to Fiona Westmont if, by some miracle, she has returned from the great beyond. After making these careful investments, I spend some of yesterday's profits on a Chick-O-Stick for myself. I know this will make me smell like peanut butter, but by lunch, half the kids will smell like Skippy anyway.

I may be the dumbest kid in smart class, but I can double my lunch money before the morning bell stops ringing. By the end of the week I'll have enough profit to buy my poor little neighbor Danny a new Hot Wheels car at Neff's Toys. I'm tired of sharing with Tommy so I'll buy myself the latest MAD magazine at the Van Nuys Newsstand.

What, me worry?

Since God knows I'm in a hurry, he sticks me behind an old guy who decided to re-stock his wet bar at 8 a.m. He buys a bottle of Harvey's Bristol Cream, two bottles of VO, and a six-pack of Schlitz, because when you're out of Schlitz, you're out of beer. To make things worse, he asks for a carton of Lucky Strikes that the cashier seems intent on ringing up one cigarette at a time.

I've got until 8:20 to get to school, sell my candy, and land in my seat with pencil in hand for the morning spelling test. I rock from foot to foot and clear my throat loudly. I scan the headlines and try not to fidget, but I can already sense another dreaded tardy stamp will tarnish my permanent record.

The *L.A. Times* predicts McCarthy will win today's Democratic primary. Other front-page news includes something about a rocket attack on Saigon and people missing at sea in a hurricane off the coast of Florida. No mention of the Icarus asteroid currently on a collision course with Earth. Yesterday afternoon's *Herald Examiner* is covered with bad news, including a prediction that our very own Governor Reagan will beat Nixon in a mud-splattered landslide.

Sister Hope Springs said that we should have elected Nixon for governor to contain the damage when he ran six years ago. Keeping him here would have been bad for California but good for the nation. I asked her if the same logic applied to Governor Ray-gun, who she hates, but she said we shouldn't worry. A movie cowboy that played second fiddle to a chimp named Bonzo has no shot at the White House.

Candy in the bag, I jaywalk across Ventura and pass the big windows at Kerry's Coffee where each table has a little chrome juke-box that looks like it came from a Jules Verne story. For a nickel, Andy Williams and Engelbert Humperdinck will set the mood for Kerry's famous Hobo Scramble. Pater took me here once to scout locations and make Hobo jokes. The pancakes

21

were fine, but there wasn't one cool song on the jukebox. When the Martians arrive, I'll bring them here to impress them with the many ways mankind can fry an egg and ruin breakfast with two much *schmaltz*.

I zip up Kester and turn down Dickens, which is what I'll catch if I'm late for school again. A line of people waits in front of a home with an American flag and a "Vote Here" sign planted in the front lawn. Election Day is a social occasion for the little old ladies who provide ballots, Tang, and Hydrox cookies to neighborhood voters.

I slow down to be sure that Ritchie Pash, the Al Capone of our playground, isn't lurking behind the large juniper, smoking a Pall Mall and hoping to steal my candy. If I get the jump on him before he jumps me, I can outsprint him to the fence.

An angry mom in a Ford Fairlane station wagon honks at the militant crossing guards wearing orange sashes and brandishing their hand-painted stop signs like Cuban revolutionaries. Cars with no hope of beating the bell eject kids who sprint the last block before the morning lockdown. A fading yellow school bus crawls toward the finish line of this morning's marathon.

The dark corridors of Sherman Oaks Elementary school are gussied up with hand-painted election posters and red, white, and blue crepe paper. Enough tempera paint to fill a swimming pool has been wasted on stick figure elephants, cartoon donkeys, and dumb slogans. Everyone who votes in the mock election will get a sticker to wear. One kid already has two. In what is probably not an official Nixon endorsement, somebody put "I Like Dick" stickers on the door of every girls' bathroom.

I manage to arrive with a few spare minutes to navigate the canals of commerce. The hall monitors are wearing straw hats and campaign buttons. Henry Radford knocks aside the red, white, and blue sea of younger kids and makes a beeline toward me. "Got my cigar?"

"Cigar? You're too young to smoke." He's wearing a Nixon button, and I feel like messing with him. "Smoking makes your breath smell. Girls won't want to kiss you if your breath smells."

"Stop screwing around, Max. Here's your dime."

"Sorry. Inflation. Price is fifteen cents now."

"What? It only costs you a nickel!"

"Plus the price of transport. I have expenses." And losses when Ritchie Pash strikes. "You can always buy your own."

"No I can't. My dad drops me off. Now take the dime or I'll straighten your crooked Jew nose."

"My nose is only worth a nickel. Which is what you still owe me." I wave the green bubble gum cigar in front of his face. "I might chew this myself today."

"You little shit bird." Henry produces five pennies from his front pocket, and we complete the exchange. He stuffs the entire cigar into his mouth and storms off into the red, white, and blue yonder.

I sell a few Bit-O-Honeys to younger kids as I make my way toward class. Most gobble the goodies on the spot, but a few put the candy in their pencil pouches and lunch boxes. Sensing that the bell is about to ring, we all walk faster.

A teacher dressed as Uncle Sam directs behavior and foot traffic at the intersection between hallways. Yesterday, the same Uncle Sam led an assembly where students impersonated the candidates and delivered campaign speeches. It made me sad when the dorky crowd cheered some little third-grade Nixon-lover's promise to force all the hippies into a giant bathtub and then pull the plug.

I didn't mention this to Nana. Nixon's giant bathtub sounded a lot like the showers at Dachau. Thirty years after her liberation, she's still convinced that another Holocaust lurks around every corner.

Just as Nana and my father once washed up on these shores, I too am a refugee, exiled from my neighborhood school and any chance of making local friends. I was a second-grader just minding my own business when I was plucked from Wonderland Elementary and enrolled in this educational experiment that has now been declared a complete failure.

The bell begins to jangle, its hammer beating out a warning. Abandon hope all ye who enter these classrooms. The shrill noise will last for exactly seven seconds, long and loud enough to rattle our brains and wake Rip Van Winkle. I have just enough time to race into my classroom and drop into my seat before the clattering stops.

"Please rise for the Pledge of Allegiance." Dr. Blast doesn't waste a second.

When I was transferred here, Sherman Oaks School, SOS, had a radical principal named Mr. Butler who wanted to try something different. He was a free thinker with a walrus mustache and the crazy notion that if kids were treated like humans they would act like humans. Butler teamed up with the UCLA School of Education to test a theory that so-called smart kids will learn because they want to, not because they are forced to. Cram them together like neutrons and you'll get an explosion of brilliance. He abolished the school dress code and traded in his gray suit and skinny ties for turtleneck sweaters and plaid sport coats. Mr. Butler brought in a couple of cool teachers who were young and wore miniskirts on Fridays.

"I pledge allegiance to the flag of the United States of America..."

It turned out that what inspires anyone with a brain has the opposite effect on school district officials. It's amazing that the

24

SOS experiment lasted for three minutes, but Mr. Butler managed to keep it alive for three years.

The final bomb fell when members of the Board of Education came through to observe "the experiment," looking in on us as if we were zoo monkeys. Their safari was perfectly timed for the day Agnes Hamlin, the redhead genius who always smelled like milk and Cheerios, was trying to reassemble a chicken from the bones left over after making soup. In another corner of the steamy room, Ben Chang was putting the final touches on a weather balloon and basket contraption designed to send an Easter Peep to the edge of space. He got flustered to the point of crying when grilled by one of the board members and came off as a blithering idiot instead of the smartest kid I'd ever met. Fortunately for him, unfortunately for the future of elementary education, Curt Van Owen, class clown, chose that moment to create a loud distraction with an energetic Professor Fingleheimer dance in the doorway.

The district was too square to trust Principal Butler. The writing was on the wall when they brought in a cavalry of new teachers and deputized the worst of them, Miss Malajusto, to enforce discipline as our new vice principal. Butler was gone a week later. In her first school assembly, Malajusto said her job was to get us ready for the real world, a place with no room for a bunch of sissy brats and smarty pants. Time to buck up and stop thinking our poop smelled like perfume.

"… and to the republic for which it stands..."

Butler's brief revolution ended with a government takeover when Maleficent Malajusto brought the Age of Aquarius crashing back to Earth. The cool teachers disappeared, the turtlenecks receded and after three years of freedom, we lab rats receded back into the sewer.

"…one nation, under smog, invisible, with liberty and justice for all."

"I heard that, Strauss." The first man I've ever seen in front of a classroom has a Ph.D. and insists that we address him as "Doctor." Dr. Blass, aka Dr. Blast, is a Malajusto man with a NASA buzz cut and squeaky wingtips. He did not come from the UCLA School of Education or, in fact, the current decade. His rumpled brown suit looks as if it hasn't been pressed since 1952.

~ ~ ~

I was under my table when Sally Geller passed me a note saying, "Where's Fiona???" in perfect cursive with lots of swirls and loops. This was a very bad sign. If Sally doesn't know where her best friend is, foul play must be to blame. I shake my head and tuck back into my fetal crouch.

The only silver lining to this cream of mushroom cloud is that Fiona Westmont was not present to witness my disgrace during the drop drill. Nobody has seen or heard from Fiona in a week, including her sidekick, confidant and interpreter, Sally Geller, the only person with whom Fiona shares complete sentences. There are whispers on the schoolyard that Fiona threw herself from the Griffith Observatory because Gregory Peck never answered her love letters. I've also heard that she has taken ill with mumps, measles, polio and chicken pox, but polio has been eradicated and we've all had the other three by now. Another rumor is that her parents' theater, The Playhouse, went bankrupt after their latest show flopped, so they hijacked a plane to Cuba to escape from critics and creditors.

Fiona Westmont was too perfect for this world. She was mysterious as a silent movie. Boys teased her for being so different. None of us were sure who she was, and I doubt she knew, either. Sadness ran through her like a Mississippi River of sorrow, draining her heartland into a gulf that I could never cross. She was tragic enough to be Jewish.

The only reason I held her interest, slight at best, was because I promised her a role in my father's movie. I told her that "Trotsky in Love" would soon be a major motion picture. This was a lie, but I wanted her friendship badly. I think there's a loophole in the Ten Commandments for minor stuff like this.

For Fiona, every day was a screen test, every minute a performance. She wrapped herself in elaborate outfits from the Thirties and Forties. One day she was Ava Gardner, the next, Joan Fontaine. If it weren't for Fiona, none of us would have heard of Greta Garbo or Marlene Dietrich. Fiona was always ready for her close-up.

Her friend Sally Geller kept us stargazers informed of Fiona's daily character changes. "Show some respect, Katharine is still brokenhearted over losing Spencer!" On the anniversary of Errol Flynn's death, Fiona draped herself in black, covered her face with dark lace and spent the day crying. She came to school on her own birthday in a strapless wedding gown and, through Sally, insisted we throw cafeteria rice to celebrate her imaginary marriage to Charlie Chaplin. Once, during a Santa Ana heat wave, she wore a floor-length fur, elbow gloves, hat and hose. I'm not sure who she was supposed to be that day, but she did it without breaking a sweat.

Elegant. Aloof. Timeless. During recess, she would float on high heels while I stomped around in my dirty hiking boots. I never saw her eat at lunchtime. She would lean against a eucalyptus tree and puff candy smoke from a cigarette holder she claimed once belonged to Grace Kelly. She never spoke in more than a whisper. Now more mysterious than ever, even Sally Geller wonders what happened to the wonderful Fiona.

I know, but I'm too ashamed to tell.

The die was cast the day I asked her to be my special friend. To my surprise, Fiona let me put a Saint Christopher medallion around her angelic neck, though she refused to let me kiss her cheek. "I'm saving myself for Douglas Fairbanks," she said and turned to stare longingly into an invisible camera. But he was long gone, and one day later so was Fiona, dissolved into silver molecules that floated away on the hot, dry wind.

For the record, the permanent one, that medallion was not my idea. I overheard one of the Notre Dame boys explain that true friendship requires a saint medal so one afternoon, on a day without Hebrew school, I jumped off the bus to visit the church store. The old nun minding the medallions saw I was confused and guided me toward Christopher, patron saint of travelers.

But now Fiona's gone. The only silver lining is on the back of the medallion she might still be wearing. I know it's silly, but my heart is so broken it's running on one ventricle. When mom left for Jesus, I took a vow before God to never love again. Now I promise to become a Vulcan like Mr. Spock and live out my days in pursuit of truth, not feelings. Emotions are illogical, love most of all. Losing my mother should have taught me, but I'm a slow learner.

Dr. Blast and Miss Malajusto are right to punish me; they just have the wrong reason.

As I wait to be paddled by the principal, I consider becoming a Catholic so I can pray to the patron saint of idiots to be forgiven for scaring Fiona away. I stew in fear and self-pity until I overhear the school secretary mention that Fiona moved to New York City where her parents have joined an experimental theater troupe. "They'll probably perform in the nude," she says, nose deep in her files among which, no doubt, are the stained pages of my permanent record.

New York can't be that far away. I'll find her somehow. Fiona and I will meet again in this life, not the next, perhaps on the set of "Trotsky in Love."

Strengthened in the knowledge that Fiona has not joined Douglas Fairbanks in Hollywood Heaven, I step into Malajusto's office to face the music. I am ready to bite the bullet and meet the paddle Malajusto calls the "Board of Education." Instead of a few quick swats, she prolongs my suffering by ordering me to write "Good citizens do as they are told" five-hundred times in that perfect cursive that only the perfect girls can master.

I wonder how many times the British told George Washington that good citizens do as they are told.

Malajusto gives me until Friday to deliver the document. Since there's no hope for improving my chicken-scratch cursive, I'll have to blow this week's candy profits to bribe a girl with a corrupt heart and steady hand to be my scribe. At this price, a couple of swats would have been preferable.

I slink back to Dr. Blast's inferno just in time to grab my lunch bag and venture out into the wilds of the schoolyard. Late to the party, I'm condemned to sit at the dumb boys table. Today these mental midgets are debating whether Barbara Feldon — Agent 99 on *Get Smart* — is cuter than Barbara Eden from *I Dream of Jeannie*. I suggest that this is a false choice, just like the argument over Ginger versus Mary Ann on *Gilligan's Island*, but nobody is interested in my point of view. Like old men on a park bench, these dopes have the same argument every day.

None of them wants to talk about the election, the comet hurtling toward the Earth, or the need to start a revolution against Malajusto. No one is interested in my lunch, so I leave it safely on the table and wander over to the milk station.

The usual rabble is waiting in line to buy milk to accompany the delights or abominations packed in their lunchboxes. Regular milk costs seven cents, chocolate a dime. A trusted older student, the milk monitor, wheels the cart into the lunch area and solemnly dispenses little cartons of moo juice as we shuffle forward.

I gather my pennies and enjoy the smell of dry heat rising off the asphalt. Sunlight filters through the rustling eucalyptus leaves. I imagine Fiona's draped silhouette backlit by the golden rays.

Zoran Parsnik, a recent immigrant from a country where fun is illegal, starts chanting "Boris! Natasha! Kill Moose and Squirrel." Cartoon is the only English he knows.

Off in the distance, I see Malajusto patrolling the schoolyard in a knee-length gray skirt and matching tweed coat. Despite her attempt to impose a strict dress code, boys' hair is inching south faster than the girls' hemlines are receding. I can almost hear the sharp words our feared principal has for everyone. Whenever she sees kids flirting on the playground, she says, "Another card-carrying member of the sexual revolution." Boys who fear getting hit by a hard, speeding dodge ball are "yellow-bellied sap suckers." She told Ben Chang, the Chinese kid whose grandparents probably built the railroads, not to use the office phone because he might "Wing the Wong number." I learned the words "brazen" and "hussy" from hearing her dress down a second-grader in plastic Beatle boots. Any boy in bell bottoms is a "sailor" which is pronounced with a lisp and accompanied by Malajusto smoothing one of her penciled-on eyebrows with a spit-wet pinky. Boys with long bangs are "faggots." Skinny girls are "Twiggy." Fat kids are doomed.

I need to save money, so I forgo chocolate for regular milk and return to the dumb boys' table to eat my cream cheese and jam on Wonder Bread sandwich. It's a good thing I like this

30

concoction because it has zero trading value with the knuckle draggers debating bologna versus salami. Last year, these guys discussed nuclear physics but sixth grade and the new regime has left us a few clowns short of a circus.

I see Sally Geller adrift on the playground. For the first time in memory she exists as a separate person, not just an appendage of the fabulous Fiona. I watch her wander aimlessly between the four square courts and tetherball poles and feel responsible for her grief. Curt Van Owen runs up behind Sally, pulls her hair, and does the Professor Fingleheimer dance in a circle around her. After one orbit, she slaps him so hard I hear the echo from across the playground. He runs away with Sally in hot pursuit.

I bite into my Granny Smith just as someone streaks past me. It's Ritchie Pash, Boss Tweed of the schoolyard, running at top speed in loose-fitting cowboy boots. He shouts a battle cry and dives onto the milk cart like a flying squirrel. The milk monitor twists aside, and the cart takes off rolling, then tumbling and sending coins and calcium in all directions.

It's as if all rules have been suspended and all consequences are on hold until the coins stop spinning. Every kid within shouting distance joins the fray, jostling for the nickels, dimes, and pennies spinning along the pavement. The thin layer of cellophane that stands between us and barbarism is ripped away. It's lunchtime in the kindergarten of good and evil.

Even the good kids stuff undeserved windfalls into their pockets. The distraught milk monitor, a Jehovah's Witness who deserves better, tries to restore order. Neither he nor his God can contain the larceny. Outlaws are everywhere, too many to chase. I pick up a couple of nickels that roll by me.

"Help! Police! Robbers!" a goodie girl shouts and the others join in screaming bloody murder.

31

The poor, defeated milk monitor picks a few remaining pennies from a white puddle. Trembling, he tries not to cry as he trudges away to face the certain wrath of the cafeteria matron whose dislike for kids is worse than her Friday fish sticks.

The schoolyard returns to normal for about one second, and then the sheriff arrives with her goodie girl posse. A burst from Malajusto's whistle is enough to vaporize spilt milk. She storms in and rounds up every kid within twenty yards. One by one we must turn our pockets inside out. Coins clatter as they hit the asphalt. I'm caught in the dragnet and found guilty when I refuse to say where my candy profits came from.

A pair of glass click-clack balls shatters in the distance. I wish I'd had the nerve to go talk to Sally Geller instead of surfing this stupid crime wave.

We criminals are questioned individually. The weak are offered a plea bargain to turn snitch. Nobody dares rat on Ritchie Pash, the only person on Earth scarier than Miss Malajusto. I can't tell her about my morning candy business, so I plead the fifth and she confiscates my hard-earned coins. Adding insult to robbery, she hits me with another five hundred lines of "Good citizens do as they are told" due in perfect cursive by Friday morning.

The milk monitor returns to the crime scene and seals his doom by fingering Ritchie Pash. When other kids nod in agreement, Ritchie offers a Robin Hood defense and shows no remorse. Malajusto expels him for two days and promises to dance on his grave when they "peel his barbequed butt off the electric chair."

The ringing bell is the signal for us to line up behind our classmates, boys left, girls right. Some idiot tries to start a round of "pass the poke," but today the poke stops with me.

Unlike most days when I can honestly say I've learned nothing, today I'll take home a few important lessons: drop drills are pointless, most kids are criminals, and Fiona is alive. Since Nana Hannah survived the Nazis, I won't tell her I also learned how innocent bystanders can become a mob and how quick I was to join.

Monkees and Nazis

The walk back to the bus stop is more dicey than usual.

"Kike!" Ritchie's expulsion means he's ahead of schedule to harass me as I leave the school grounds.

"Heard it before, Ritchie." He usually doesn't hit me, but today I'm a bit worried. He's the type of lawless kid who doesn't care if you wear glasses. "Loved the milk wagon job today."

"Hebe! Yid!" He takes a final drag on a hand-rolled cigarette he stole from his father and flicks it at me. "Wop! Dago!"

"I'm not Italian. Sheesh! Get your insults straight."

"Christ Killer!"

"That's better."

"Penny Pincher!" He sends a small coin, probably a penny, whizzing by my head. I know he'll kick me if I pick it up. It's the perfect ending to a perfect school day.

I consider dashing into the Army recruiting depot on Ventura Boulevard, a few doors down from the La Reina Theater where *Rosemary's Baby* is playing. Perhaps I can enlist for as long as it takes to avoid Ritchie and atone for my role in the milk mob incident. I'm too young for Vietnam, but maybe there's an installment plan for future wars. Enlist now, die later.

Ritchie loses interest in killing me so I short cut through Neff's Toys to look at the Hot Wheels cars. I grab a green Beatnik Bandit that I could sell for a profit and ask Mr. Neff to hold it for me until next week, but he points to a sign that says "In God we trust, all others pay CASH." So much for being a regular customer.

The cost of having a thousand lines of "Good citizens do as they are told" ready by Friday has nearly bankrupted me. I'll have to raise my candy prices. I can't afford five cents for the raw egg in a dime-sized Orange Julius. I wander over to inspect the Greek's offerings at the Van Nuys Newsstand on the corner near my bus stop.

The Playboys and girlie magazines are up on the top shelf where only grown men can see them. The comics are at my eye level. I thumb through a twelve-cent copy of Archie and Veronica until a Greek shadow looms behind me and says, "No pay, no read." That's the thanks I get for all the Superman comics I've bought here. For the record, the permanent one, I prefer Betty to Veronica, but today I feel like Jughead.

I wish I had my transistor radio with me. Hearing the Real Don Steele would cheer me up after a day like this. I'd rather be listening to KHJ than the dull churn of afternoon traffic. I want to hear The 5th Dimension and find out if Tiny Tim is still in the Top Ten.

Jack, the afternoon bus driver, doesn't sing or play mouth trombone, but he knows everything imaginable about baseball. I used to pull cards from my collection, and he would amaze the riders by reciting every fact and statistic no matter how obscure the player. But baseball lost my interest when Sandy Koufax, the only Jewish player, retired. Driver Jack lost my respect when he started making snide comments about spoiled ghetto kids and unpatriotic longhairs. His "Nixon's the One" button makes me lose interest in his daily tirade about the L.A. Dodgers' pitiful starting lineup.

I hope Bobby Kennedy wins today.

The rear bench is a good place to sit cross-legged and watch San Fernando's big valley roll by. I used to pretend the bus was a spaceship back when I was a kid. Now it's my own personal

Yellow Submarine. Each window is like a color TV that plays nothing but commercials.

A blind man boards with a golden retriever guide dog. I've never seen either of them before. The dog seems happy to have a break and curls up on the floor to catch a few winks. The warm diesel fumes are making me sleepy, so I move forward to get a closer look at the dog. I make high-pitched squeaking sounds whenever the door opens or the bus stops, but I'm unable to wake the blind man's dog. Poor pooch. It must be hard to be so well behaved all the time. He'll never know the joy of chasing a ball, barking at a cat, or wrestling on the floor with a kid like me.

The blind man's eyes roll around in their sockets as he listens carefully to the door opening and closing, the change jingling in the coin counter, and the bus grumbling through traffic. I watch him nod like a bobble-head doll and realize that this is how he takes in the world around him. Sound. Smell. Vibration. He scrunches his nose and nods, unaware of how odd this looks. He has no idea that the rest of us keep our faces frozen, noses forward, and heads steady.

Nothing else of interest comes along until we approach the Big Donut Drive-In, where a camera crew is wrapping up a shoot. I suppose it was only a matter of time before someone realized that a place with a hundred-foot donut is a good location to film a cop show. A pair of real cops stops traffic so a big white TV truck can back into the street.

"Why are we stopped?" the blind man asks. He senses something out of the ordinary.

"Damned longhairs are everywhere these days," Jack says.

Indeed, longhairs are milling around the donut stand wearing striped bell bottoms and colorful, puffy troubadour shirts. It's as if half of Laurel Canyon just descended with a mountainous case of the munchies. Or maybe KHJ is throwing a

Big Kahuna party at the Giant Donut stand. I race from window to window, but I don't see KHJ's official Mustang convertible.

"Who's out there?" the blind man asks.

"Maybe it's one of the presidential candidates," I say.

"President of Faggot-land," Jack says. The donut stand usually has a cup of coffee and a mixed half-dozen ready for Jack to grab as the bus passes by. He's mad that the film crew has disrupted this important delivery. He's mad that ungrateful beatniks have taken over the world that he helped save in the last war. "Why don't they get a job?"

"Is there a problem?" The blind man rocks his head from side to side with a toothy grin that doesn't match the distress in his voice. "Is something happening here?"

"What it is ain't exactly clear," I whisper.

The bus idles while a mess of chopped Harleys roar away down Riverside Drive. I see a "Hell's Angels" patch on the back of a leather jacket. The riders look like modern Vikings come to pillage North Hollywood. The sidewalk swarms with TV extras dressed like Renaissance minstrels. Across the street, the Der Wienerschnitzel parking lot is full of bouncing teenyboppers in head bands and hot pants being corralled by cops and yellow tape.

I hear Nana's voice in my head insisting it should be "Das," not "Der" Wienerschnitzel.

I hurry back to look out the rear window as the bus finally crosses the intersection. The big donut has been converted into a peace sign with a big pink gorilla perched on top. I pinch myself hard enough to verify that I'm not dreaming, but still can't believe my eyes. This has to be a hallucination. I just saw the Monkeemobile.

It finally hits me that this is no cop show. There's only one program this zany and colorful. The Monkees were just on location at the Big Donut Drive-In! This is monumental news.

Bigger than the Great Schoolyard Milk Robbery. Bigger still than today's presidential primary. This is so huge that I won't be able to brag about it because nobody will believe me. For once I'm in a hurry to get to Hebrew school. *Mach schnell!* I need to scoop anyone who might have seen this from the back seat of their mother's Buick. I need to break this story before it breaks away.

I leap out at the next stop and dash into the candy store on the corner of Burbank and Laurel. Uncle Irv, the store owner, listens to my disjointed story of giant donut peace signs, gorillas, guide dogs and Monkees. To get rid of me, he agrees to extend credit for a pack of strawberry Hostess Snowballs and a small carton of chocolate milk—brain fuel for the next two hours. I promise to pay him back on Thursday.

"Thanks, Irv! Gotta go!"

"Advance warning." His thick Polish accent hints of pickled herring and epic suffering. "Today would be a good day to behave like an angel."

I race to my Hebrew class only to hear Sammy Jacoby already telling everyone about the Monkees. We are expected to believe that they wolfed jelly donuts together. "Davy Jones was glazed as my cinnamon twist! Michael Nesmith was torqued out of his wool hat!

Nana says that the best lies are half true, and most kids seem more than half convinced. I almost believe Sammy's story until I remember who's telling them. If there was a Bar and Bat Mitzvah Class of 1968 Oscar for fibbing, Sammy would win. I can't believe this rich brat will be my B.M. partner in October.

"Micky Dolenz jammed a donut hole back in his cruller and called it a stone-nut. I laughed so hard I almost tossed my fritter."

I never thought I'd be so glad to see our Hebrew teacher, but it comes as great relief when she throws a wet blanket on

Monkee mania. Miss Cormi—rhymes with "bore me—" is fresh off the boat from Israel. She seems to hate us all, which is unfair. Most of the kids in my class are good eggs, fine and upstanding young citizens who will soon be Bar and Bat Mitzvahed as adults within the congregation. We will get good grades, go to college, marry within the faith and still manage to disappoint our mothers.

But good eggs are often eclipsed by bad apples. Bad apples smoke on the bus. Bad apples steal the milk money. They grow up to start wars, vote for Nixon and tear gas students. The good eggs might inherit the earth, but only after the bad apples turn it to compost.

I've noticed that the worst of the bad apples don't fall far from the wealthiest trees. Their fathers are successful lawyers and businessmen. Their mothers serve on committees. These are the kids with Adidas and bell bottoms, color TVs in their bedrooms and swimming pools in their backyards. The rich kids think I'm well off because I live south of Ventura. They don't know that I live south of Ventura in an old A-frame cabin. Nana says it's not what you have, it's how you use it. When I'm around rich kids I do my best to use what I don't have.

Miss Bore-me always starts class with a word exchange where she points to an object, names it in Hebrew, and we teach her the English counterpart. Today she points to a light switch, makes us repeat the Hebrew word three times and then beckons to the class. Everyone waits for Sammy Jacoby to serve up a choice translation.

"It's called 'shit.'" Sammy doesn't disappoint.

"What?" Bore-me moves closer. "Repeat?"

"SHIT!" Sammy yells to be heard over our snickering. "It's called a SHIT!"

Wham!

Cormi smacks Sammy across the cheek with a sudden dose of Old Testament wrath, imported directly from the source. The slap hits so hard and fast it triggers a small sonic boom. Before Sammy can draw a breath, the coat closet door swings open and out jumps Dr. Miriam Jakowitz, our temple's Director of Education. Dr. Jakowitz, aka DJ, leads Sammy away by the ear.

A sting operation! This must have been what Irv the Candy Man was hinting at. DJ must have leaked her intentions when she stopped at his shop to buy cigarettes and tranquilizer darts.

"Let that be a lesson to you," Bore-me says in better English than I remember her capable of. I've noticed her vocabulary making rapid progress over the last couple of weeks. Maybe she has a local boyfriend. Maybe he's a goy friend. "Don't forget," she reminds us, "I fought in the Six Day War."

Sammy was never a serious challenge to someone who could assemble a machine gun blindfolded.

We slog through an exercise in Hebrew cursive, attempting to learn the secret code that looks like random squiggles. I can barely write English cursive, so mastering the art of Hebrew scribbling seems especially pointless. The good news is that class will end early so we can attend a special assembly. The bad news is that we have to attend a special assembly. This usually means watching some documentary about the joys of kibbutz life followed by a lecture about what a bunch of pussies we are for not moving to Israel.

I stop by the bathroom on the way to the auditorium, not because I need to, but because Nana always insists you should never pass a toilet because it might be hours before the next opportunity. Menthol tobacco smoke hangs in the air.

"Oh, it's just you." Sammy peeks from a toilet stall. "You should have said something. I flushed half a cigarette 'cos I thought you were a narc."

"Just need to visit Betsy Mush." We all love the Hebrew word for bathroom because it sounds like a girl's name. "Sorry about your ciggie."

"Just for that, you get Shoshana."

"She's your girlfriend, not mine." Shoshana is the dreaded last toilet stall. It's named after a girl in our class with crusty white lips, blue cat eye glasses, and a collection of drab pinafores from the pioneer days. She has the nauseating habit of sitting in class and licking the buttons on her fuzzy green Girl Scout sweater when she isn't just wiping her wet nose on the sleeves. The only injury worse than getting stuffed into the Shoshana stall is when Sammy adds insult by throwing water into my stall and killing the lights before running away laughing. I promise vengeance from my darkened throne.

I find my way to the auditorium and linger outside until the lights have dimmed enough to hide my wet shirt. I slip in and take a back row seat next to crusty-lipped Shoshana who puts her arm around me as if I'm her new best friend. I want to shake her loose but I'm afraid she'll raise a ruckus. DJ has just finished introducing a movie and Asher the custodian wrestles with the projector until the film loops settle down. I worry about what Shoshana might try in the dark.

10, 9, 8 … test pattern … click, click, click …

Today's entertainment is a documentary about the liberation of Auschwitz. Within seconds I'm ready to upchuck my chocolate milk and Hostess Snowball into Shoshana's lap. A wobbly aerial shot captures a long train track, smoke stacks and gas chambers. Piles of glasses, mountains of hair, a room full of gold fillings. Starving prisoners too skinny to be scarecrows. Deep hollow eyes, too exhausted for tears. Trembling gray hands reach out to us.

We have seen Holocaust films before, but nothing quite like this. This is a thousand times worse than anything my

41

grandmother ever told me about Dachau. It's a million times worse than the nightly news from Vietnam.

I moan at seeing the pile of rotting naked bodies. Shoshana covers her eyes and folds forward, all sniffles and tears. I pat her back and say it's okay, but it really isn't. Her grandmother died in one of the camps. Her father ate shoe leather to survive. Like me, Shoshana is growing up under the long shadow. No matter how tightly she closes her eyes, these images will haunt her forever.

"And now," DJ announces as the lights come on, "we have a very special guest. Mrs. Bella Pinsky, Survivor of Auschwitz, will share her experiences with you."

Pinsky. Auschwitz. Poland. It strikes me that the liberating army in the film we just saw was Russian. The footage was shot by the Soviets who also shot a lot of Nazis during the war. It's easy to forget that we were all on the same side once.

"Thank you, Doctor Jakowitz," Mrs. Pinsky steps up to the microphone. She is a small woman the same age as Nana, though she looks much older. She is dressed like all the old ladies in the congregation: a frumpy green skirt and suit coat, a small hat with a fake flower, and an enormous purse with which she can undoubtedly defend herself. "*Shalom*, children."

She proceeds to tell us her story, a tale of such brutality, sadness, and unbearable loss that even the bad apples turn to mush. Her father was shot the day the Nazis invaded. She saw friends and neighbors dragged away, never to return. She saw a pregnant woman beaten by a soldier. A Jewish baby was tossed in the air for target practice. *A baby!*

"I barely remember the day the Russians marched in to liberate Auschwitz. I was so weak at that point, so close to death's door that I fainted and woke up days later. How I survived the war is a mystery only God can explain. Why I survived is no mystery: I survived to bear witness that this must never happen again."

Bella Pinsky has made it her mission to share her story in schools, churches, and congregations across Los Angeles. Unlike the few survivors and refugees I've met through Nana, Mrs. Pinsky is still seething. She is haunted by ghosts and memories. Her anger makes perfect sense to me. The real mystery is how my grandmother ever found a way to be happy.

"Never forget that Germany was once a civilized country where our people had lived for hundreds of years. You may think Hitler can't happen here, but that's exactly what Germany's Jews thought before *Kristallnacht*."

What if Hope Springs was right? What if Nixon is the American Hitler?

"What is our answer to Hitler?" Mrs. Pinsky asks. "How to guarantee our survival in a world where no one will lift a finger to defend us? The answer is simple, children. Israel. Our homeland is the only place Jews can be safe. We must populate and defend Israel, the Promised Land. Our answer to the Holocaust is clear."

The auditorium is silent. No one fidgets. No one breathes.

"For me, the war will never end." Mrs. Pinsky chokes up for a second and then finds the strength to finish. "The war continues as long as there are Nazis living among us. Nazis right here in Los Angeles. We must not rest until every last Nazi is brought out of the shadows and into the sacred light of justice. *Todah rabah.* Thank you, children."

Applause gushes like water from an overflowing lake of tears. We cheer for Mrs. Pinsky. We cheer for the Promised Land. We cheer with a new sense of purpose. My class, this year's Bar and Bat Mitzvah cohort, will stand tall. We will make *aliyah* to the holy land. We will enlist in the Israeli Army. We will defend Jerusalem.

An idea emerges through the fog of tears and applause. I have been looking for a *mitzvah*, a deed of consequence or act of service to perform for my big B.M. Most kids raise money for Hadassah, dedicate some trees to be planted in the desert, or perform some forgettable act of charity that is secretly funded by their parents.

Not me. I will do something that no kid has done before. My deed of consequence will be the greatest *mitzvah* ever. When I enter the community of adults on the day of my big B.M. even the *alter kockers* will raise their bushy eyebrows and say, "*Oy*! A true *mensch*, this one."

Thank you, Mrs. Pinsky. There may not be many ex-Nazis hidden among us, but I happen to know exactly where one of them lives. With God as my judge, I will capture this villain and bring him into the sacred light of justice.

Hope Springs

It's Friday evening and the canyon is slipping into twilight as the sun sets beyond what the Chumash once called the Western Gate.

Nana is about to light the Sabbath candles when Hope Springs peeks through our open door looking like a loved one just died in her arms. Her broad curls are furrowed into tight cornrows, eyes cloudy as if she's been underwater.

"*Shabbat shalom, Hopeschen,*" Nana puts aside the box of strike-anywhere matches and gives Hope a hug. My grandmother remembers horse carriages and gas lamps. Hope's ancestors were slaves. Soon both women will see a man walk on the moon. Nana lived through two world wars that burned across her own front yard. The only way she makes sense out of all she's seen is to say that God keeps a big zoo.

Hope joins us at the piano, which doubles as an altar for our weekly ritual. She's been here before and observed silently from a distance. Tonight she puts her arm around me and huddles with my family. Fearing that the moment might evaporate, I inhale as much of her sadness as my lungs can hold.

My grandmother lights the candles, then covers her deep blue eyes with bony hands. "Welcome dear Sabbath, bride of twilight." In self-imposed darkness she prays silently at first and then recites the ancient words to bless the newborn candle flames. Her tiny, angular frame is softened by the flickering light. She lingers over the blessing as if waiting for God, with whom she has a personal relationship, to answer. He is as real to my grandmother as Hope Springs is to me. I want to hold on to both women forever. I worry they will disappear like matchstick smoke.

Abraham, Martin, and John. And now Bobby. John's younger brother. Hope once said her great-grandfather was freed by Lincoln. MLK's words haven't stopped echoing and Bobby Kennedy's last breath is still in the wind. For Hope, this is personal.

I know Hope from my weekday perch on the back seat of the Blue Bomber. She listens to the news and debates politics with Pater during the morning ride. Between MLK's assassination this spring and Bobby's murder this week, there's no wind left to fill her sails. Over the past few months, I've watched Hope change from optimistic to angry to deflated. Standing next to me, her arm weighs heavily across my shoulder, as if she might sink without my support.

"There was darkness, there was light. The seventh day ..." Nana finishes the blessing and wipes a rare tear away. The flames dance and greet their short lives with all the heat they can muster. I name one candle Martin, the other Bobby. Both flames burned short and bright, bringing light to the world before being snuffed out by darkness.

Where was God when they were shot?

While Pater blesses the wine, I send up a prayer for Hope, a prayer to the God of Sarah, Rebecca, Rachel and Leah. I can't soften Hope's sadness, but I can help her feel at home. She holds me close as if I'm all that keeps her from drifting away.

Hope was the first person I thought of when I learned that Bobby Kennedy had been shot. Pater and I were driving downhill when someone on the radio mentioned Bobby's surprising election victory and the horrific shooting. After his victory speech, a speech that Hope witnessed, Bobby detoured through the Ambassador Hotel's kitchen and was greeted by a gunman. When we heard the morning news that Bobby was in the hospital, Pater was so stunned he almost drove through a stop sign.

I knew Bobby wasn't going to make it when Hope didn't show up at the Canyon Store the morning after the election. Bobby was her summer antidote to a toxic spring in which Martin was killed, the news from Vietnam kept getting worse, and ghettos went up in flames across the country. Hope needed Bobby's win more than he did. I couldn't shake the image of her walking into the ocean, disappearing forever, straight through the Western Gate.

"Amen." Pater takes a sip of the sacramental wine and passes the old goblet that Nana brought from Germany. We sing the *She'ma* and even my brother Tommy, ever vigilant against the uncool, joins in. Most of the time prayers are just words that we repeat without thinking, but tonight, the ancient chant anchors me.

"Hear o' Israel: The Lord our God. The Lord is One."

This is the prayer written on the scroll inside the *mezuzah* mounted by our front door. It's hard to believe that Abraham's simple words were ever considered revolutionary, hard to fathom that the notion of just one God was once blasphemy. Our neighbor Mumu Marie believes in the Holy Trinity, which to my count equals three Gods. Abraham's one big God could just be the sum of many little gods the way a flock of small birds can appear to move as one big cloud. Nobody really knows. I don't even know if my father believes in God or if he just does this to make Nana happy. I know she believes. She says God exists in order for life to make sense.

"Maxie?"

Pater nods a request to bless Nana's home-baked challah. Unfortunately, this peels me away from Hope. Maybe she thinks it's weird to bless a loaf of bread, but it's just giving thanks. I pretend to have difficulty with the Hebrew and keep one eye on

Tommy to make sure he doesn't muscle in on my spot under Hope's wing.

But Tommy's distracted by his uncooperative hair. He looks like the Dutch Boy paint mascot. He strokes a strand into place and, when that doesn't work, he pulls it behind his ear, only to have it spring loose.

I finish the blessing, and Pater breaks off a chunk of Nana's fresh challah to share. The crust is golden, the bread light and fluffy inside. Perfection. The smell fills me with memories of a world I never knew, a world where entire villages smelled this way on Friday afternoons. I will forever associate Friday with the warmth of Nana's braided challah.

I invite Hope over to join us around Pater as we gather for his weekly blessing. She puts her arm around me again. I can feel the beat of her broken heart.

"The Lord bless you and keep you. The Lord make his face shine upon you ..." My father lets the Hebrew words linger as if casting a spell to heal the world.

I have heard this blessing almost every week of my waking life. Sometimes I find comfort in the words. Tonight I find comfort standing next to Hope and sharing my father's blessing with her. She needs it more than I do.

At the end of the blessing Pater adds, "And may God rest the soul of Bobby Kennedy, now a beloved memory."

I wonder if God is happy to have Bobby with him in heaven or if he, too, is brokenhearted over having to take him away so early.

Our silence is interrupted by Hope's sniffle. She takes refuge in the kitchen and offers to help get food onto the table, but Nana evicts her, saying that's what kids are for.

"I'll help wash the dishes later," Hope says.

"Tommy will wash the dishes." Nana nudges Hope toward our small dining area. "God owes us a miracle this week." She grabs my ear as I try to sneak by.

"Hey! This is supposed to be a day of rest," I say, but I'm handed a noodle kugel before any further grievance can be filed. Tommy grabs the roasted chicken platter only to get yanked back into the kitchen.

"Nothing worse than a naked chicken," Nana says as she adds broth.

For now, the only thing worse than a naked chicken is a dead one swimming in prune juice. Nana tosses dried fruit in almost everything she cooks. It's a holdover from the old country, where a fresh orange was such a luxury that she still eats the peel. Hunger is everyone's ancestor, she says. Still not convinced that we live in a land of plenty, she stockpiles dried fruit to keep us free of rickets during what masquerades for winter in Southern California.

Hope sneaks back into the kitchen and snatches a bowl of roasted potatoes dusted with paprika, a spice from the old country that makes things look pretty but does little for flavor. Nowadays, half of the girls at Wonderland Elementary School are named Paprika. Tommy says they will grow up to be pretty but tasteless.

We all bounce around like electrons until finally settling in around the table.

"From the mythical northern land of Sonoma." Pater wrestles a cork from an unwilling bottle of red wine. He fills a glass of wine for Hope even though she's only twenty years old.

"The place where the children of farmworkers pick library books instead of grapes?" Hope surfaces from her funk long enough to bait Pater.

49

"Exactly," he says. "The earthly paradise where the Sun Maid Raisin girl skinny dips with Caesar Chavez in the California aqueduct."

"Are raisins part of the grape boycott?" I ask. "I miss having raisins in my lunch bag."

"Wine is exempt," Tommy says. He tries to grab the bottle, but Nana's quick to slap his hand and refill her own glass.

"It's OK," Pater assures himself. He holds up the label for all to see. "This wine pre-dates the boycott. Next week I'll switch to French."

"I'm sure the French farmworkers are happy," Nana says. "They were happy to make wine for the Nazis."

"Let's not start in with the Nazis." My dad is the only one in the family who's allowed to say this. He was my age when they came knocking.

"*Acch.* The way this world is turning ..." Nana mutters.

I get up and slap my new Simon and Garfunkel record on the turntable. This is an improvement over last week when Tommy tried to pass off the band "Cream" as Sabbath music because "Disraeli Gears" sounds like a Jewish album title.

"How can you say the She'ma one minute and call Clapton God the next?" I asked. "Besides, if Clapton is God, why did he choose a drummer who plays like Satan?"

"Jews don't believe in Satan," Pater insisted. "We believe in the messiah."

"I believe in Ginger Baker," Tommy said, invoking one of his drummer idols.

"Ginger?" Nana asked. "I'll bet his mother's called Paprika."

"Who are we listening to?" Hope asks, bringing me back into the present.

"*Bookends.* Simon and Garfunkel," Tommy says. "I saw them at the Monterey Pop Festival last summer."

"New York navel gazers." Hope is never shy with her opinion. "If they self-absorb anymore they'll dissolve."

"All singer-songwriters are self-absorbed," Pater says, not because he believes it but because he heard me talking about becoming one and wants to discourage the idea.

"I love this album," I say. There's no way I'm giving ground on this. I've listened to *Bookends* twice already today. The songs flow and swell with mysterious lyrics and angelic, echoing voices. Garfunkel might be self-absorbed, but I have a sense that Simon's singing to me and me alone.

"These guys are boring," Tommy says, because he likes to insult stuff I like. He stuffs a potato in his mouth and moves in for the kill. "Why don't you put on your favorite Monkees record, Maxie-poo?"

"Wouldn't you rather hear The Archies, Tom-tom Teenybopper?" As a recent Vulcan, I'm still cool with sarcasm. I race Tommy to the hi-fi to defend my right to choose the music once and a while. "Maybe we can listen to your Captain Kangaroo record."

"That's Captain Beefheart, you numbskull."

"Do you like The Byrds?" I ask Hope. Maybe she can tip the balance in my favor.

"Saw them at Monterey, too," Tommy says, his mouth never too full to remind us how cool he is.

"Yeah, yeah. You saw everyone at Monterey." His running away to San Francisco last summer is still a sore spot. There's not much affection around here for the Summer of Love after he left his heart and half his brain in San Francisco.

"Even I like The Byrds," Nana says. "I love how they chirp in harmony."

"The early Byrds get the worms," Pater says.

"The early worms get eaten." Tommy walks over to the turntable and pulls out his favorite abomination: "Freak Out" by Frank Zappa.

"Zappa isn't Sabbath music!" I insist.

"Bullshit," Tommy says. "Zappa is the direct word of God."

"Dad! Tom-tom said bullshit."

"So did you, Maxine!"

"Act your age, not your shoe size."

"No music and no more fighting," Nana says.

"Why am I being punished?" I demand.

"Nobody's being punished." Nana turns to Hope. "Do you see anyone being punished?"

"Yeah. Me," Hope says.

Nana tries to offer everyone more peas, and Hope surprises us by saying yes the first time.

"Hope, Hope, Hope. You did that all wrong." Pater imitates an old man, an *alter kocker*. "Here's how it's supposed to go: Do you want more peas? No, I'm stuffed. How about I give you just a few? No, they were delicious, but I couldn't eat another bite. C'mon, you're so skinny, and vegetables will put hair on your chest. Fine, fine, but you're to blame if I die of such happiness."

Hope laughs and wipes half her peas onto my plate. "Don't need any more chest hair."

I wonder for a second if ladies get chest hair and avoid looking at Tommy for fear that he might start his "Max almost has one pubic hair" rant. Fortunately, he's busy tapping a three-on-four pattern on the edge of the table. His feet are pumping imaginary drum pedals, vibrating the creaking floor joists. If an earthquake hit right now, no one would notice.

"What are you doing this summer?" Pater asks Hope.

"Think I'll go to Prague."

"I thought you were going to Chicago for the convention," I say.

52

"No point now," Tommy mumbles, reminding us that the cops didn't beat out all his brains when he got busted during a teen riot on the Sunset Strip a couple of years ago. "Gene McCarthy can't win it and Humphrey is a robot. Besides, Prague is the most happening place in the world."

"Exactly." Hope drains the last of her wine and refuses my father's attempt to refill her glass. "I think I'll rejoin the boycott."

"Sure?" he hides the label.

"Really," she says. "Three times no."

"Prague!" Nana says as if spitting out something she was choking on. "Czechoslovakia is a horrible place. Awful people. Short and shifty with crooked noses."

"That's Jews, Nana."

"Communists," she lets the word dangle as if it just came out of her nose.

"The Russians helped defeat the Nazis," I mention. World history is always good for stirring up controversy at the dinner table, and Mrs. Pinsky's talk at Hebrew school reminded me of something we want to forget: The enemy of my enemy was once my friend. "The Russians liberated Auschwitz, you know."

"Wonderful person, that Josef Stalin. A real mama's boy."

"The Czechs are creating Socialism with a human face." Hope says.

"Human face and Russian boots." Like Hope, Nana has strong views and doesn't mind sharing them. She ladles out amily banter served in the traditional manner: barbed and steaming.

"Ask the Vietnamese how they like American boots," Hope says. "I think Czechoslovakia's the only place on Earth with a shot at getting it right."

"They've got a shot at getting shot. What they'll get is a Soviet invasion." Nana isn't exactly lightening the mood. "Anyway, I'm sure you'll be a big hit over there."

"What she means is that you'll be the first black person they've ever seen," Tommy says with thick Germanic exaggeration.

"Did I say that? I didn't say that." Nana looks around the table. "Did I say that?"

"It's okay, Mrs. Strauss," Hope says, smiling. "I know your great-grandfather owned slaves."

"Slaves? He barely owned a silk worm."

Tommy stops drumming on the table for a second. I'm glad he's not teasing me anymore, but baiting Nana isn't much of an improvement. "Nana's voting for George Wallace."

"*Acch!* Enough nonsense. I'm not voting for anybody. Bunch of stinkers, all of them." Nana pronounces it *shtinkers*.

"If you don't vote, you can't complain," I say, happy to get a word in, even if it's stupid.

"Maybe our good friend LBJ will end the war on his way out of office." Pater knows Hope hates LBJ. She thinks he killed Kennedy. John Kennedy. Geez. Now when we talk about dead Kennedys we need to specify which one we mean.

"LBJ? Lint for Brains Johnson? That triple-chin redneck can't even win his own War on Poverty," Hope says.

Hope accepts a second piece of lemon sponge cake without negotiation. I don't have the heart to tell her that prune juice is the secret ingredient that makes it so moist. I feel good seeing Hope smile even if it's as thin as the powdered sugar Nana sprinkles on anything she doesn't smother in paprika. The cake absorbs our words, and for a while our mouths are too full to talk. Which is a good thing in this house.

After dinner, Nana enlists Tommy to help clear the table. Pater tells Hope she can stay with us if she needs a place to crash when she comes back from Czechoslovakia.

"You can stay here now," I say, not looking at my father for approval. I wish Hope would spend the summer at our house and not go to Prague. What's in Prague that we don't have in Laurel Canyon? If Hope just spent the summer here I'm sure she would fall in love with us. Maybe Pater could adopt her so I can have a big sister to beat up my dumb brother. Given enough time, I might even find a way to make her like Simon and Garfunkel.

But I know Hope is leaving. America has drained her batteries. She needs to recharge somewhere. Anywhere.

Seeing that Tommy's distracted with dishes, I follow Hope over to the record shelf.

"There's something I need you to take care of," she whispers to me, maintaining eye contact until satisfied that I'm really committed. She pretends to inspect and then slips an envelope into the Don Ho Christmas album. "In case I don't return."

"Okay," I say. At first, I feel drunk with happiness. Drunk as last Passover when I had four glasses of wine. But my happiness is quickly eaten by fear. What does she mean about not returning? Is someone out to get her? Is she planning on staying in Prague forever? Her eyes reveal nothing as I slip the record back among the others. "It's safe with me."

Hope nods and flops down on the couch and opens the copy of *Time* with a long-haired teenager in sunglasses on the cover. To drive home "The Generation Gap" headline, there's a reflection of his angry father in the lenses.

"What about the Beatles?" I plop down next to her. "Do you like the Beatles?"

"Navel gazers."

Mumu Marie
and the Man Who Cuts Legs Off

Banana Face Jane pushes her stingray up the street and clatters back downhill. She's got Ace playing cards clothes-pinned to her front forks so they snap and click loudly against the spinning spokes. Mary Jane, MJ, calls this her motorcycle, which would be cute if she weren't a buck-toothed fourteen-year-old who still rides with training wheels. Nana calls her a late bloomer.

A few of us have gathered across the street from my house, enjoying the cool cushion of Mumu Marie's Forbidden Front Lawn. Little Danny, Grumpy Chuck's grandson, slings insults as Banana Face clatters by. Our goal is to so enrage Mary Jane that she throws down her bike and chases us uphill. Only five years old and Danny already knows more cuss words than I do. It's a race to get MJ's goat before Mumu Marie chases us off this precious patch of spongy green dichondra.

Mumu Marie is the only person in the canyon with a front lawn, and she wages chemical and holy war against bugs, weeds, and kids to keep it groomed to irresistible perfection. Her lawn took years to perfect and requires eternal vigilance to defend. Last week, a bearded hippie leading a small lamb at the end of a rope hiked up our street and stopped to rest on the Forbidden Front Lawn. He was dressed like Jesus, but this didn't stop Mumu Marie, more Catholic than the Pope, from turning her sprinklers on him.

Pater said Marie should have treated that hippie better, just in case he was the second coming she always warns us about.

"Two donuts short of a dozen!" Little Danny yells as MJ clatters by. The other kids giggle. "Two eggs short of an omelet!"

I resist a sudden urge to feel sorry for her. I know it's bad to tease a late bloomer, but its summer and I'm bored.

Banana Face struggles uphill and then races down Wonderland Avenue with her pigtails and handlebar tassels flapping. She gets off the bike at the stop sign because the training wheels make it hard to turn around on the slope. MJ knows that if she ignores us long enough, Dialing for Dollars will break for commercial and Mumu Marie will come out to smoke a cigarette and give us the business.

"Banana Face, Banana Face, you just lost the human race!" Danny sings but in spite of his best efforts, Banana Face just rattles by again. The other kids lose interest and leave to destroy an anthill one of them found in the canyon. Their departure turns out to be perfectly timed.

"You should be ashamed of yourselves." Mumu Marie appears in a cloud of smoke that could choke a skunk. Pink curlers cling to her head like tentacles. A terrified little Jesus dangles on her shining crucifix, struggling in vain to avoid getting crushed between her big wobbling breasts. Mumu launches into some classic fire and brimstone, banishing all summer boredom as she fumbles around to find the sprinkler key. "Jesus will punish you in hell!" she shouts.

"Tell Jesus to turn on the sprinklers," I say. A flood is preferable to going to hell on a hot day, but we've hidden her long metal sprinkler key, so neither is likely.

Distracted by Mumu's cursing, I don't notice Mary Jane sneaking toward us. Late bloomer, maybe, but she was clever enough to ditch her noisy bike before creeping back uphill. She pounces on Little Danny just as Mumu locates the sprinkler key I stashed in her juniper.

"Your mother's a street walker!" Banana Face Jane mashes Little Danny's big head into the Forbidden Front Lawn.

Mumu spouts more hellfire and damnation because the God of her people seems more worried about crushed dichondra than a kid's broken neck. The Father, the Son, and The Angry Mumu wobble along the porch, zories flapping. She brandishes the metal sprinkler key like a royal scepter and curses our filthy souls.

Her loud phone rings before she reaches the edge of the porch, a miracle that probably needed both of our Gods to intervene.

"Marie, Marie! Dialing for Dollars is calling," I say, but she just gives me the finger and shouts that the Holy Ghost has special punishment reserved for Christ Killers. "I'm not afraid of ghosts," I say, but it's not true. Laurel Canyon is full of ghosts and I'm afraid of them all. "Better answer your phone in case today's your lucky day."

"Game shows are run by Jews," she says, slamming the screen door. "That's why good people never win." But torn between a chance to split our skulls or break the bank, she disappears into her living room to finish her TV dinner and kneel before the jackpot.

Once the threat of cracked skulls and hellfire has vanished, I turn my attention to prying MJ's mitts loose from Danny's neck. Fortunately, Danny's made of tougher stuff than the rest of us. A beating from MJ is a ticklefest compared to what his Grandpa Grumpy Chuck can dish out. He rolls across the lawn no worse for the wear and dances away laughing, while Mary Jane and I wrestle until she runs home in tears, covered with grass stains. Danny and I run downhill and stash her stingray behind a neighbor's hydrangea.

Ah, summer, how I love you. I hope every day will be this glorious.

"I gotta go home," Danny says.

"Wait! I got a secret mission for you, Danny boy. Chance to be a hero."

"You mean, like an astronaut?" Danny's pumpkin face lights up, front tooth missing, freckle farm on each cheek. He looks like Alfred E. Neuman.

"Better." He's torn between racing home for a lunch and finding out what historic caper I've got planned. When Mrs. Pinsky said there are still Nazis among us, I realized that one of my neighbors is one of them. With Danny's help, I will penetrate the armed and fortified bunker of Mr. Klaus Shreidermayer, aka Shreddermauler, aka the Man Who Cuts Legs Off, the Laurel Canyon Nazi.

The Man Who Cuts Legs Off got his nickname by threatening kids who walk tightrope-style along the low wooden fence in front of his house. He scares us so we make a game out of taunting him. I'm not sure where Shreddermauler is from, but he sounds German and my grandmother doesn't like him. In addition to threatening kids with amputation, Shredder drives a Volkswagen hatchback and has a nasty little schnauzer-poodle named Schnoodle. If that's not the profile of an ex-Nazi, I don't know what is.

The Man Who Cuts Legs Off is old enough to have been a German soldier. Maybe he loaded my grandfather, Otto Strauss, into a boxcar. Maybe he shot him. Nana knows from German records that my *Opa* was arrested and loaded onto an eastbound train, but even the meticulous Nazis have no record of what happened afterward. Maybe the brave soldier Shreddermauler threw my grandfather's half-dead body into a ditch along the railway line.

Shredder makes a point of keeping to himself, as if solitude could hide a horror show's worth of past crimes. No wonder

Nana Hannah avoids him. Maybe she thinks he's a Nazi. Soon I'll have proof.

Bringing a Nazi to justice will be the second biggest *mitzvah* in Jewish history. Busting a fugitive Nazi will make those other kids' Hadassah donations look like the Sunday funnies. When this story breaks, my hands will be immortalized in the Jewish section of Grauman's Chinese. Operation Pinsky is not without risk but "Danger" became my middle name when I realized that Klaus Shreidermayer was an escaped Nazi. My friend Mark the Mailman all but said so. Almost. At least, he's dropped some very clear hints, and I'm not stupid.

I like walking with Mark the Mailman in the summertime because he's the only adult besides life guards who can wear shorts at work. The other perk, for me at least, is that Mark knows everything about everyone in the neighborhood because he delivers their magazines, bills, and postcards.

Mark says that if he had been less of a goofball in high school, he would have gone to a better school than Da Nang University. Sometimes while we walk he tells me stories about lost patrols and tunnels full of Viet Cong. I'm still not sure if he's joking when he looks up into the trees and says, "If I'm ever hit, don't let Charlie rob the mail train."

In addition to the artists, musicians, and oddballs that live in Laurel Canyon, Mark says there are lots of lonely widows, though he's not talking about my grandmother. Besides, Nana fears men in uniforms and doesn't consider herself a widow. Not officially. She doesn't know what happened to Otto Strauss and often talks about my missing grandfather as if he's still alive. She believes, or wants to believe, that he survived somehow and is lost in the shadows behind the Berlin Wall. Mark's carried many of her letters of inquiry and delivered the disappointing responses to our door.

Still, Nana holds on to hope. She says hope makes us human.

Mark lets me push the mail cart even though it's against regulations for civilians to handle the post. It's probably against regulations for Mark to smoke pot in his mail truck, too, but tidbits of gossip about the neighbors buys my silence. The more Mark smokes, the more he talks, which is how I got the poop on Shreddermauler.

It turns out that the Man Who Cuts Legs Off gets a letter from Germany on the first day of every month. Mailman Mark says the envelope and return address look official, which can mean only one thing: Shreddermauler is still on the fatherland's payroll. I need to get my hands on one of these letters. Since I can't rob the mail truck, I decided to sneak into Shredder's bunker to find the smoking Luger.

I spent the first few weeks of summer watching Shreddermauler. He's almost a hermit so I came up with a plan worthy of "Mission Impossible." He never leaves his house except to take his dog out for a poop, and these excursions don't leave me enough time to poke around the grounds.

Earlier today, I snuck along the ravine and fed Schnoodle some Ex-Lax through a break in the back fence. I figured, rightly so, that the fat old pooch would gobble the sausage and not notice the surprise inside. Once the laxative hit, Schnoodle got sick and Shreddermauler raced off to the vet.

D-day.

Little Danny is small enough to fit through the doggie flap and spring the inside lock to Shreddermauler's back door. He's also young enough to do anything an older kid tells him. When the kitchen door creaks open I step inside the dark house. I walk lightly across the linoleum in case it's booby-trapped. The yellow beam of my flashlight sweeps across Shreddermauler's well-stocked wet bar.

61

"Screwdriver? Harvey Wallbanger?" Danny often mixes drinks for his grandfather's poker buddies. When Grumpy Chuck wins big, Danny gets off without a beating. Old Chuck once told me that Danny makes a perfect martini. He also said that early morning is the best time to drink because "that's when you're still sober."

Danny's mother, Carly, flew the coop after Chuck slapped her once too often. Somehow, in her haste to escape, she left her son behind. Maybe she forgot giving birth to him since she was barely sixteen at the time. If anyone knows where the kid's father is, they aren't saying. Mumu Marie once said that Grumpy Chuck was Danny's dad but that makes no sense at all. When she's not quoting the Bible, Marie gets her facts from the National Enquirer.

Girl Gives Birth to Own Grandmother! Preacher Explodes During Sermon! Martians Invade Laurel Canyon and Nobody Notices!

We've got an hour at most to ransack SS headquarters and find the smoking guns before Shredder returns with his Nazi lapdog. Danny looks under the furniture and through the lower cabinets; I peek behind a painting of a clipper ship, thumb through some books and feel along the walls for any secret compartments.

"Wow!" Danny says, waving a sketchbook. A loose page falls to the green carpet. "He draws pictures."

"Not what we're after." The problem with kids is that they're so young. Hard to keep them focused on the mission. "Remember: we're trying to find soldier stuff. Gold coins. Maps. Dead people."

"Neat-o!"

I look through some bills and envelopes on the kitchen table but can't find any letters from Germany. A copy of *Life* magazine with pictures of James Earl Ray and Sirhan—"The

Two Accused"—on the cover makes me cringe. Are these Shredder's heroes?

"Hey!" I whisper to Danny and place a shushing finger over my lips. There's a noise beneath the house, something or someone in the crawl space. I hold my breath and concentrate for a few seconds, but it sounds more like a skunk than the boa constrictor Grumpy Chuck claims to have turned loose a couple of years ago.

The curtains are drawn but sunlight sneaks in around the edges and reflects green off the curved old Zenith television in the corner. Dust motes drift like fish food in an aquarium. A dark couch, an easy chair with matching footrest— the place seems normal except for one thing: no records. No hi-fi. Not even a radio. This is a house without music. A house, Nana would say, without a soul.

We work our way to the bedroom where I check under the mattress and ferret through a chest of drawers. I'm hoping to find an old uniform, a snapshot or medal. Maybe Hitler wrote him a personal commendation for letting a boxcar stuffed with starving Jews die of "natural causes." Maybe my grandfather was one of them.

I'm starting to worry about the time. How long have we been in this dark old house? I need proof and I need it now. Something to show that the old Kraut once separated the weak from the strong, extracted gold fillings with needle-nosed pliers, or cut legs off for gruesome experiments like the so-called "doctor" in the Auschwitz documentary.

My heart skips a beat when the house creaks, shifting in the heat. I listen for another few seconds, but all I hear is the whistle of a Helms bakery truck making its daily rounds. If we can get out of here quickly, I'll buy Danny a glazed donut.

But Shreddermauler is too smart to leave a smoking gun in plain view. A quick pass through the obvious hiding places

63

turns up nothing but socks and underwear. I shine my flashlight into the bedroom closet and find a few skinny old ties hanging alongside some gray slacks and white shirts. Black V-neck sweaters, no turtlenecks. He seems to live in a world before color, either the most boring man alive or a master of dull disguise.

I scan the corners with my light. Say what you want about this murderer, he keeps a clean closet. Not even a cobweb. I'm about to give up when I notice a trap door to the attic.

Bingo.

"Up you go, Danny boy. Up, up and away!"

Danny scales the shelves like a monkey. He pushes open the hatch and climbs into the secret abyss. I pass him the flashlight, and a second later, his round face peeks back at me from above. "It's scary up here."

"Be brave like Tom Terrific."

"It's hot."

"Hurry, then."

I stay busy below but there's nothing in the hamper but undershirts and towels. Nothing in the linen closet but sheets. The bathroom cabinet looks like a commercial for Pepsodent.

I can hear Danny crawling around in the attic. It doesn't sound like he's finding anything bigger than a termite. We're running out of time, and I'm running out of patience. I know this man is a Nazi. Why won't he just admit it and face the oompah music? I shuffle back into the living room and nearly trip over the sketchbook that Danny dropped. Kids! Why can't they ever clean up after themselves? I gather the scattered pages absentmindedly until one catches my eye and I realize these drawings might be what I'm looking for. This is not a collection of landscapes and fruit bowls. These sketches are snapshots from a guilty man's conscience. Soldiers. Fires. Fear. Lacking photos to celebrate his Nazi deeds, Shreddermauler reproduced them from memory.

Mitzvah accomplished. Almost.

I hear a car pull into the driveway. Shreidermayer's VW hatchback sputters and falls silent. The car door slams. Schnoodle yaps at the front door. The key is turning.

Why are Germans always early?

I can't leave Danny stranded in the attic but if I stay here, we'll both get caught. I told Danny to be brave, now I have to run. If Shreddermauler finds Danny, off go the legs. If he doesn't, the kid will bake in the summer heat. Either way, Grumpy Chuck will finish off whatever Shreddermauler leaves behind.

I know what my father will say if I get caught, if I get arrested, if they throw me in the slammer. He'll say, "How could you do this to your Grandmother?" or "Don't you think she's had enough pain in her life without you adding more?" Pater's number one rule is that we are not allowed to cause his mother any grief. She's suffered enough. Anything I feel like complaining about is a drop in the ocean compared to what Nana's lived through. As long as she remains silent about her scars, I can't *kvetch* about my scrapes and scratches. Nana's tough, but my getting caught red-handed robbing a neighbor's house will push her over the edge.

I debate grabbing the sketch book but it's too big to hide so I grab the fallen page and stuff it in my back pocket. I toss the book onto the living room table. It seems to hover for a second, held aloft by the breeze from the opening door. I need to run, but time freezes long enough for me to notice the TV *Guide* with Barbara Eden from *I Dream of Jeannie* on the cover. If I had a genie, I'd burn all three wishes to get us out of here alive.

Do I abandon Danny or add my legs to Shreddermauler's bone pile? Do I send my grandmother to an early grave? Am I an eagle or a duck? Given the choice between heroism and survival, I sprout chicken wings, fly through the kitchen and pretend to be entering by the back door just as Shredder enters through the front.

"A raccoon, a raccoon!" I shout loud enough to startle the old man and alert Danny that the jig is up. "A raccoon in your house!"

Schnoodle races in barking and snapping. He recognizes me as the source of this morning's misery.

"*Vat de chell are you doink here?*" Shredder says. He sounds just like the little German soldier on "Laugh-In" who doesn't know the war is over.

"I saw a raccoon in the canyon." I'm scared to the point of puking but this wild fib is all that stands between me and never standing again. My Vulcan side is nowhere to be found. I think I hear Danny lower the trap door to the attic, but I don't know which side of it he's on.

"It went through your yard and jumped through the doggy door."

"You little liar!" Shreddermauler isn't buying it. "I should cut your leg off for this."

Leg. Singular. At least I'll be able to hop away. I inch backward down the steps and bump into Danny, who has just materialized behind me. He really is Tom Terrific. Cat burglar. Bartender. Banana Face-heckler. This kid has real talent. Danny reaches down to calm Schnoodle and looks up at Shreddermauler as if this is just another summer day on Wonderland Avenue. "Raccoons eat dog food. Haven't you noticed dog food missing lately?"

"Raccoons!" I say. "Raccoons are thieves."

"You are thieves!" Shreddermauler stumbles toward us, gray hands twitching like crab claws. None of his steak knives looked big enough to cut my leg off, but I don't want to wait

66

around and find out what else he's got. "I suppose the raccoon just opened the door and let you in?"

"I followed him in!" For a split second, Danny seems innocent as a kitten.

"Danny is the bravest kid I've ever seen," I say. It's true, but not for this reason. He's brave for surviving his drunk, violent grandfather. He's brave for waiting on the corner every night in case his AWOL mother happens to street-walk by. He's brave for having escaped from Shreddermauler's hot attic. "Danny chased that raccoon around your house and back out the door. He's ..."

"Tom Terrific!"

"Get the hell out of here," Shreddermauler yells. "Never come back or I'll—"

"—CUT OUR LEGS OFF!" We run laughing across the steep backyard, legs intact. I give Danny a one-up over the fence and we disappear into the ravine like Secret Squirrel and Mighty Mouse.

Shredder shouts something at us in German that sounds like, "Go poop in the ocean and wipe your butt with a bubble," but the curse lasts so long that I'm out of range by the time it ends.

"Gotta go!" Danny panics. He's late for lunch, a major sin. Getting strangled by Mary Jane or chopped to bits by Shreddermauler is nothing compared to what Grumpy Chuck can do with a leather belt.

"See you later," I say. If I had one wish left, I'd find Danny a better home. "Good job, Tom Terrific."

With any luck, and Danny's overdue for some, Grumpy Chuck will be snoring on his La-Z-Boy when the kid sneaks back into their old log cabin. Chuck claims that his father, Great Grandpa Grumpy, built the house with his bare hands back when Laurel Canyon was crawling with wildlife and mountain men. Danny says Chuck still hunts 'possum in the canyon.

Danny's shriveled old granny is from some dusty place where ladies carry a full glass of "refreshment" at all times. She always reeks of perfume and booze. Her white hair is stacked in a glowing pile atop her tiny, twitching head. Granny rarely says anything because Grumpy is dumb and opinionated enough for the both of them.

Nana Hannah won't allow me inside their house. She's opposed to drunks, guns, and child beaters. This summer she's been sneaking snacks and praises to Danny. She says he's a sweet, unlucky kid and that God will take care of him.

I hope she's right. God needs to act soon before Grumpy Chuck goes too far. God must see that Danny deserves better than to be raised by hillbillies. If only Danny's mother hadn't run away. If only his grandparents didn't beat him. If only God was paying attention.

The Mamas & the Nanas

I run home hoping Shreddermauler will let the incident pass. Little Danny is too young to be tried as an adult, but I'm old enough to have known better than to break into a neighbor's house. Nana will be brokenhearted. Pater will never forgive me. If old Shredder presses charges, I'll live out my days breaking rocks on the chain gang.

But instead of a black–and–white–with–a–cherry–on–top police cruiser, there's a green dune buggy in our driveway. The "Stop the War" bumper sticker could be an undercover cop's attempt at a disguise, but the tie-dyed scarf wrapped around the roll bar seems a bit too playful for the LAPD.

I don't want Nana to notice my post-robbery jitters, so I take time to inspect the magical car and give my hummingbird heart a few measures to tick back to *allegro non troppo*. I'm soon relieved to hear Tommy's muffled thumping in the garage. His back beat gradually overcomes the sound of my own pounding pulse.

The buggy's tiger-striped interior looks like a booth from Sambo's restaurant. The steering wheel is a peace sign, and the 100-mph speedometer suggests this jalopy is packing more horses than the Wild Wild West. I can't resist climbing into the front seat to pretend I'm zipping through the asteroid belt. The dashboard trim glows as if painted with radium.

The old Blue Bomber pulls up the driveway just as I round Jupiter. It's a hot day, and, lacking air conditioning, Pater's got the windows rolled down and the radio set to the station that

69

plays all news, bad news, all the time. A thin layer of dust coats the windshield.

"Greetings, earthling!"

"Nice car. A real creampuff. Did one of Danny's little Hot Wheels grow up?" It's one of those Pater questions for which no answer is needed. What he's really asking is what the deuce I'm doing in this little green coupe.

I notice Mumu Marie across the street, crouching over the microscopic weeds that threaten her front lawn. She's watching us from the corner of her eye, no doubt adding the candy-apple-green metal flake freakmobile to her list of grievances against my family. I wonder if she's already told Nana about the Banana Face incident.

The Bomber's back seat is filled with brown paper bags which I must help unload. "Arms out, Beetle Bailey," he says, which is what he calls me when issuing orders. Pater loads me with grocery bags. I trudge up to the front door and kick it open with such authority that the cabin shakes like a wet dog. Shuffling into the front room, I nearly trip over three women sprawled on their bellies across the knotty pine floorboards.

"Up!" My grandmother commands. She arches her back and raises her head and feet into the air. "Hold!" The other two try to maintain the position but the bigger gal crumbles quickly. Nana remains rigid until the skinny lady with the long blond ponytail wobbles and flops. "Down!"

Fatty groans. Skinny exhales loudly. Nana sits up and points to her abdomen. "We are strengthening our diaphragms," she says. Except that she says it like, "*Ve are scthr-r-r-eng-ten-ning our di-ah-fr-r-rams.*"

"Every girl needs a strong diaphragm," the blonde says.

"I'll stick with the pill," the big one says, laughing at a joke I don't understand. She rolls over onto her back and smiles like someone who expects me to recognize her. "Hey, kiddo! Anything good in those bags? I've got the munchies."

"Tang. Fritos. Cap'n Crunch."

"Max! We don't eat that junk," Nana says.

"Too bad." The big woman looks like the host of a kid show I used to watch.

I navigate my load around the corner to the kitchen and root through the bags to see if there's anything interesting beside the wholesome squirrel food Nana feeds us. Sure enough, Pater snuck in a packet of Fiddle Faddle. I hide the snack under the sink where my brother won't find it and hurry back to figure out why Nana is rolling around on the floor with two hippie chicks.

"Good, Joni," Nana Hannah says to the blonde. Except that it sounds like, "*Goot, Choni*." Pater came to America young enough to lose his accent, but my grandmother's is so thick she could star on "Hogan's Heroes." "Now sing!"

The big woman has given up, but Joni is still practicing the breathing exercise on the floor. She holds the arched position and tries to hold a note but it doesn't last long before she slumps back to the floor and looks up with sky-blue eyes.

I forget all about being a Vulcan and fall into the hole my mother left behind. I want my father to marry Joni. Right now.

"It's like yoga for the voice," the big one says. Have I seen her on the "Smothers Brothers" show?

"*Stimmt!*" Nana says, forgetting that some Californians don't speak German.

"That means 'right' or 'exactly'," I say, showing off for Joni. I've seen her buying cigarettes at the canyon store. She looks like a hippie fashion model, but I guess she's also a singer. I hear muffled tom-tom rolls coming from the garage. As long as Tommy stays in his groove, he'll stay out of mine. I want Joni all for myself.

71

"Come on, Cassie," Joni says. "Give it another try, Mama."

Cassie. Mama. Now I know. The big woman is Cass Elliot of The Mamas & the Papas. Tommy saw them last summer in Monterey. Next to The Byrds, who he also saw at the pop festival, they are the biggest rock group this canyon's ever known.

My wiry little grandmother looks smaller than a pickled herring next to Mama Cass. Nana calls her Naomi for some reason and encourages another go at the diaphragm exercise.

"Arghh!" Mama Cass rolls onto her ample belly but can't even raise her ankles. "Sorry, but I'm built for comfort."

Joni takes the cue and starts singing an old blues song. Naomi, Cass, or whatever her real name is, picks joins in with enough power to vibrate the floorboards. We're soon in earthquake territory.

As he passes through the room carrying the grocery bags I've long since forgotten, my father, a cantor's grandson, scats a coda in his best Louis Armstrong voice.

Cass laughs and gathers Joni into a hug, and they help each other up from the floor. Nana applauds and the canyon ladies— rock star and goddess—laugh like little girls. Nana puts her hand on Joni's stomach. "This is where good singing strength comes from."

"In that case," Cass rubs her tummy, "I don't need a microphone."

I'm suddenly aware that Tommy's drumming has stopped. *Please God, don't let him come in here and ruin everything.* He can have the Fiddle Faddle. I don't want to share this perfect moment.

"Hold this note." Nana sings a tone that would be at home around middle C on the nearby piano.

Cass, clearly a rebel, sings a folky harmony which could have easily gone bluegrass until Joni adds a nearby note that

72

moves the chord in a darker direction. Cass drops into bass and our living room feels like the inside of a speaker cabinet. When Joni runs out of wind, it becomes a contest between Mama Cass and grandmama Strauss to see who can hold out the longest. They lock eyes and hold their tones until Nana gets louder just to drive home who rules the musical roost.

"How do you do that?" Mama Cass gasps for breath.

Nana's not winded at all. "When you sing from your diaphragm, it's like having an endless reservoir to draw from." Except, of course, she says this with her heavy accent which, added to the fact that she just outlasted the younger women, adds a bit of don't-argue-with-the-Valkyrie authority. "That exercise will help you build strength."

"It's also a great way to polish the floor," Pater says. He's back with the last grocery bag. "You're welcome to practice here anytime."

Cass ignores my silly father. "That was a nice harmony you were singing, Joni."

Joni grabs my nearby guitar, a piece of junk that Pater bought in Tijuana. She retunes it to some eerie open chord, and she sings a few notes that weave between the vibrating strings. My inner Vulcan goes up in smoke, and I realize two things: One, she is the most beautiful woman I have ever seen. And, two, she isn't human. Joni is perfection from another world. She is all that is flawless and too angelic for this foolish planet. She would be a perfect big sister. I'm happy she hasn't noticed my un-cool clarinet sitting on the piano bench.

Joni strums a haunting chord that can't decide if it's major or minor. She frets a couple of positions, gets a pattern rolling off her long, perfect fingers, and chants an odd melody while looking off into a dimension where sound exists independent of time and space.

"You have a good ear," Nana says. "Interesting voicings."

73

"I had polio as a kid," Joni says, waving a left arm that looks perfect to me. "I always found normal chords uncomfortable to play."

"You still don't play by the rules," Cass says.

"That's the pot calling the kettle!" Joni laughs and tosses back her ponytail. She strums a bit and chants a melody that sounds like a prayer.

"I'd love to have you join my temple choir," Nana says and looks at me. "You would make God smile on Yom Kippur."

"Religion's not my bag, but Cassie's Jewish." Joni laughs. Big white teeth. High cheekbones. Shiksa goddess. California perfection.

"I'm an atheist, thank God," Cass says.

"If it wasn't for God, atheists would have nothing to believe in." Nana has an endless supply of Old World wisdom, but I haven't heard this one before.

Cass Elliot has the most contagious laugh I've ever heard. It emerges from deep inside her and overflows like champagne. There's no way not to laugh along when she lets loose. By the time the giggling stops, I've moved her to the top of my list of replacement mother candidates. Pater should marry her. Now.

"Here's another tuning I like." Joni diddles with the low strings and then tries to wind up the high E, but it snaps with a sharp thwack. "Oops," she says. "I'm sorry, sweetie."

What I want to say is "If you convince Cass to marry my father, you can cut those strings to ribbons." But I manage to get ahold of my runaway thoughts and repeat one of Nana's one-liners. "If a string breaks, don't fret it."

"I'll tune the rest of the strings to an open G." Joni fiddles with the tuners and then strums a folksy sounding chord. "Now you can play like Keith Richards. You know who he is, don't you?"

She doesn't wait for an answer. Which is merciful because I was about to reveal my complete ignorance by saying he plays with The Mamas & The Papas until I realized that she's strumming a Rolling Stones tune on the five-string guitar.

"Five strings, three fingers, one *putz*," Cass says.

"Cass!" Joni feigns embarrassment. Her big teeth shine like stars. "There's a rabbi present."

"Part-time Cantor," Nana says. "Like rabbi, but more fun. As penance, you now have to sing with my temple choir."

"*Shemah Yisroyel!*" Cass belts out two of the six words in the most important prayer in all of Judaism, the affirmation that there is only one God and he likes us best. "Sorry, baby. That's all I've got."

"You could do a Jewish version of 'California Dreamin'." Pater has been listening from the kitchen doorway. He breaks into a thick Yiddish accent and sings, "*Schlepped* into a *schul*, I found along the way…"

"Nice," Cass says. She and the goddess are now halfway out the door "Thanks for the voice lesson, Mrs. Strauss."

"Hannah. Call me Hannah."

"I'm going to spend more time on my tummy," Joni says.

"Singing, not sleeping, *dah-link*," Nana says.

I hear the dune buggy's motor choke and idle. A minute later, someone slips a record album through the gap at the bottom of our front door. It's got a "Demo – Not for Sale" sticker and hand-drawn picture of Joni on the cover. I slap it on the turntable and wait for the amplifier tubes to glow.

~ ~ ~

Later that night, I'm up in my loft, lying in bed listening to my transistor radio. Wolfman Jack is broadcasting on XERB from Tijuana, spinning records, selling miracle cures and howling like a man who gargles with fishhooks and razor blades. I'm trying to replay the Shreddermauler incident, but it's already hazy in my head.

Then I remember the sketch that I stole. I climb down from my loft at the tip of our A-frame and find it in the back pocket of the pants I threw on the floor. I climb up to my crow's nest and pull out the flashlight I keep in case of earthquake, fire, or nuclear war. The sketch is a pencil drawing of soldiers gathered outside a burning house with broken windows. Light from the flames reveals the scared face of a kid hiding behind a tree. Smoke and shadow mix in a fearsome cloud.

I want to believe that Shreddermauler is one of the soldiers but the more I stare at his sketch, the more something nags at me. What if he's not one of the soldiers? What if he's the victim? What if he's the kid hiding from the soldiers? I yank my earphone out by the wire and sit up on the edge of my bed. If Mr. Shreidermayer is a good guy, then my big *mitzvah* just went down the toilet.

But Shreddermauler can't be a good guy. He drives a VW. He has a nasty little S.S. lapdog. If he's so innocent, why does he keep to himself, alone and angry in a house without light or music? Why does he plant spiny cactus around his bunker? What about those letters from Germany the mailman told me about? And why threaten to cut off our legs? Where does an idea like that even come from?

I can still hear static and the Wolfman howling through the dangling plastic ear phone. Music pulsing from a rebel station. Songs about cars, school, money and girls. Songs about freedom. Songs of peace and protest. The summer soundtrack of 1968 is blasting over the airwaves, but for some reason I've still got the Voice of America from 1942 bouncing around in my skull.

The year is more than half over. Why I am still locked in the past? The Holocaust was twenty-five years ago. Why am I lost in its shadow? Shreidermayer was thirty, maybe thirty-five when the war ended. He's not the kid in the picture, but that doesn't mean he's the soldier.

I needed him to be guilty. I wanted to condemn him. I wanted him to hang, but the only thing hung is my own personal jury.

Tomorrow I'll start raising money for Hadassah.

Jail Bait

I've got my ears stuffed with toilet paper and my head jammed inside a kick drum. I'm helping my brother, Tommy, test and adjust his new double bass pedal, the one I helped to make for his eighteenth birthday. His band, Jail Bait, is practicing later today.

"Kick it again," I shout and receive a round of chest-compressing triplets in response. Tommy thumps joyously while I watch the throbbing mallets beat on the vibrating skin.

"Anybody home?" Tommy's grasping the power of double bass. With my head in the drum he's grasping that power too well. "Are you still down there?"

"Sounds like thunder." I extract my face from the line of fire before my skull implodes. "Now move your flat feet so I can mark the pedal settings."

"I wish my feet were flat," Tommy says. "With flat feet I could 4-F right out of the army."

"Pity you have no physical disabilities, Tom-tom."

"I have you, Maxine."

"Too bad the draft board doesn't give deferments for above-average siblings. Now stop moving your stinking feet or I'll cut your toes off." I can't believe I'm almost quoting Mr. Shreidermayer.

Tommy cooperates barely long enough for me to scratch a couple of tick marks that capture the settings we've been working on all morning.

This double bass birthday pedal was hatched in the workshop where Carlito hides from his wife, Mumu Marie.

When I'm not wandering the canyons or spying on ex-Nazis, Carlito's shop is my favorite place to visit. He's a machinist at the General Motors plant out beyond the Van Nuys airport. Unlike my dad, Carlito's handy and knows how to make stuff.

I smuggled one of Tommy's old single-mallet pedals out of the garage and snuck past Mumu Marie. She disapproves of the shop with its noisy machines and Snap-on Tools girlie calendars where Carlito spends his free time avoiding her and making Hopi Kachina dolls. Marie says that the Kachina dolls are abominations unto the Lord. Idolatry, pure and simple. If Jesus wasn't always watching, Mumu would probably strangle Carlito with her rosary.

When the two of them argue, which is often, it's loud enough for the whole canyon to hear. Ozzie and Harriet they're not.

I like watching Carlito work. I like watching the beechwood spirals fall from his lathe as the Hopi gods emerge. He talks a lot about growing up in New Mexico, which Marie says is like growing up Okie with taco sauce. She says Mexicans aren't real Catholics and that Jesus will punish them for believing in magic. I don't understand why Mumu's heaven depends on sending everyone else to hell.

Carlito made me wear goggles when he cut the steel for Tommy's pedal. He says that his milling machine is accurate to a thousandth of an inch — overkill for rock and roll, but Tommy appreciates the workmanship. My brother's a precision player, not one of those boneheads who drums like a wind-up bear.

I've learned to keep Tommy's equipment adjusted because the thought, no, fear of being a pipsqueak whiz kid at my father's high school has me considering all possible escape routes. In case high school doesn't work out, Plan B is to become a roadie. Running away with a travelling band sounds a lot better than being a pintsized genius in a teenage freak show.

79

Crisscrossing the nation in a thundering eighteen wheeler, yakking on the C.B. radio, eating toast and crispy bacon at truck stops sounds a million times more fun than cramming for a math test.

I'll keep the band's equipment in shape so they can get lost in the music instead of being distracted by blown tubes and wobbly hi-hats. I'll keep the Doctor Pepper cold and deal harshly with any promoter who shortchanges us. The band is called Jail Bait for a reason, so I will protect them from jiggly teenyboppers and would-be groupies.

Once again, the truth is that I was born too late. I'm about five years too young to hit the road. The redwood forests and the New York islands will have to wait until I'm old enough to hobo it. In the meantime, I can help Tommy get his gear set up right and hope the gigs go well.

I'm too young to enter the dens of iniquity where music is played. Only on rare occasions am I allowed to see his shows. I'm condemned to wait in the kitchen and have my hair tousled by mini-skirted waitresses in go-go boots. One time at the Whisky, I snuck out into the crowd just as a barefoot hippie girl stole a beer, downed it in one gulp and danced on stage.

It probably helped to be drunk at that show because Jail Bait's music is too weird to decipher sober. The only reason any club gives Jail Bait an opening slot is that Tommy has earned a few favors sitting in as a substitute drummer for bands with last-minute personnel problems. By that, I mean last-minute drummer problems. Tommy may be the only drummer in L.A. who isn't a complete flake, but he's still young, so give him time.

Drummers are people who like to hit things with sticks, which is why so many are in jail. Guitarists are a dime a dozen, but good drummers will always be in short supply. If Tommy can stay out of Vietnam, he'll never run out of gigs.

80

If he can make it to twenty-one without being arrested, the Sunset Boulevard riot incident will be stricken from his permanent record. Tommy almost lost this battle when he was accused of arson a few weeks ago. It wasn't his fault, but he was the only one old enough to face charges when the band performed in floor-length Lady Godiva wigs at Gazzarri's. This was supposed to be some kind of commentary on hippie hair run amok, but the stage almost caught fire when Tommy's wig flew into a hot floor light.

Fortunately, the fry cook knew how to use a fire extinguisher. The crowd remained calm because they were too stoned to understand that the smoke and flames weren't part of the show. Jail Bait is now banned from Gazzarri's, but the surviving members claim that gig is the stuff of legend.

The Rock and Roll Treehouse

I'm throwing a worn tennis ball against the garage door, trying to get my brother's attention while he practices rolls and paradiddles, drumming with headphones on.

I chuck a smooth fastball, one so straight and solid it could have spared me the shame of being picked last for every team sport requiring mastery of round objects. My one perfect pitch smacks the strike zone right in between backbeats. All at once, the drumming stops and Tommy disengages from behind the used Slingerland kit he bought with last year's session money.

"Stee-rike three! You're outta there!" I shout, but Tommy is squinting into the daylight and doesn't even see me. The best pitch in the history of baseball goes unnoticed.

Tommy walks out into the scrubby hillside known as our backyard. He disappears through a missing plank in the back fence without acknowledging me. In spite of the teasing and torture he subjects me to, when it comes to letting Tommy run wild in the woods, I am my brother's keeper. If it weren't for me, he would have been eaten by coyotes a long time ago.

"Where ya going, Doctor Traps?" I catch up easily because he's standing still. I grab a handful of acorns and toss a few into the underbrush to scare away squirrels that coyotes might find appetizing. Grumpy Chuck has shot all but the meanest possums in the canyon, but I toss another acorn just to be sure.

"Can you hear it?" Tommy asks.

"No, but I know a gopher who can really dig it." I listen for a second, but despite playing loud music his hearing exceeds a dog's. So does his near-complete lack of common sense.

Ignoring the possibility of rattlers, Tommy picks his way through the chaparral and down to the arroyo, which hasn't seen water since January.

"What's the scene, Jelly Bean? What's the plan, little man?"

Tommy shushes me. Which is good advice. Whatever he is listening for won't include rattlesnakes. I remain on red alert, tossing acorns onto the trail ahead while he tracks whatever his fruit-bat sonar has locked onto.

Tommy's head pivots and scans. Still ignoring me, he locks on to a signal and heads up toward Lookout Mountain, where the musicians and crazy people live. On still nights I can hear jangly guitars and strained falsettos drifting down the hill, but today, *nada*. As we ascend single-file along a deer trail, I begin to hear the prey Tommy seeks. The soft, distant tinkle of what sounds like a lost ice cream truck draws us forward.

Tommy runs ahead, but I'm distracted by a rustling behind us. It could be a falling branch or a feral cat, but it might also be the coyote that's been trying to catch me since I was knee high. I gather a fistful of stones and pepper the brush to let all intruders know that I'm the one to be feared.

"Ouch!" Little Danny emerges from behind a bush. He's rubbing his head where one of my stones connected with his round noggin.

"Why are you following us?"

Danny shrugs and skips up the trail. He has a new welt on his arm.

"How'd you get that one?" I ask, but I already know his answer will be a variation of "I bumped into something," or "I don't remember." The truth is that Grumpy Chuck probably beat him with a belt or a switch or whatever else was handy.

"Where ya goin'?" he asks.

"I was following Tommy until you tried to bushwhack us." I feel bad about having hit him with a rock. He probably thinks the whole world is allowed to beat him. "Now I don't know which way he went."

"I know," Dan says. He heads up the trail and takes the left fork. "He's going to the rope swing house."

We emerge onto a hillside above the old Tom Mix cabin, across the street from the haunted ruin where Houdini's mansion once stood. We sneak under an old wooden fence, avoid a patch of poison oak, and descend toward a noisy and colorful garden party.

Living in the canyon has made me immune to the strong, crisp Vicks Vaporub aroma of pine and eucalyptus, but today I'm hit with the sweet smell of night blooming jasmine in broad daylight. I sniff a bit more and detect wisps of incense smoke rising through the laurel and sage.

We scramble down a hillside pockmarked with caves. Caves with hippies in them. Nana Hannah says the hippies are the Thirteenth Tribe of Israel. Pater says if that's true, Laurel Canyon must be Mt. Sinai. I say a burning bush is the last thing we need on this dry hillside. God, if you're still out there, please send rain.

There's music coming from the house, so it's a safe bet Tommy's already inside.

A topless chick wearing nothing but hip huggers and a peacock feather earring waves to us. The earring and everything else about her is big enough to see from a distance. The breeze rustles a big sycamore, sending dappled light strobing over her bare torso. She's in her late teens and looks a lot like Annie, our former baby sitter who transformed overnight from upstanding Catholic girl to under-aged groupie. Maybe it was Annie I saw the other day riding shotgun in that rock star's convertible.

"Danny?" A curly-haired gal approaches us from the patio. She's wearing what must be a home-made dress that looks like a

84

giant coffee sack. Danny ignores her and wanders over to play on the rope swing.

I notice a group of nude sunbathers lying like spokes of a wheel with flowers piled at the hub. A human mandala? The wheel of karma? God's giant donut? Like much of what passes for normal in Laurel Canyon, it probably seemed like a good idea at the time

"Danny, it's me!" The coffee sack bears the word *"mala,"* a Spanish warning that this girl might be evil. Danny fears no evil, but I still want to protect him. "Who's that?" I ask.

"My mom." Danny mutters as he swings by me.

I don't recognize her, but then nobody's seen Carly, Grumpy Chuck's daughter, in a couple of years. She wasn't a hippie at the time, but, then again, neither was anyone else. Danny must have been three or four when she disappeared, younger than I was when my mom went to Jesus. We have missing moms in common, but like Danny's welts and bruises, we never talk about it.

Tom Mix, the old silent film star, must be rolling in his grave as the music from inside his cabin gets louder and weirder. It sounds like a battle of Teen Fair bands with everyone playing at once. I'm torn between looking for Tommy and standing guard over Danny in case his supposed mother is having a bad trip.

"Excuse me, Miss." I want to ask her a question that only Carly would know. Like, why did you abandon your kid to his psycho grandfather?

"Hi, Maxie!" She flashes me a gray-toothed smile, free of guile and orthodontia.

Knowing my name seems as good a proof as any that it's really Carly underneath those wild curls. Grumpy Chuck's wayward daughter is not much older than Tommy, but she looks to have aged ten years in the last two.

"Honey, Mommy's almost ready to take you back."

"Go away!" Danny keeps swinging, avoiding eye contact the way kids do when trying to hide their feelings. I can see that he's about to cry.

"C'mon, sweetie." There's just enough gravity for a tear to fall.

Danny turns his face and keeps swinging. He didn't ask to be her son, and Carly didn't ask to get pregnant. He's an old man's punching bag. She's a flower child in a coffee sack without a penny or a plan.

"Danny, come here," I say. He stops swinging and slouches over to where we're standing. "You never told me your mom was up here."

"Nobody can know," he whispers.

"Why the secret?"

Danny looks away.

"I'm so happy you found your mother," I say, but my train of thought derails. I wish I could find my mother. Staying mad at her is the only way to prevent hurt from taking over. Carly may be flakey, but at least she wants to be with her kid. "Aren't you happy to see her? Why is your mom a secret?"

"Because," Carly says, "we're all just a little bit afraid of Grandpa, aren't we, honey?"

Danny's nose drips. "Says he'll kill us."

"Now, honey, we know Grandpa doesn't mean that," Carly says without conviction.

"He hates everybody except John Wayne." Danny's moist eyes soften. "I wish I was John Wayne."

"Just a little while longer, honey. I'll have you out of there soon," she says. "Can I push you on the rope swing now?"

Instead of enjoying a mother-and-child moment, Danny runs downhill and races into the cabin.

Carly drops into a squat. She pulls her arms inside her dress and starts to cry. "I don't know what to do."

I don't know what to do either, but that's never stopped me before. Standing around listening to Carly cry isn't making things better. I'm on the verge of crying, too. Nana says tears spoil the soup, which is why she never cries. Nana ran out of tears a long time ago. Poor Carly. I never imagined that motherhood could bring such heartache. I crouch besides the slumping sack and pat what I think is Carly's back. "We'll figure something out."

"Don't tell Chuck you saw me here."

"Don't worry."

"Worry? That's all I do these days. Promise not to tell Chuck. Promise?"

"Okay."

"No. Cross your heart. Say it!"

"Cross my heart, hope to die, stick a needle in my eye."

When is a promise not a promise? Would Danny be better off living in this hippie commune with Carly than remaining at the mercy of his drunk old granddad? Danny's current situation is bad, but I'm not sure if this Technicolor mental institution would be any better. Grumpy Chuck beats him, but who knows what might happen on Carly's side of the looking glass?

I'm curious about what's going on in the cabin. I leave Carly in her coffee sack and walk past a bearded man wrapped in an American flag and not much else. He waves his arms and shouts verses to no one, an escapee from the Cocoa Puffs box. Maybe the old Tom Mix cabin is really a low-security insane asylum. Any minute now, big German nurses with long syringes will round up these looney tunes.

I enter to an immediate assault on my ears. The cabin seems host to an outlaw mariachi gang waging war with bent trumpets and trash can lids. A cartoon theme song rings from the far end of the long hall. Self-proclaimed musicians compete for dominance in what can only end in mutually assured destruction. Waves of distortion shiver the ceiling timbers.

The strange wall of sound now beckons people away from their human mandalas and poetry circles. The great room fills with tribal dancers, spinning tops in capes and caftans, a quilt of flesh and fabric, buzzing like bees. This would be an easy place to get lost for the rest of the decade.

A skinny man — half Groucho, half Cuckoo Bird — is flapping his arms at the center of the room. He's wearing elbow-length gloves and waving a fluorescent baton that traces glowing trails under the black lights. Wiry black hair, deep-set eyes and dark goatee give his face a carved and crazy look. A devil-shaped Gibson SG is slung like a samurai sword across his back. Day-Glo Groucho and the Armageddon Orchestra play a symphony for an alien invasion. Music for the end of the world.

Orange cigarette tips pulse like distant stars. Eyes and teeth glow as if detached from their faces. A barefoot man in a bright white toga spins through the crowd, and a drifting balloon bounces off my head.

There's a canyon legend of tunnels connecting the Tom Mix cabin to the burned-down Houdini house across the road. If the tunnels exist, I'll bet they lead directly to the inferno I saw in a Jehovah's Witness comic book. It's too dark, chaotic and crowded in here to find anyone and Danny is small enough to disappear below the hemlines.

I weave around the spinning space cadets and whirling dervishes. There's no sign of Danny, but I do see my brother's bell-shaped head bobbing at the far end of the room. Tom-tom Tommy's gone completely native. Lost in space on Planet Groucho, he's planted behind the most elaborate drum set west of the Mississippi. He's flailing with all fours, sending out shimmering cymbal crashes and rolling waves of thunder across the great room. Slowly, one by one, nearby musicians succumb to the rhythm.

At this moment, and I know it won't last, I can't help but love my brother. Only Tommy could find order in this musical anarchy. The steady tick-tick of his hi-hat is like a rescue beacon that keeps me from drowning in this churning river of noise. At first, his steady backbeat seems out of place in a room where everyone is marching to their own drummer. Tommy nudges the stampede into formation until Guitar Groucho joins the roundup and herds the room toward a common groove. Groucho nods at Tommy and they conspire with fills and fragments that gradually fall into orbit.

And on the eighth day of creation Man created music.

I get close enough to recognize Groucho from one of Tommy's album covers. Now it all makes sense: This is the House of Zappa. Frank wiggles his Fu Manchu, winks a dark eye at me and unhinges the strangest licks I've ever heard. Zappa's left hand blurs as he folds, spindles, and mutilates his red guitar. Bent strings squeal while Tommy's triplets ricochet around the room like gunfire in a canyon.

Hypnotic light bounces off the many mirrors. This is how space aliens will conquer us if they haven't already. Patterns swirl across the walls and ceiling. People bob and spin around me as if I'm standing at the center of a merry-go-round. I'm searching for the door when coffee-sack Carly floats by in a whoosh of burlap.

"Where's Danny?" I tug on her wrist.

"He'll be okay." She smiles and pulls me into the dance.

I resist her attempt to twirl me. "Have you seen Danny?"

"Don't be so uptight, Maxie." Carly lets go of my hands. "Learn to trust the magic," she says before spinning away.

But the only true magic I trust is the time-bending rhythm flowing from Tommy's giant drum kit. Reflections off his cymbals shine like sonic pulsars, casting shadow and light across the undulating field of flower children. This is one of the increasingly rare moments where I find my brother more amazing than annoying.

Tommy drums because he must. Drumming is his mission on Earth. Drumming and driving me bananas.

Disappearing Danny

Danny's gone missing and his grandfather thinks I'm to blame.

Chuck is always angry. Angry to the point of bursting a major artery.

He's angry at the hippies, the commies, the Jews and the Negroes. Grumpy Chuck says it's just a matter of time before a black plague destroys America. I know this because his five-year-old grandson told me. According to Little Danny, old Chuck is armed, on alert, and ready for the race riots. Any day now, the ghetto fires will spread like cancer, climb into our canyon, and leave nothing but smoke and ash.

I've heard Chuck ramble about similar subjects. It happened in '29, it will happen again. The gold standard is the only thing between us and the next great depression. What good is paper money? When the economy collapses, the only true currency will be ammo, whiskey, and Playboy magazines. Bullets, booze, and boobies. When the time comes, shoot to kill. Especially those goddamned hippie nut jobs and pansy-ass liberal fruitcakes.

Grumpy Chuck recently added a "This Truck Protected by Smith & Wesson" bumper sticker to complement the ones that say "George Wallace for President," and "America: Love it or Leave it." Danny claims that Chuck plans to bolt a howitzer to the hood of his El Camino. He says that Chuck has a fully-stocked fallout shelter cut into their backyard. Chuck believes that only Christians will survive the race war. His Bible says so.

Grumpy Chuck will probably finish himself off before anyone else does. Instead of going out in a blaze of glory, he'll slam a few drinks, doze off, and drop a lit Tiparillo into the folds of his La-Z-Boy armchair. When his house catches fire, the exploding ammo and gunpowder will make the American Revolution look like a Sunday picnic.

Chuck has a large vocabulary for everyone who isn't white. According to Danny, who heard it from Chuck, who learned it from his pappy, who heard it directly from Jesus, the country is being dragged downhill by all the spics and spades, cholos, beaners, dagos, wops, micks, yids, A-rabs, frogs, limeys, reds, pinkos, russkies, canucks, krauts, polacks, nips, japs, chinks, gooks, faggots, spearchuckers and jigaboos who are stealing jobs from freedom-loving, red-blooded Americans.

Chuck scares me. He's an angry man who drinks too much and thinks too little.

Pater was forcing me through my Torah tropes when Chuck's sharp door knock interrupted my misery.

"Danny here?" Chuck slouches like a dustbowl cowboy in our doorway. His gray hair is slicked up into a poor man's pompadour. A tight cowboy shirt is tucked into a pair of shrink-to-fit Levis that never did. His El Camino idles in our driveway like a snoring bloodhound. "Seen him lately?"

"Nope. Not today." I'm wearing my best poker face and hoping it doesn't crack. Looking away would arouse suspicion so I stare directly up at Chuck. If eyes are the windows to the soul, then Chuck's is bloodshot. I wish I was tall enough to hide the *mezuzah* on our door post, though I doubt Chuck would know what it means.

"Gone missing." Chuck scowls at me, his face puckered with wrinkles. He smells like smoke and sawdust. "Did he mention anything to you?"

"About what?" Pater steps up. He once called Child Protection Services on Chuck during a beating the whole canyon could hear. The so-called authorities gave Chuck such a stern warning he stopped beating his grandson for a whole week. The ceasefire may have been Danny's best week ever, but I'm sure Chuck made up for lost time after the authorities lost interest.

"Have you checked the tree fort?" I can't hold the poker face much longer so I risk a smile. "You know that little Danny. He's probably off playing cowboys and Indians in the canyon."

"Naw. Stuff is missing." Chuck fumbles with a bent Tiparillo but can't find his lighter. He fishes in his pockets for a pack of matches but his boney fingers come up empty. "Took a duffle bag."

"I'll be happy to go look for him," I offer a diversion to throw Chuck off the trail. "Danny's been talking about camping in the woods. I'll bet he'll be back for dinner."

Chuck hooks his thumb through the big buckle he probably beats Danny with. "He ain't camping, and you know it."

I do know it. But Grumpy Chuck doesn't know that I know. He doesn't know half of what I know, and I intend to keep it that way. I don't care if Chuck whips off his belt and starts swinging it right now. I won't flinch and I sure as shoe polish won't talk. For every minute I keep Chuck standing here, Little Danny is one mile closer to freedom.

"Would you like to come in and call the police?" Pater's offer surprises me at first, but then I raise the stakes.

"I know a couple of FBI agents," I say. It's almost true. I mean, everyone in the canyon knows about the two wing-tipped G-men assigned to keep an eye on things around here around the Canyon Store. Long-haired musicians and hippie chicks in tube tops that fit like tourniquets must be a real threat to the nation because that's all our local FBI agents seem to care about. "Should we bring them in on the case?"

"Think I don't have a phone?" Chuck glares at us as if trying to decide which is worse, a Jew, a kraut or both. "If I find out you're behind this …" he points his bent mini-cigar at me.

93

"Are you threatening my kid?" Pater puts a hand on my shoulder.

"If the shoe fits, wear it, Pinko."

"Don't you ever threaten us," Pater says. "Get off my property and don't ever come back."

"This ain't your property."

"Get the hell out of here."

Chuck scowls for a second, then stomps off into his El Camino and guns the engine. Sparks fly when the trailer hitch strikes the road at the bottom of our steep drive.

"Wow, Dad." I've never seen Pater so ready to punch somebody. "Thanks for sticking up for me."

"Never give in to bullies, Max. Never."

"So...let's get back to that Torah portion!" I say, but Pater isn't buying my sudden conversion. He's had to pull so many teeth to make me study Hebrew that the tooth fairy has unlisted her number. He gives my shoulder a Vulcan squeeze and spins me through the door.

It seems like the wrong time to mention that I went back to find Danny's mother at the House of Zappa the day after Tommy's big jam session. I asked around for her, but nobody seemed to know who I was talking about. Curly-haired girls in burlap are a dime a dozen up there. So every day this week I returned to the old cabin on Lookout Mountain, waited in the garden, and watched the freaks float in and out of the house.

Carly finally wandered by, but was reluctant to talk. Reluctant in the sense of "Please, don't ever come here again" reluctant. But I persisted because I couldn't stand to see one more welt on Danny's arm or hear one more crazy story about Grumpy Chuck's plan to convert his chimney into a missile silo.

Carly said she needed more time, a month or so, before she could rescue her little boy.

"Child Services is about to put Danny in foster care," I lied. God must be pretty busy these days, and it's still a couple of months before the Day of Atonement, so this fib probably won't count against me. "If you want to see Danny again, you need to move fast."

"Once I have my beautician's license I'll be able to take care of him."

"License?" Any fool can have a kid. To cut hair you need a license. "If you wait any longer, you'll need an undertaker's license."

Carly's face tenses up. "I'm gonna do makeup and hair for the studios."

"The studios? Chuck works for Universal. He'll be asking around, looking for you. Sooner or later—"

"We'll change our names."

"Danny's just a kid. He'll say something at school or in the store. If you want to be safe, you need to leave town."

"You don't understand, Maxie." I try to vaporize Carly's tears with my laser eyes, but she's soon crying as if she's the one getting beaten. "Once I've raised some scratch I'll share a pad with some other girls. As soon as I'm earning real bread I'll take care of Danny."

"Danny can't wait any longer. He's in danger, Carly. You need to do something now."

She covers her face with her hands, whimpers that she's doing the best she can but she's flat broke and needs time to get her act together. Mostly she's scared. Short on cash, long on fear. "It's worse than you ever imagined. Chuck isn't just Danny's grandpa, he's …"

Holy cow. If Mumu Marie was right about this, I'll need to rethink all the other crazy stuff she says. Nana says I need to learn how to walk by a pile of poop without kicking it to see what's underneath. Maybe someday I'll stop kicking. Even the

95

National Enquirer would find this too sick to print "Seriously? He's...?"

"I'm so ashamed." Carly says, "That's why I can never go back. Please don't tell anyone."

"It wasn't your fault, Carly."

Carly buries her face in her hands. "I feel so worthless."

"It's going to be okay," I say, though it probably isn't. This is a weird wet hairball that can never be untangled. Grumpy Chuck should be rotting in prison instead of raping his own daughter and beating her kid—jeez!—their kid. Not sure what else to say or do, I hold her while she sobs and trembles. Eventually my Vulcan side comes up with an idea. "Where would you go if you couldn't stay in L.A.?"

"'Frisco." She gasps for breath. "But I don't even have bus fare. I'm in debt up to my eyeballs."

San Francisco. Tommy's favorite town. If you want to disappear, that's the place to do it. "How much would you need to get started up there?"

"Huh? What are you talking about?"

"Getting out of Dodge, Carly. A couple of one-way tickets on the next Greyhound outta here. Two weeks at Motel 6 while you look for work. How much would that cost?"

Carly rubs her eyes and nods toward the big cabin. "These people know people. They go back and forth between here and 'Frisco all the time. There are plenty of places to crash up there."

"Yeah, but now you'll have a kid in tow. You can't just leave him on a park swing while you braid hair. Maybe it would be better if you put him up for adoption."

"How could you even think that?"

Bad idea, Vulcan side. Now she's crying so much I may need to build an ark. I should have known better than to get between a mama bear and her cub. Kids need their mom. I guess some moms need their kids.

Carly may not have been first in line when God was handing out luck, and she may have come up a bit short on brains, but she's Danny's only hope. I do a quick calculation and offer up a hundred bucks of my anticipated B.M. winnings that I'll have to borrow from Tommy. With enough blackmail, I should be able to get it interest-free. A hundred bucks should buy Danny and Carly enough time and distance to break free from Grumpy Chuck's House of Horrors.

"You don't have to pay me back, but you do have to promise me something."

"What?" She wipes her nose on the sleeve of her peasant blouse.

"Swear to God, hope to die? Stick a needle in your eye?"

"Yes."

"Say it."

"Swear to God." Sob. "Hope to die." Sniffle. "Stick a needle in my eye."

"Now, cross your heart, spit shake and pinky swear that you will take care of Danny. He's a good kid. You should feel proud of him."

"I promise. I promise."

We lock pinkies and look into each other's eyes. I'm not sure she'll remember anything I said, but she got the gist of it. What Carly lacks in book learning she makes up for in street smarts, and that's probably worth more in this case. As for *chutzpah*, she's got that in droves, whatever droves are. Any girl who's been through what she has and hasn't flipped her wig is probably going to pull through.

"The day you get that hair dresser license—"

"—Beauty Operator … I graduate in two weeks."

97

Carly and I will need to watch for a moment when Chuck's at work and his poofy-haired wife leaves the house to stock up on vodka and toenail polish. I'm not sure how I'll get Danny ready, but he's always down for adventure so it shouldn't be a problem. When the time comes I'll enlist Tommy to drive them to the Greyhound station, which reminds me that I'll need to check the departure schedules to be sure they get out of town before Grumpy Chuck can draw his Colt 45.

"The day you graduate is the day we put the plan in motion. Till then, mum's the word."

"Mum," she smiles. "I'm his mum."

"You'll be a great mum, Carly. All you need is love."

"Got plenty of that." She smiles. Finally.

That's what I didn't tell Chuck when he came looking for Danny. Maybe I'll tell Pater someday. Father may know best, but this isn't a TV show. For ten cents a day you can save a kid in Africa. For the cost of a Schwinn ten speed, you can save a kid in Laurel Canyon.

Tentatively Untitled

Pater wants to call his movie "Tentatively Untitled." He's been working on the screenplay so long that I've lost track of the story. At this point, I don't think he knows what it's about, either. Every day, he wakes up early to sip coffee and tap on his Smith Corona. He keeps a notepad in the car to jot down ideas at traffic lights. He dictates to me while driving.

"It needs to be larger than life." Pater wants to tell the world a story but doesn't think his own experiences are interesting enough to share.

"What about your life? Seems to me escaping the Nazis is pretty large."

"Nothing really new there." Pater says.

"How old were you when you got on that boat to Israel? Ten?"

"It was called Palestine at the time."

"Your father disappeared. Your mother sang opera to survive Dachau. Your extended family was wiped out. Call me crazy, but I see a movie in there somewhere. Why not write about that?"

"I'm into the future."

For a while "Tentatively Untitled" was about a car salesman who grows tired of hawking sedans and station wagons to snooty suburbanites. One day, he drives a used car off the lot and heads off to find America. He picks up hitchhiking servicemen, vagabonds and folk singers until the car breaks down somewhere in Texas. From there, he hobos around, drifting through what Pater calls "America's changing landscape" until he lands in the middle of Martin Luther King's big march on Washington.

This version of the story was heavily influenced by having Hope Springs in our car every weekday morning. Once she moved on, so did the movie.

The next version was about two unlucky sailors. After years of entertaining fellow navy men, they come to Los Angeles to make it in show business. But the world has changed twice while they've been away at sea, and nobody is interested in the song and dance *shtick* they have to offer. They're chasing a dream but find only nightmares.

The two confused sailors are fish out of water. They get ejected from every movie studio, bar, and bed they land in. Monday night, they drink the Hollywood Roosevelt Hotel lounge dry until they are thrown out by the barkeep. Tuesday night, they get so unruly at the Chateau Marmont that the cops are called to drag them away. On Wednesday the Sunset Hyatt House lives up to its "Riot House" nickname. By Thursday, it's clear as gin that the sailors are less interesting than the parade of characters wandering in and out of their mishaps and misunderstandings.

Many of what appeared to be secondary characters, the extras, reappear wherever the sailors go. The sailors continue to fade into the background as the mixed-up lives of the extras take center stage. Pater hopes the audience figures out the real story as the unlucky sailors continue to miss the point.

I still think the story of how Pater was shipped away to escape the Nazis and how Nana survived and eventually found him would be more interesting. But what the heck do I know? I'm just the kid in the back seat taking notes as Pater weaves through traffic, shooting ideas in all directions.

Pater attempted to do some field research for this story, stopping at bars and happy hours after work to observe drunks in their native environment. Unfortunately, he got thrown out of a lounge at the Sportsmen's Lodge for snapping Polaroids of the patrons. A drunkard followed him into the parking lot and threatened to break Pater's jaw unless he shredded the prints. The Sportsmen's may be the Bar Mitzvah capital of the San Fernando Valley on Saturdays, but it's No Man's Land on Tuesday afternoons.

After Pater abandoned ship on the sailor story, the action moved from dimly lit, red velour-covered lounges to bright and tacky diners. This new direction was good for me because it translated into soggy waffles and scrambled eggs at breakfast joints around town. Worried that the rabbi might smell pork on our breath, Pater imposed a "no bacon on Saturday" rule.

This change in direction should have been a big opportunity for me. I was hoping the two of us would hang out, rap and break bread together, but Pater was more interested in eavesdropping, taking notes, and snapping Polaroids. Unlike the Sportsmen's, people at Denny's, Sambo's and Du-par's enjoyed having their pictures taken.

I gave up trying to distract my father into taking more interest in his offspring until one morning when inspiration struck like a grease fire. After visiting a couple of identical blue-roofed IHOPs, I came up with an idea that Pater found interesting enough to pay attention to me.

"Do you know about the Theory of Relativity?"

"Sure. Dead cat in a box with the little gremlin who moves the molecules."

"Sort of." He's confusing Schrodinger's cat with Maxwell's demon, but I know better than to rub his nose in it. Pater was a sociology major, which might explain why he now spends his spare time eavesdropping at the IHOP. "Einstein said that an observer inside an elevator or a train without windows can't say for certain where he is or how fast he's moving."

"What do you think, Maxie? You're at least as smart as Einstein."

"All I have in common with Einstein is that we're both Jews who ride bikes."

It doesn't take an Einstein to see that the IHOP orange juice isn't fresh-squeezed. Why do they always advertise 'fresh-squeezed' when it's really from concentrate? Pater pushes his glass aside and signals for the waitress, but she's flirting with some big tipper by the cash register. "I dunno. Maybe you're right. Maybe I should just write about Nazis. Why not? Everyone else does."

"No. Wait. Listen: Every IHOP is identical, right? You can't tell one from another." I clink my knife against the bottomless coffee pot to make sure Pater's paying attention. I want him to understand that the Theory of Relativity is alive and well at the International House of Pancakes. "Once you're inside an IHOP, you could be anywhere. There's no way to know which one it is or where you are."

"Why not look out the window? I see Van Nuys Boulevard out there, so I know this IHOP's teetering at the edge of hell."

"Why are you allowed to say words that I can't?"

"I'm a screenwriter. Besides, 'hell' is in the Bible."

I can't tell if Pater was following what I was saying or veering off onto one of his endless tangents. "IHOP relativity is just like the guy in a train. He can't say for sure if it's the train or the scenery that's moving."

Pater seems to be spacing out again, eavesdropping on the conversation in the booth behind him. Was he always this trippy? It makes me half-crazy and might be what drove my mother away. I wave my hand in front of his face to cast shadow puppets onto the movie screen in his mind. "Tell the truth. Was I adopted?"

"Huh? Oh, yeah, a squirrel delivered you in a little basket. What you're saying about Einstein might make a good ambient conversation. Maybe the waitress and the bus boy can argue about relativity in the background."

"Yes, but right now I'm in the foreground and I'm trying to tell you something important." I pound my fist on the table just hard enough to turn every head in the restaurant. People look at me. *"Spare the rod, spoil the child,"* they're thinking. I glare back at a disapproving old biddy until she takes refuge in her bottomless coffee cup.

Pater doesn't notice the sudden hush. He stabs a silver dollar pancake and pops it in his mouth. A puff of powdered sugar coats his nose. "While the two main characters debate something mundane, I could have a kid explaining relativity to an adult."

On the off-chance he can still hear me, I continue with my pitch. "I'm thinking that IHOPs could be like tunnels. You walk into one in, say, Pasadena, have your meal, think nothing of it and when you walk out, you're in — I don't know — Hong Kong."

"They have IHOPs in Hong Kong?"

"It doesn't matter. Bakersfield. Fresno. San Berdu. The point is that your two heroes discover a secret Martian plot to take over the Earth with a connected series of identical pancake houses."

"Wait. There's Martians?" Pater slathers some jam onto a silver dollar pancake, rolls it like a little cigarette, and swallows it whole. "When did 'Tentatively Untitled' become sci-fi?"

"Never mind. Forget the Martians."

"Wait! Maybe my protagonists don't even realize that they are changing locations because things look the same everywhere they go."

"Bingo! Collect two hundred dollars as you pass 'Go.'"

"And Martians are trying to immobilize the Earth by making us fat from pancakes and Aunt Jemima!"

"There you go," I say, but I'm not sure where he's going. Maybe he's just poking fun at me. "Did anyone ever tell you that you're easily distracted?"

"You know how when we used to drive down Van Nuys Boulevard and every shop and every block was different? What happened to the old toy store and the newsstand and that little fruit market? Nowadays there's a Ralph's, an IHOP, and a McDonald's, on every corner. You're right. It's like the aliens invaded and nobody noticed. Every 7-Eleven could be a portal, part of a secret network connected through tunnels or those *Star Trek* beam-up things."

"Transporters?"

"Martians don't need to land everywhere at once to conquer the planet. They only need to take over the IHOPs."

"They already have," I whisper and arch my eyebrows towards the waitress, who arrives with our check even though we're only half-done eating. She calls me "honey" and looks the same as every other waitress we've encountered over the past few Saturdays. "They're already here."

"We need to alert the FBI," Pater drains his coffee cup, scans the check, and slaps a five onto the table.

Carnival of the Animists

It's the fifth of July and Friday night service number five. I need to attend ten Friday night or Saturday morning services before my big B.M. I prefer Fridays since they're shorter and the music is better.

"You're going the wrong way." Instead of heading into the valley, Tommy turns right at the bottom of the canyon. His Ford Econoline van is empty except for a snare drum vibrating like a drunk rattlesnake. We pass Du-par's Restaurant and bounce down Ventura Boulevard on bald tires and bad shocks. "Hey! Wrong way, Corrigan!".

"Maybe. Maybe not." Tommy turns and winks. He has Nana's warm blue eyes, though his are more devious. "Find us some tunes there, Charlie Tuna."

I fiddle with the loose knob on the scratchy AM radio, but nothing satisfies Tommy's impossible taste until I zero in on a weak station playing big band music.

"Cool!" Tommy wrenches the volume knob so fast it spins onto the floor and rolls under my seat. The bent antenna whips up a stew of static and swing. Music from the past arrives like light from a distant star, faint radio waves from a world long gone. "That's Gene Krupa, greatest drummer ever."

We turn right on Cahuenga and rumble toward Hollywood. It's hot in the van and my window doesn't open. The motor fumes are at smog-alert levels in this rolling soup can. I'm plotting my escape when we turn into the parking lot of the Pilgrimage Theater. It's a temple of sorts, but not the one I'm supposed to be attending. Nana will kill me when she discovers that I didn't go to *schul* tonight.

Tommy reaches for a duffle bag I hadn't seen earlier. "Quick! Change clothes," he says and throws a pair of my Sears Toughskin jeans and a striped tee-shirt at me.

"Why? Are we going to rob a bank? This is getting weird, Tom-tom."

"It's going to get weirder. Trust me."

Trust isn't in my vocabulary tonight, but I climb back to change and consider the possibilities. If his plan is to pull a bank heist, at least I won't be tried as an adult. With any luck, all of tonight's pending crimes will be erased from my police record if I make it to eighteen without further incident.

I follow Tommy not because I trust him but because I worry that without my good influence whatever scheme he's hatching might turn out even worse. We join a group of people dodging traffic and crossing the street toward a giant deco angel.

"The Hollywood Bowl?" I try to read the marquee but Tommy is tugging my arm and pointing at the hillside.

We weave through a honking maze of long-haired drivers trying to wedge their dented jalopies into the few slivers of open asphalt left in the parking lot. For a second, we're caught in the headlights of a brightly painted VW Microbus. Fluorescent peace signs and a vivid paint job, blaring music and burning weed and motor oil suggest that this crowd has not come to hear the Boston Pops. A dark flock of Hell's Angels cuts through traffic like sharks through a school of lesser fish. Their choppers cough and fart.

"Up, up and away!" Tommy leads me past the colorful tribe milling around the main entrance. After a quick quarter-mile we head up into the thin woods downwind of the big Bowl. The faint smell of eucalyptus mixes with pot smoke that's thick enough to alter my DNA. We ascend through the tribe of hippies, bikers and college students who seem to have taken up residence along the wooded perimeter of the Bowl. I stick close

106

to Tommy so as not to get tangled in the suede fringe and sideburns.

"Uppers. Downers. Reds, whites, and blues for the Fourth of July." The hungry-looking dope dealer is probably not what Hubert Humphrey meant when he said that small business is the heart of the American economy. "Acid? Windowpane? Mother's little helper?"

I would have been my mother's little helper if she hadn't gone to Jesus. Instead, I'm drifting with her idiot son through some kind of outdoor drugstore. There's no potion strong enough to make me forgive my mom for leaving or pardon Tommy for *schlepping* me to this illegal circus. As dopey ideas go, this is a prize winner.

Many of these forest children appear to have settled in for the evening, perhaps longer. Maybe they live in trees the way I live in a house. If this is evolution, I'm not sure which direction we're headed. Some people are wrapped in Mexican ponchos, others in Navajo blankets. A few pup tents strung between the skinny trees complete the sense that we've stumbled into an Acapulco gold rush camp.

I follow Tommy to the top of an incline that looks down over the side of the Bowl. We're about two-thirds of the way back from the stage, a decent spot from which to watch the show, but just as I dig my heels into the hillside, Tommy says, "Let's go!" and jumps into the breach.

The way he nails the landing suggests he has done this before. Tommy looks up and signals frantically for me to join him. "You're taller!" I say, but he's already disappearing into the crowd.

Gravity calls.

"Come here often?" I catch up with Tommy and smack him hard and square on the arm.

"All the time." He pulls his hair into a short pony tail and lets it spring back into place. Hair is obviously important here and his Doris Day doo fits in nicely. "Follow me. We'll get front-row seats."

Another bad idea.

I'm not sure who we are here to see, but judging from the blue glow of amplifiers stacked across the length of the stage I doubt it's the L.A. Philharmonic. The Hollywood Bowl is designed for an orchestra to be heard without amplification. Tonight's tower of tweeters and wall of woofers suggests that this hallowed ground will soon be desecrated with decibels.

The house lights dim out and to my surprise, KHJ Boss Jock Charlie Tuna comes out and announces, "Ladies and Gentlemen … from Los Angeles, California … The Doors!"

The Doors? Seriously? Those beach bums are almost my neighbors.

The cheering crowd adds to my amazement that a Laurel Canyon garage band made the leap from half-price Tuesday — Girls Get in Free! — at the Whisky to Friday night at the Hollywood Bowl. I have half a mind to demand a refund until I remember that we snuck in to this adult kindergarten. I look for escape routes, but Tommy's pulling me past an old, overwhelmed usher down to the next section.

This crowd is far more pagan and way more enthusiastic than the congregation I was supposed to spend the evening with. Unlike the regulars at temple, many of these people seem to be having a religious experience before services have even started.

For a moment, the crowd is louder than the band. People are standing on the benches shouting and raising their hands to heaven. If there's an exit nearby, I'll never find it. Praise the Lord and pass the earplugs.

The band wastes time trying to tune but finally gives up and launches into a song. Enough people sit down for me to see the stage, but now I don't see Tommy. The crowd seems friendly for now, but a mob like this will eventually need a virgin to sacrifice so I remain on high alert.

The Doors have a new album and some catchy radio hits that they seem determined to disown tonight. In spite of the Great Wall of Woofers, the band isn't too terribly loud. Which is a gift because they're not too terribly good.

The screen door must have been wide open when the guy on keyboard snuck in. If this faker with the white boots and ringmaster muttonchops can be famous, then Asher Levi, the organ player at our temple, is Ludwig van Mozart.

The best performer in the group is the stagehand struggling to keep the drummer's gear from falling off a raised platform. If timing is everything, the drummer is in urgent need of some. I wish he'd give Tommy a chance to show this crowd what real drumming is about.

The guitarist seems to have just discovered minor chords. He's dressed in black, probably hoping nobody can see him. Thankfully, nobody can hear him. He has enough amplifiers to sink the Sixth Fleet but only enough electricity to power the string of Christmas lights dangling behind the band.

Jim Morrison, self-proclaimed singer and shaman, paces around in tight leather pants and a jeweled vest with golden trim. I have trouble not seeing him as the druggy guy who lives behind the Canyon Store and wanders down to buy beer and cigarettes from time to time. He emerges from a trance long enough to shout, "We want the world, and we want it now!" but doesn't offer any clue as to what he intends to do with it. Does he even know he's on stage? Jim appears ignorant of the fact that sixteen thousand people are wondering why they came here tonight.

The band breaks into a polka, a song about a whiskey bar, the one that should have never hired them in the first place. The tune sounds like an Israeli folkdance I learned at the Jewish summer camp where my dad works. I'm disappointed that Morrison isn't dancing with a wine bottle on his head but maybe he's reserving that for the big *Hava Nagila* encore.

If I wasn't so desperate to find Tommy, I'd sneak into the ladies room and stuff my ears with ten-cent tampons. But my pockets are empty. I don't even have a dime to make a phone call.

I know that my dumb brother is trying to get as close to the stage as possible. He wants to soak up whatever rock and roll magic propelled these nuts from high school dances to the big time. Unlike the Doors, Tommy's band has real talent. If kooks like the Doors can pack the Bowl, Jail Bait could someday fill the Grand Canyon. Then again, maybe talent doesn't matter. Maybe fame just falls from the sky like stardust.

Morrison is about to fall off the stage. He prowls, preens, and shouts incoherent poetry. A gal in a nearby aisle tears off her top and throws it at the stage. The bandana wrapped around her forehead helps keep her brains from leaking out her ears as she gyrates and waves her arms.

I take advantage of the confusion to climb over a low rail and descend to the next section.

"Cancel my subscription to the resurrection," Morrison yells. It strikes me that Morrison may be crazy, but he's not stupid. If people want to treat him like the messiah, why argue? The world is lucky that Jim Morrison's army is too stoned and ragtag to march very long in any one direction. All it would take for this organized chaos to turn into a Nazi rally would be for Morrison to shout *"Sieg Heil!"*

I glance behind me to be sure that the crowd hasn't transformed into thousands of beady-eyed Shreidermayers. I zoom in on the one dark face, hoping to find Hope Springs in the crowd, but this isn't her kind of scene. Hope went to Prague to join a real revolution. If she thinks the Beatles are navel gazers, then the Doors are lost in their own belly button lint.

A swollen half-moon rises above the Bowl and looks for a better planet to orbit. NASA should do the world a favor and send Morrison to Mars. As long as he acts like someone just passing through our galaxy, a star blinded by its own light, why not indulge him? Help him hitch a ride on the next comet out of here.

"Wake up!" Morrison screams, probably at himself. I wish I could wake up, but I feel trapped in his nightmare. The stage pulses like a black hole that wants to swallow me. The crowd sways, the music swirls, and Jim's poetry is enough to make anyone not on drugs lose their marbles.

I look up and recognize the face of Jim Morrison's girlfriend, who I know from an ice cream episode at the Canyon Store. She was blocking the aisle, trying to decide between Rocky Road and Rum Raisin, so I suggested she buy one of each. She's been friendly to me ever since, and now she's heading toward the stage

"Hi, Pamela!" A smile covers the entire southern hemisphere of my face. The north is invaded by puppy eyes so big they eclipse my forehead.

"Lost, sweetie?" She extends a hand and walks me past the usher. Strawberry blond hair bouncing, she's as radiant as Morrison is dark. Opposites attract, I guess, though I've never understood why. "Come sit with me."

Pamela leads me to the edge of the stage, and we squeeze over to the center section just as the band clicks into their big radio hit, "Light My Fire." She offers me her seat and plops down on the lap of a skinny guy who looks like one of the Rolling Stones. His face is so tight I can see his skull. He must be

111

famous because Pamela is bouncing around on his lap and he still looks bored.

I feel safe for the first time since getting separated from my dumb brother. Safe, until some knucklehead throws a lit Fourth of July sparkler on stage just as Jim sings the words, "funeral pyre." Fortunately, the man in green, the guy who keeps the drums from waddling away, is quick to stomp out any trace of spark.

At this point a merciful God would cut the electricity. Then again, a merciful God would have sent me a responsible brother instead of a complete ding-dong.

A bearded fan passes me a hand-rolled cigarette. I stare at it for a second, wondering why I took it from him until Pamela plucks it from my fingers. "Goes great with Rocky Road," she says.

The band stumbles into a dirge about an unknown soldier. The guitarist turns toward his amp and makes sounds like a wood chipper. Unfortunately, when he faces us again, his guitar is still in one piece. Next, he holds his instrument as if it's a machine gun and shoots at Morrison. Jim falls dead in an ear-shattering burst of noise.

"Have you seen the accident outside?" Morrison writhes around on stage like a caterpillar. There's something very sad about him. He seems very lonely for someone bathing in love and limelight. I'm sure he's on drugs, but I suspect he's still crazy when sober. "...I want the snakes to suck my skin...I want the worms to be my friends...I want the birds to eat my eyes ..."

Morrison cradles a single maraca as if it's the Christ child. He holds it up to bless the faithful but gets distracted when a bug lands on the stage. "Ode to a grasshopper," he announces but the tribute falls apart when he sees that the grasshopper is just a moth that, like my idiot brother, is drawn to short-lived flames.

112

People cheer, and I make for the exit. There will be no place to hide when the fans snap out of their stupor. Time to escape this looney bin before any threat of an encore.

Sunset Boulevard Detour

I find Tommy's van after wandering around the parking lot until half the cars are gone. He shows up eventually, full of energy, inspired by what must have been a different concert than the one I saw.

My ears are ringing so much I can barely hear him talking.

"Let's take a quick detour down Sunset. Are you hungry? Ever been to Barney's Beanery?"

"Just take me home."

"How 'bout we hit Hamburger Hamlet? My treat! Come on, kid, live a little. You've never seen the Strip by night."

"Temple ended two hours ago. Nana is already freaking out."

"Don't worry, Maxine. Nana Banana's been asleep for hours. Don't be a wet blanket. I think The Animals are playing at the Whisky. The streets will be a freak show."

"Not interested. Not hungry. Not talking to you, Tom-tom."

"Did I ever show you where Pandora's Box used to be? That's where I got busted a couple of years ago, the night the cops went crazy. We were just hanging out when they started swinging their clubs and dragging kids off to jail. Teen riot, my ass. The pigs were the ones rioting."

The motor turns over after three attempts to wake it. The clock on the dashboard says 1:30 but there's no reason to believe it. It's late, but not 1:30 a.m. late. My guess is midnight. "Wrong way," I say when Tommy turns down Highland toward Hollywood. "It would be smarter, faster, and cheaper to go back the way we came."

"Take the scenic route for once in your life."

"So I'm being abducted again?"

"Don't worry, pumpkin head, you'll be home in time for the Saturday morning cartoons."

"Promise me: no stops. No detours. I don't want to see the Playboy Mansion or the Chinese Theater."

"Let's drive by the Troubadour. That's where Lenny Bruce was arrested for saying *schmuck*. Can you believe it? Arrested for speaking Yiddish? Maybe they're having a hootenanny tonight."

"Home, Thomas."

"Sheesh. What's with kids these days? Okay, here's what we'll do. I'll take Sunset only as far as Coldwater Canyon. We'll take it up to Mulholland. From there it's just a quick hop, skip and jump till you're back home with your Barbie dolls."

I give Tommy the silent treatment, which has no effect because he's not listening. He turns onto Sunset Boulevard where a big Marlboro Man stands guard over a giant traffic jam. Farther down the boulevard I see what appears to be a long, banana-shaped vehicle. It's finally happened: Space aliens have invaded and nobody noticed. Nana wouldn't be surprised to learn that God's big zoo isn't limited to our little galaxy.

"Sunset Strip: The beating heart of Los Angeles." Tommy is playing tour guide. "During prohibition this place was packed with speakeasies."

"What's a speakeasy?" So much for the silent treatment.

"Illegal taverns. Gangsters like Mickey Cohen used to run gin joints and casinos right under the cops' noses."

"Cohen? A Jewish gangster?"

"Yeah, but don't be impressed. He could have been a doctor."

"Is there a weirdo convention in town? What are all these people doing in the street?"

"This is nothing. You should have seen Haight-Ashbury last summer."

"Yeah, yeah. I know. San Francisco is the center of the universe."

A car full of lowriders pulls alongside in a '57 Chevy. Purple metal-flake paint. Red tuck-and-roll. Dingle balls and more chrome than Detroit, Michigan. "Angel Baby" is etched in swirly letters across the driver's side door. Brassy music from a Mexican station squeals through half-open windows. The two Chicanos in front have slick hair and shiny, long-sleeved shirts. The girls in back have hair cascading like waterfalls over combs so tall they fill the rear window. The driver looks over, so I flash a thumbs up. He blasts his ah-ooga horn and sets the chassis jumping.

"Cool hydraulics," Tommy says.

I have the sudden sense of being a prisoner in my father's movie except that there's no background or foreground on this swirling boulevard. We are all extras searching for the story.

Angel Baby's driver takes advantage of a gap in traffic to make his tires squeal. We're left sitting in a cloud of burnt rubber and greasy kid stuff.

"Check out those pretty boys," Tommy says.

A flotilla of chopped Harleys is parked on the sidewalk. Bearded guys in leather cowboy chaps and Hell's Angel's vests with "Live to Ride – Ride to Live" patches sneer at anyone who looks at them. Some rev their engines, others polish their chrome. One big guy—the leader?—is seated backwards on his bike, making out with a young chick pressed against his sissy bar. One of his hands is buried deep inside her macramé halter top; the other is lost in her long hair. Pedestrians give them a wide berth, which forces more tourists into the street.

Someone slaps an ad about a band called the Stone Poneys on my side of the windshield. Tommy's wipers don't work, so we're stuck with it until I can lean out far enough to sweep the page away. Rock and roll is pouring from every car radio and club door along the Strip. This is Disneyland for hippies, a world so far from the suburbs that the other side of the hills could be another planet.

"I'm heading up to 'Frisco tomorrow," Tommy says. "Big free concert in Golden Gate Park. I think Janis Joplin is playing. Wanna tag along?"

"Nope." I guess I should feel honored by the invitation, but once he leaves for San Francisco he may never return. His brain didn't return after the last trip. He was a smart kid before running off to San Francisco last summer. What happened to him up there? "Did you ever take LSD, Tom-tom? That's bad stuff, you know."

"Bad stuff," he says. "Mushrooms are better."

"Don't change the subject. I'm talking about drugs, not pizza."

The banana-shaped mothership has deployed aliens dressed in white jumpsuits who walk through the crowd with big plates of tiny hot dogs. The Martians were clever enough to disguise themselves as Little Oscar and their ship as the Weinermobile, but I'm not fooled. The Earth is defenseless against such devious invaders.

"Unreal," Tommy says, and he's right. There is something not quite real about the kaleidoscope of life glowing like neon fungus in a petri dish, too strange and delicate to survive the L.A. sun.

"Tommy!" He's too distracted to notice the flashing red light behind us. "L.A.P.D. I think they want you to pull over."

"The fuzz? What do they want? I'm not speeding. Nobody can speed on Sunset."

I resist reminding him that I thought this detour was a bad idea. "Is there anything in the van that Nana wouldn't approve of?"

"Besides you?"

"Touché, Tom-turtle. I mean do you have any of that marijuana or stuff the rock musicians take? If you've got anything illegal, it would be best to let me hold it."

"Then hold yourself, Dopey."

"They won't search a kid. Besides, the only way to get that riot incident off your record is—"

"Don't worry, I'm clean, Maxine."

The cops want us to pull over but finding a parking place on Sunset Boulevard only happens in the movies. We inch through the cars and people with a siren blaring behind us. A gaggle of tourists point in our direction, excited to be getting their money's worth. *Cops! Hippies! Bikers! Wish you were here.* Tomorrow they'll catch a Greyhound back to Utah.

I'm scared. L.A. cops have a bad reputation, and there's no good reason for them to pull us over. Tommy's van is the most boring car on the road. No peace signs. No curtains. No "War is Not Healthy for Children and Other Living Things" stickers on the rear bumper. Maybe the van is too clean. That's why the cops are suspicious.

"PULL THE CAR OVER NOW!"

Tommy navigates through traffic and pulls into the Tower Records parking lot.

"Let's hit the record store after the cops split," Tommy says. "I wonder if they have the new Vanilla Fudge album."

"Tommy, this is serious. If they ask any questions, you're just taking me home after I got sick at a birthday party, okay?"

"Solid."

One cop hangs back in the squad car while the other cowboys over to the van and signals for Tommy to roll down

118

the window. He shines a bright flashlight into my eyes and then directs his beam around the interior of the van. Tommy produces his driver's license and the officer looks it over.

"Here." Tommy passes me a twenty dollar bill. "Just in case you need to catch a taxi home."

"Step out of the car, boy, or are you a girl?" Cop Number One orders Tommy.

Cop Number Two taps on my door and says, "Well, well, well. What have we here?"

Tommy's feet barely hit the pavement before the cop slams him into the van. Based on how it sounds from the inside, Tommy hit the panel pretty hard. "Hey! That's my brother," I shout and try to open my door, but my cop leans against it and ignores me.

"Stop police brutality!" someone shouts from the street.

"Off the pigs!" another person yells from the safety of the crowd that has gathered around us.

I scramble over to the driver's side and jump down to the street just in time to see Cop Number One smash Tommy into the side of the van again. My brother's hands are cuffed behind his back and his nose is bleeding.

"Hey!" My fear has vanished. I pound on the cop's back. "Cut that out! He wasn't doing anything wrong."

"Well, well, well. A dope fiend and a runaway." Cop Number Two grabs me and carries me away with ease.

"Put me down," I shout. "I've read the Constitution!"

The cop laughs and cuffs my wrists. Having neutralized any danger I posed, he opens the back door and shines his light around the van. "Feisty little shit, aren't you?"

"Go back to Russia," someone shouts, but all the attention is not helping our cause.

"Clear off, you morons!" Cop Number One shouts at the people who have gathered to watch the show and jeer. "You've got till the count of three before I declare this an illegal assembly."

"One!" says the cop. He draws his gun and the crowd takes a giant step back.

"This is still a free country, you fascists!"

"Two."

The crowd loses interest in whether or not the cop can count to three.

I hear sirens in the distance, more squad cars inching their way down the crowded strip. The cops might have been smart enough to radio for backup, but they didn't realize that my wrists are too skinny to stay cuffed. I could pull a Houdini, but I don't want to abandon my brother.

"Well, well, well." Cop Number Two slashes a hole in the snare drum Tommy had in back of the van. He produces a wad of tin foil and examines it. "Lookie what I found. We done caught ourselves a dope dealer. What we got here, Jim? Pills? Powder? Pot?"

"That's crazy," Tommy says. A strand of blood-matted hair falls across his face. His hands are cuffed tight behind his back. He smiles at me, trying not to look defeated. "You guys planted it."

"Oh, so now we're liars and we're crazy? Is that it?" He shoves Tommy hard against the van. "You're under arrest, hippie girl." Cop Number One sticks his toothy face into Tommy's. "One more smartass word outta you and I'll shut your faggot mouth for good. Nine unpaid parking tickets, five gone to warrant. Expired tags. Transporting a minor for an immoral purpose. Curfew violation on the kid. Dope in your car. How 'bout I save the state some money and we settle this right now?" He drags Tommy away and stuffs him in the back of the squad car.

I could escape, but I'm terrified for my brother. If the cops are this rough on the street, there's no telling what they might do to him without a crowd to witness. The only good news is that I'm not scared anymore. Now I'm angry. "My dad is the assistant D.A.," I shout. "You brownshirts are in big trouble."

"We'll just see about that, you little trained monkey." Cop Number Two picks me up and stomps over to the car. "Riding with a drug runner wins you an E-ticket to Juvenile Hall."

I bite my lower lip and fight the urge to mouth off.

~   ~   ~

I'm too young to throw in jail, and Tommy and I have a consistent story. Consistently boring. Once assured that I was no threat to anyone but my locked-up brother, the cops let me hang around the station until Nana and Pater come to my rescue.

The ride home is more dismal than a rainy day. Pater steams and Nana curses in German about Tommy's bad judgment. When I ask her to translate a couple of choice phrases, she breaks into English to convince us that the USA is the Fourth Reich.

"It's time to leave," she insists. "We need to get out of this country before it goes to the dogs."

"I like dogs," I say, hoping she might give in just to cheer me up.

"We should move to Canada."

"We're not changing countries again," Pater mumbles. "Once is enough, and I've done it twice."

Germany. Israel. The USA. For once Pater's math holds up. But Canada sounds friendly and Tommy would be safe from the draft there. "It's almost the same country," I say. "Isn't anyone worried about what's happening to Tommy in jail?"

Silence. No one speaks for the rest of the weekend.

It turns out I was right to be worried. Tommy looks half-dead when we finally spring him Monday morning. His face is bruised. Bags under his eyes. Worst of all, the cops gave him a buzz cut, standard procedure to keep hippies from smuggling head lice into the halls of justice. During his arraignment, the courtroom is full of people I would never want to share a cell with.

"Thomas Strauss," the judge gives Tommy a quick once-over and doesn't like what he sees. "How do you plead?"

Tommy opens his mouth to speak but no words come out. My big brother looks so tiny standing before the bench. I want to jump up and defend him. I want to explain to the judge that we did nothing wrong; that the foil package was planted; that traffic fines, dangling tail pipes, and expired license plates are small potatoes. That a bit of mercy sends a stronger message than a harsh punishment. Sensing my restlessness, Nana squeezes my wrist.

"Excuse me, your honor." Pater doesn't have the money for lawyers and he's too proud to ask Jesus for help. I hope all those "Perry Mason" reruns come in handy. "What are the charges?"

The judge seems bothered by this question. He folds his dishrag eyebrows into a scowl and reads a list of offenses long enough to get Tommy deported. "Unpaid tickets gone to warrants. Expired vehicle tags. Contributing to the delinquency of a minor. Possession of contraband with intent to sell. Failure to stop when so ordered."

"A word, your honor?" Pater approaches the bench to negotiate away the more outrageous charges, but the judge isn't having any of his permissive parenting.

122

"The final charge is failure to report to a selective service induction center when so summoned."

"What?" Tommy didn't see this one coming.

Nobody did, except me.

"Defendant will be silent."

"I was never summoned!"

The judge bangs his gavel, just like on TV. He gives Tommy the stink eye and says, "Even if half these charges are dismissed, you're still in a world of trouble. So here's the deal, son. Bring me evidence that you've been inducted into military service within sixty days and I'll drop all charges."

"And if I don't?"

"I'll throw the book at you, and you'll still end up in the Army. Your terms or mine, son. Either way you're going to straighten up and serve your country."

Frustrated and defiant, Tommy pleads not guilty to all charges. A court date is set for a month from now. In the meantime, he can go free on a thousand dollars bail. The judge might as well have said a million. It may be lunch money to Rockefeller, but a thousand bucks is a fortune to us. I'm floored when Nana produces ten crisp green pictures of Benjamin Franklin to pay the bail.

"Nazis!" Nana mutters as we leave. Her eyes glare like blue fire.

We drop Tommy off at the impound lot, and Pater hands him exactly thirty-seven dollars to get his van out of jail. Once the old Econoline turns over, Tommy rolls off to the DMV and the rest of us roll home. A summer camp song pops into my head and I wisely keep it to myself.

Rolling home, get drunk!

Rolling home, get drunk!

By the light of the silvery moon…

"What a stinking mess," Pater says after we part ways with Tommy.

We crawl through workday traffic in silence and then turn up Coldwater Canyon. I stare out the window at the giant houses while Pater tells Nana that we're not changing countries and America isn't turning into Nazi Germany. "Tommy was stupid, got caught, and now he has to face the music."

"If he had any gold teeth, they would have pulled them out," Nana says, still angry as a hornet. "I wouldn't be surprised to find numbers tattooed on his wrist."

"Things will be okay," I say, though I don't believe it.

"This isn't a TV show, Max." Pater sounds weary enough to crawl back in bed until 1968 is over.

"It's just like 'Perry Mason,'" I insist. "The cops didn't follow basic procedures. They planted evidence and searched without a warrant. That just happens to be unconstitutional, by the way. That thing about the draft summons is fishy, too." I don't mention that I've already spoken with a lawyer I know who said that the Sunset cops are notorious for ignoring the rules. "And what's with that haircut? Tommy needed that hair for his music career. I say we sue for one million dollars in lost income!"

"Ever the optimist, Maxie." Nana turns and smiles at me like I'm a dumb kid. "That's what I love about you."

"I spent half the night in that precinct. Every kid they dragged in was accused of having dope wrapped in foil. If Hope Springs were here, she'd organize a sit-in. Can't you see? It's all fake. What is this, the Wild Wild West?"

"The wild West Coast," Pater says. He turns right on Mulholland, where a lot of the cool old houses are being torn down to make way for marzipan mansions with high hedges and ornate gates.

"What was that stuff about never seeing the draft summons?" Pater makes unavoidable eye contact across the rear

124

view mirror. He holds it so long I worry he'll miss the next curve.

"Sorry?" I was hoping he'd missed this little detail. A car crash would be preferable to this conversation. "Uh … maybe one day when I was delivering the post with Mark the Mailman … maybe it was *Shabbat* and I saw a letter for Tommy that kind of worried me … maybe I set it aside and kind of forgot about it?"

Nana shoots me a stern glance. Stern in the German sense where the word comes from. Pater eyes me again in the mirror.

"I swear! I was going to deliver it." I feel like crying at this point. Crying over my own stupidity. Crying for Tommy's stupidity. Crying for all the stupidity in this stupid world. "I didn't mean to get Tommy in trouble. I just forgot."

Silence confirms that this is all my fault. Yom Kippur is right around the corner, but there's no way I can ever atone for this. God is going to open the Book of Judgment and throw it at me. Who by fire? Too easy. Who by water? Too quick. Who by wild beast? That seems about right. Maybe I should start fasting now so the canyon coyotes won't find me worth the trouble.

A moment of silence in my family is like an hour in anyone else's. Usually we're all talking at once, but now Pater's driving a little too fast and Nana's breathing a little too loud. It's hot in the car. I can't seem to get enough oxygen even with the windows open. This would be the perfect moment for an asthma attack. Who by sneezing? Who by wheezing?

The Blue Bomber turns right on Laurel Canyon, and I know better than to ask if we can stop in at the Canyon Store for a Creamsicle. Besides, Jim Morrison is probably in there buying cigarettes, and I never want to see him again. This whole mess is his fault. Two minutes later we turn onto Wonderland Avenue.

"Well," Nana says. She believes my story but that doesn't fix anything. "We just explain the mistake to the draft board. Tommy shows his college registration and that's that."

"Uh..."

"There's more?" Pater pulls into our driveway. He's gripping the steering wheel tight enough to twist it off. "Could it possibly get any worse at this point?"

"Well..."

"So? *Nu?* Maxie?" Nana hasn't removed her safety belt. The car has stopped but she's still bracing for impact.

"It's just that ... I don't think Tommy registered for college." In fact, I know he didn't. After barely graduating high school and hating every day of it, his plan was to move up to 'Frisco and join the rock and roll circus.

"He missed the deadline?" Pater is too weary to raise his voice. I can almost hear one side of his broken heart attacking the other.

"I thought he told you."

"*Oy vey,*" Nana slumps back into the seat as if she plans on staying there a long time.

G-Men

Cartoons are over. It's a hot Saturday afternoon, and I'm lying on the cool living room floor reading *Mad* magazine. The Beatles are on the cover with a bearded guru who looks a lot like Alfred E. Neuman. "The Chimps," a send up of The Monkees, seems like it was written just for me.

Nana Hannah is practicing scales and running finger exercises up and down the piano. Her left hand works the bass notes while her right hand raises an old Disneyland coffee cup to her thin pale lips.

Frontierland! Adventureland! Tomorrowland! Nana thinks Walt Disney is the messiah. Pater says that Laurel Canyon — Canyonland! — is a suburb of Disneyland. We've got plenty of costumed characters and no shortage of Mad Hatters. All we lack are flying elephants and spinning tea cups.

The Disneyland mug isn't Nana's finest piece of pottery. That prize goes to a pair of delicate tea cups with matching porcelain saucers. She says her parents used to drink tea every day after supper. Her memories, like porcelain, are all she has of them. She lost everything — her house, her parents, her brothers — the tea cups, like my father, are all that survived.

Her left hand keeps the bass clef busy while she drains her cup of good-to-the-last-drop Maxwell House. She says the Israelites may have been too rushed to let the bread rise, but Moses didn't leave one drop of instant coffee behind in Egypt. Nana refuses to drink Folgers coffee. She suspects their spokeswoman, Mrs. Olsen, the neighborhood busybody who solves everyone's problems with a fresh cup of coffee, is an ex-Nazi. Nana claims to have seen Mrs. Olsen in Hollywood driving one of those "little Nazi cars" that the rest of us call Volkswagens. Nana's hatred of VWs is what led me to suspect Mr. Shreidermayer.

If I'm opinionated, I inherited it from Nana. She likes the Monkees but distrusts the Beatles. She likes long hair on boys but thinks girls look better with pixie cuts, so I shoot right up the middle to drive her crazy. She loved JFK but is threatening to vote for Nixon because he's tough on commies. "I've earned the right to be inconsistent," she says when my father points out that Humphrey hates commies, too.

Nana and my father argue over election-year politics every night during dinner with Walter Cronkite.

"Nixon won't stop communism or end the war," Pater insists after Nana defends Nixon to get his goat.

"Kill a Commie for Your Mommy," I say, quoting one of Grumpy Chuck's bumper stickers. I'm tired of the same conversation every night. Let's get this election over with so we can argue about something else. "Better Dead than Red."

"Tricky Dick is a paranoid nut," Pater insists. I think he misses Hope Springs. Nana's less fun to argue with.

My two remaining ancestors should be able to agree that paranoid nuts are easy to spot. Both of them had firsthand experience with the biggest nut Germany ever produced. Maybe the reason they argue about the future is because the present is slippery and it's hard to talk about the past. Nana lets a detail slip every now and again, but most of what I know of her story I've picked up from stray comments and loose puzzle pieces. I know that her husband, my grandfather Otto Strauss, was carted away during the *Kristallnacht* raids for refusing to let the brownshirts enter his home.

"Is this the thanks I get for serving the fatherland?" he demanded when Nazis pushed opened his front door with the butt of a rifle.

The Nazis didn't care that my *Opa* Otto had marched to the Russian front in World War I. They didn't care about his Iron Cross for bravery, his commendation from Kaiser Wilhelm or the Strauss family crest dating back to the fifteenth century.

Maybe Mr. Shreidermayer was on patrol that night. Maybe he kicked down doors, smashed windows and dragged Jewish men away to the death camps. My thoughts are swirling with images of Nixon, Hitler, and Alfred E. Neuman when a firm knock rattles the front door.

"Are we expecting anyone?" Pater looks up from the crossword puzzle he's been working on. He is home for a weekend between camp sessions.

"Me? I'm grounded, remember?" Grounded forever. It will take from now until Yom Kippur to atone for this summer's crime spree. Breaking and entering. Getting arrested on Sunset for being out after curfew. Misplacing Tommy's draft letter. My most recent act of treason was calling Mumu Marie the "Spanish Inquisition" right to her face.

I can't wait for summer camp to start.

A knock at the door sounds like someone we don't know. Maybe it's the Fuller Brush man. A friend or neighbor would just pop the door open a crack or whistle through the mail slot to see if anyone was home. The Jehovah's Witnesses have given up on us since that time Pater came to the door in his underwear and invited them in. Today's visitor is probably an encyclopedia salesman. I toss *Mad* aside and sleepwalk to the entrance.

Two men in suits are perched on our thin front porch looking very serious.

"FBI."

"Like on TV?" I ask. They remind me of Bill Gannon and Joe Friday, the cops from *Dragnet*. I look around to see if there's a film crew on our street. "Do you have shoe phones?"

"Are you here alone?"

129

"Dad," I shout into the house, "FBI are here."

The music stops mid-scale. The *L.A. Times* rustles as Pater folds his crossword puzzle. Gannon points to the *mezuzah* on our doorpost. When Friday nods knowingly, I realize that we might as well have lit a big neon sign that says "Jews Live Here." Not quite as obvious as our lack of Christmas lights in December, but it's there year-round if you know what to look for. If that little prayer box is supposed to bring good luck, it just stopped working.

"Gentlemen?" Nana appears with the same stern voice she uses to tell me that *Mad* magazine will rot my brain.

But my brain is flashing back to a time before I was born, to the moment when the storm troopers dragged my grandfather away. Nana puts a hand on my shoulder, more to steady herself than calm me down. She gets understandably nervous around cops and authorities. I want to tell her that this is Laurel Canyon, 1968, not Berlin, 1938, but there's still time for history to repeat.

"Can I help you?" I ask.

"How's tricks, Kiddo?" Gannon says, identifying himself as the nice guy in whatever game is about to unfold. I recognize him from the parking lot of the Canyon Store, where he keeps an eye on the rebels and rockers who stop to buy smokes and Baby Ruth bars. These two FBI hacks have a cushy assignment watching girls in halter tops bounce down the produce aisle instead of figuring out who really killed JFK.

My father was the same age as I am now when he got a similar visit on *Kristallnacht*. When one of the brownshirts shoved Nana and tore her dress, my future dad wedged himself between his mother and that ape. "If they take you, *Mutti*, I'm coming too," he said. If push comes to shove, I will do as my father did.

"You really should lock your front door, Ma'am. There are all kinds of weirdoes in these parts," good cop Gannon says.

"Yes. Of course. We'll be sure to do so from now on." Nana tries to shut the door, but Friday jams his foot in it.

Nobody locks their door in the canyon, there's no need. The local weirdos aren't dangerous, and until today, the FBI had never invited themselves in.

I sense Nana stiffening. From the corner of my eye I see Pater coming over to join us. In 1938, my young father led worse thugs on a brief chase around the house until one Nazi cornered him and the other whipped out a gun. That's when Nana did pretty much the strangest thing I've ever heard of: She launched into a full-throated, *fortissimo* rendition of the "Queen of the Night" aria from Mozart's *Magic Flute*.

"I can break glass, too," she told the stunned brownshirts.

Her voice has faded over the years, but it's still powerful enough to rattle the windows. I cover my ears when she practices her high trills. The shattering glass of *Kristallnacht* played like an orchestra behind Nana belting out opera. Her high F-note sent the Nazis back into the street holding their ringing ears.

Then they came back in force.

Kristallnacht, the dress rehearsal for the Holocaust, was a flaming success. Nana and Pater never again saw my grandfather or the other Jewish men dragged from their families. After hocking everything that wasn't broken, she paid ten times the normal price to book my father's passage to Palestine. A day after his departure, the Nazis returned to ship her off to Dachau. For the next five years, playing Mozart for the officers was the only thing that kept her from the gas chambers. To this day, she refuses to sing The Magic Flute.

Nana never learned her husband's fate, and it would be years before she and my father were reunited. I hope she lives forever, because I know that Pater's greatest fear is to lose her again. He now joins us at the door as if summoned by the invisible bond that links the two of them.

"Do you know a man named Karl Strauss?" Joe Friday asks. I want to ask if they learn to talk like robots at the Police Academy, but instead file the question in my overflowing folder of stupid things better left unsaid. I'm waiting for him to add, "Just the facts, Ma'am" but he's not playing this to the letter

"I'm Karl Strauss," Pater says.

Nana squeezes the back of my neck with enough pressure to suggest she will snap it like a wishbone if I say anything.

"What can I do for you gentlemen?" Pater says. He tries to step outside, but the G-men are blocking the door. Maybe they're worried he'll escape. I notice the slight bulge under their jackets.

Friday pulls out a pencil stub and writing tablet, just like the one Pater uses for his screenplay ideas. Maybe this scene will make it into *Tentatively Untitled*. "Do you know a girl named Hope Springs, Mr. Strauss? Student of yours, maybe?"

"Could be. Lots of kids pass through my office."

"Lots of radicals at your school?"

"All kids are radicals."

The Feds don't like this answer as much as I do. My relief that they aren't investigating my break-in at Shreddermauler's house spins into worry for Pater and Hope Springs. I haven't seen Hope since she left for Prague. What could she have done to attract the attention of J. Edgar Hoover's flat-footed henchmen?

"She was arrested for trespassing a year ago," bad cop Friday continues. "Trespassing on government property."

"Is that illegal?" Pater asks. "Isn't government property owned by the citizens?"

"She was arrested for inciting a riot to overthrow the United States of America," Friday says as if a simple USA would not have gotten the point across. "She jumped bail. We have reason to believe she's hiding here."

"Here?" I ask but Nana cuts off the air to the back of my windpipe before I can ask these guys if they're plumb crazy or what.

"Do you know the penalty for falsifying voter registration forms?" Friday produces a sheaf of papers with our address written in Hope's hand. "Or do all these twenty-one-year-olds live here, too?"

"What on earth?" Nana asks in heavily accented disbelief.

I'm glad that these agents are wearing baggy, bargain-basement J.C. Penney suits because tight-fitting police uniforms would make Nana Hannah so nervous she might blast *Madame Butterfly* into their faces. Even meter maids give her the heebie-jeebies. She wouldn't let Tommy join the Boy Scouts because they reminded her of the Hitler Youth.

"Have you ever heard of the Weather Underground, Ma'am? Black Panthers?" Friday asks as if rattling off ice cream flavors. "SDS? Yippies?"

"Gentlemen," Nana says, "I think you should stop smoking marijuana."

I would laugh out loud if she weren't still squeezing my neck. There's just enough oxygen in my brain to feel another great rush of love for my spunky grandmother. I have never felt more proud of her than at this very moment. Hannah Strauss is *chutzpah* personified.

"Do you have any I.D., Ma'am?" Friday asks. "We need to verify that you're in the country legally."

At this, Nana's had quite enough, thank you very much. She steps outside with the G-men and slams the thick pine door so hard that the house shakes. I manage to push the door open and squeeze past my father. "If they take you, Nana, I'm coming too."

"Nobody's going anywhere, except these two." She takes a calm, deep breath, the kind an opera singer draws before belting out a high note. Her words have a sharp German edge that cut through the hot, still afternoon. "I did not survive the Nazis only to be harassed by Laurel and Hardy. You boys have exactly three seconds to get the hell out of here."

Friday looks directly at my father and says, "It's a shame about your son getting arrested. Too bad you couldn't help him the way you've helped so many others to shirk their patriotic duty. We wish him well in Vietnam, sir. "

"One, two …" Nana's V-2 rocket is ready for horizontal blast off.

The men step off the porch and nod with a smug look that suggests we'll see them again. They click their wingtip shoes down the front walk and drive away in a black Ford Fairlane.

J-Camp

Camp Bess Weinberg, aka J-Camp, occupies a small rustic canyon on the coast of Malibu just this side of the Ventura county line. J-Camp is a noble attempt to tame, civilize and influence Judaism's next generation, but the truth is that we all go nuts with sudden freedom and surging hormones.

My father spends half his summer here as the assistant director. I started off as a camp brat, a mascot for older kids and a magnet for bad words and misinformation I was too young to hear. Now that I'm one of the cabin kids, I try to have a good time without drawing attention to my last name. This year, I couldn't wait to escape from the heat, the house, and the nightmares about Shreidermayer.

The camp bus left the parking lot of Wilshire Boulevard Temple on Saturday afternoon, one week after the G-men came to our door. Kids were a bit shy until we rolled onto Pacific Coast Highway and someone started singing "John Jacob Jingleheimer Schmidt." A few songs later, we were singing loud enough to escape the gravitational pull of the so-called real world

Does six and six make nine?
Does ice grow on a vine?
Is old black Joe an Eskimo in the good old summertime?

Most of these kids come from far wealthier zip codes than I do. They sport white tennis shoes, wire-rim glasses and polo shirts boasting little embroidered golf players. Rich parents send their lucky offspring to J-Camp for a few weeks of fresh air and modern Judaism. They hope this will build character and keep the tribe from dissolving in the surging waters of the New World. Our parents don't realize there's no worse influence on a kid than another kid.

There are a few other outliers, losers like me who still wear Keds sneakers and don't live in Brentwood or the Palisades. I'm able to float between the cliques, but I feel most at home among the underprivileged riffraff who will never ski or learn to play golf.

Howie Bergman is too uncoordinated to do either. He's got a bushy Jew-fro on top, and a pair of suede waffle stompers on bottom that will be dirty as goats within a week. Like most of the boys, Howie has yet to lose his baby fat.

For better or worse, mainly worse, the girls are in full bloom this year.

I'm not happy to see Darlene Ginsburg, future Olympian, astronaut, U.S. President and Nobel Prize winner back at camp this year. Her aura is so brilliant it leaves everyone else blind. When she's not setting camp track and field records or winning the talent show, she's chewing up hearts and spitting out the pieces. I'm sure that if I look up "annoying" in the Funk and Wagnall's, it will show her picture.

Texas Terry, who claims to be the only Jew in Dallas, looks very cute in her hip huggers and striped tube top. I love her drawl, especially when she says stuff like, "The rest of y'all are the ones with funny accents."

Freddy Lazar, sex pervert, seems weirder than last year. Maybe someday his brain will catch up with his hormones, but for now he's just a caveman in cutoffs. Freddy spends the bus ride telling a whopper about getting shot at by an angry neighbor who discovered Freddy in bed with his nymphomaniac wife. According to Freddy, nymphomaniac means the same as horny. He's what Nana would call a "teller of

136

tales," which is polite for nonstop liar. She says he'll either grow out of it or become a politician.

Amy Buchberg, former earth princess, spent the first half of last year's session communing with nature and the second half covered with poison oak rash and calamine lotion. This year she's wearing enough makeup to paint a battleship. Girls in the know claim she stuffs her bra.

Aaron Wexler, the third-fastest swimmer in the state, got on the bus late and had no choice but to sit next to me. He grunted a hello and then ignored me for the rest of the ride. I pretend not to care about Aaron's indifference, but the truth is I really want him to like me. It's a foregone conclusion that he'll go to the formal, end-of-session banquet with Darlene Ginsburg, Miss Perfection, USA. She and Aaron swim laps in the same gene pool. They are destined to marry and raise perfect children in a perfect house with perfect pets in their perfect backyard.

Amazingly, nobody gets sick on the bus this year. There's nothing worse than starting a two-week session with barf-soaked shoes. Last year, a kid lost his lunch on the bus and was nicknamed "Puker." We never learned his real name, and he didn't return this year.

We arrive at camp and are herded into the stone amphitheater to meet our cabin mates and counselors. After my minor freakout at the Hollywood Bowl, I know better than to sit in the front row. Two hundred hungry and hormonal Jewish kids could go native faster than I could ever escape the stampede.

From up in the nosebleed section, I can see that our counselors continue to get more colorful. Each one has a special talent. Harvey the Hippie is our music coordinator because he knows every song Bob Dylan ever wrote. Harvey plays guitar, piano, and banjo, the least Jewish instrument imaginable. Musclebound Morrie is our fitness coach. He always wears tight-fitting gym clothes, even to Saturday services. His little sister, Big Bones Bertha, is the art instructor. Last year Morrie did twenty-five push-ups with Big Bertha on his back. This year, she will crush him.

I see Ruben Fineman, the drama coach whose claim to fame is a bit role as a *Star Trek* space alien that nobody can verify. Jonathan Wolfson looks like a heartthrob from the cover of *Tiger Beat*, but he's really just the Rabbi's rebel son. I see the counselor we called "Hoodlum," sitting alone at the top of the amphitheater. He's adjusting his completely unnecessary leather jacket and combing his James Dean hair. Besides serving as humanity's last defense against the rising tide of hippiedom, Hoodlum's main contribution is having invented the zorch, a bedtime favorite.

To make a zorch, you take a long plastic laundry bag and knot it every six inches along its length. Hook one end over a metal clothes hanger and let the other end hang loose over a small trash can full of water. Turn out the lights and set the free end of the knotted bag on fire. As the melting drops of flaming plastic fall into the water they make a strange *zorch!* sound. If the cabin doesn't burn down, it will smell like burning tires when the show is over.

A few years ago, all the counselors were clean-cut. Now, for the most part, they are hippies. Jewish hippies who have been to music festivals, riots and love-ins. They will bring us up to date on the antiwar movement, underground slang, and Mick Jagger's latest dance moves.

A new, long-haired counselor who calls himself "Free" looks like Geronimo's grandson. His bare chest is tan and visible under his Farmer Johns. His perfect physique has not gone unnoticed by the more advanced girls, many of whom have high school boyfriends with cars and armpit hair. Free is perched next to Mimi, the Israeli who teaches Jewish folk dance.

"Over, under, high, low. Here we go: quick, quick, slow!" We're all eager to dance because it gives us an excuse to hold hands and bump into each other.

Old Rabbi Wolfson sits on the stage next to my father. They both look us over, the rabbi presuming our innocence, my father knowing in advance of our guilt. Wolfson's eyes are soft and folded, and he's got the same compassionate smile that he had last year and the year before. The rabbi's nephew, Mark Spitz, will be swimming in the summer Olympics in Mexico. Rabbi says that God made a few of us into good swimmers in case the parting of the Red Sea didn't work out as planned.

After Pater makes a few announcements and the rabbi offers a blessing, we race up to our cabins to thumb wrestle for the best bunks and the least annoying neighbors. Once unpacked, we stretch out on our thin mattresses, stare up at the corrugated roof, and tell lies about the year since we last saw one another. It's always interesting to see what new fads and unnecessary gizmos show up in kids' duffle bags and foot lockers. This year, Clarks Wallabee shoes with sponge soles are on everyone's feet but mine. A few kids brought transistor radios, but we're too far up the coast to pick up anything but static.

~ ~ ~

The weather is generally sunny, but our first beach day coincides with the only overcast morning of the week.

Kahuna, nobody knows his real name, is our leader for all things H_2O except toilets. He reminds us that we can burn even when the sun isn't shining, so we are all required to cover our noses with glow-in-the-dark zinc oxide. Kahuna teaches us to be junior lifeguards in the pool, then he rescues us from rip tides on the beach. He's a self-proclaimed Jewish beach bum who wears nothing but "Hang Ten" clothes and dispenses West Coast wisdom like, "Never turn your back on Neptune." He's our only counselor from UC Santa Cruz, the only school where you can major in acid trips.

Beach day is the weekly roundup when we venture beyond camp to see if Amy Buchberg's left boob will bounce out of her top like it did last year. On the sands of Zuma and County Line we seek answers to life's great questions like does God exist, and what makes a Frisbee fly. A day on the coast is fun for most of us, but there's always some pigment-free princess who burns to a crisp in spite of her Coppertone. Every session produces at least one hyper-sensitive kid who is allergic to sand fleas or pukes after swallowing a mouthful of seawater.

This year Texas Terry brought an NBC beach towel with last year's TV schedule on it. It's well known that Jews must wait an hour after eating to avoid drowning from cramps, so we gather around her towel to digest our bologna sandwiches and argue over *Flipper*, *Get Smart* and *Please Don't Eat the Daisies*. Terry insists that there won't be a *Monkees* third season, but I don't believe her. How could there not be another season of the best show on TV? I learn that nobody else watches *Star Trek* and now feel more Vulcan than ever.

At the end of the day, one of our counselors has the great idea of forming a massage circle. She manages to seat sixty kids into a circle where each of us massages the shoulders of the kid in front. She insists on alternating boys with girls, which generates a lot of giggles and pinching. When the kid behind me decides to use beach sand as a massage lubricant, the circle spins off into noogies, tag, and towel-snapping.

Arts and crafts. Theater, dance, and music. Swim and sport. Our days are filled with activities designed to educate, entertain, and leave us no time to make out. In the evenings we have campfires where we sing and perform skits for each other.

At last Saturday's campfire, the counselor we call "Hoodlum" told a terrifying story about a fugitive named Jim Haggerty who hid out in the same canyon that we are in. Armed and dangerous, Haggerty was wanted for a laundry list of unspeakable crimes, which Hoodlum described in graphic detail. No amount of reward money ever convinced a bounty hunter to attempt his capture.

"He was wounded in a shootout with federal marshals. One bullet is still lodged in his calf, so he drags his foot and makes a scraping sound when he walks." Hoodlum limps around the campfire, glaring at us with dark, angry eyes. "If you hear Jim Haggerty shuffling through the woods, your only hope is to run. Don't look back. Whatever you do, don't look back."

Perfect. I had just stopped having nightmares about Shreddermauler and the H-bomb and now I have Jim Haggerty to worry about. It doesn't help that the counseling staff is unanimous that Haggerty is still at large. If they're trying to scare us, it's working.

The night of Hoodlum's story, a group of older boys snuck out after curfew, fanned out across camp, and made Jim Haggerty leg-dragging sounds around the perimeters of all the other cabins. Fear of Haggerty makes some of us more religious.

The only safe place is our wooded chapel, nestled in a grove of tall sycamore trees. God himself could find religion here. We sing songs like, "Turn, Turn, Turn" and "Blowin' in the Wind." Even the scratchy old Hebrew prayers sound good at camp. Rabbi Wolfson's sermons harken back to a time when stories had morals even if people didn't. He often talks about how a mild-mannered Dutch fisherman saved him and his parents from the Nazis. "You can never tell who the heroes are," he says.

In spite of Jim Haggerty, or maybe because of him, camp flies by at warp factor nine. No sooner did we arrive here than it is already our last Friday. We'll have one more Shabbat service, pack our trunks, and then finish the session with a formal banquet, aka the J-prom.

I'm probably the only one who dreads J-prom's soft music, slow dancing and candlelit awkwardness. Everyone is supposed to dress fancy and invite a date, which chalks up two strikes against me. This year, I'm borrowing some nicer clothes from a cabin-mate so at least I won't show up in Toughskin jeans and a Charlie Brown shirt like I did last year. I'll leave my Encyclopedia Brown glasses on my bed and try not to squint. I'll sit at a table with the other misfits and pretend to be happy when some sympathetic counselor asks for my hand in a pity dance. I've instructed my father to ignore me.

I try not to think about tomorrow's banquet. It's Friday night in the here and now and J-prom is still twenty-four hours away. The only thing that could save me from the prom would be if Russian subs attack Malibu. If they strike soon, I won't have cleanup duty after dinner tonight.

My father usually makes a few announcements before we sing the after-dinner blessing. The only announcement anyone listens for is who won today's best camper award which, for obvious reasons is never me. Tonight, Pater skips the best camper award and just reminds us not to flush entire toilet paper rolls unless our parents want to plumb Malibu.

After the announcements, it's my cabin's turn to clear dishes and clean the mess hall. I look around the dining room, hoping to find the least disgusting table, but tonight's spaghetti-and-meatball extravaganza was a tomato-sauce hurricane. It didn't help that we sang "On top of old Smokey, all covered with

142

cheese. I lost my poor meatball, when somebody sneezed." Now the floor is dotted with meatballs. The sticky tables need some serious elbow grease.

I'm scraping melted cheese off a chair when I notice two familiar-looking men enter the hall and wait by the door. For some reason, and it can't be good, Friday and Gannon, Laurel Canyon's resident FBI agents, are here. Instead of wearing their rumpled JC Penney's suits, tonight they look like the Beach Boys' parents in La Costa polo shirts tucked into belted plaid shorts. Good Cop Gannon wears sockless topsiders. Friday's still in wing tips. If this is their idea for how to blend in, they're off by a decade.

What are the G-men doing here? What tore them away from spying on rock stars and hippies in Laurel Canyon? Are they here to arrest my father? Is Tommy in some new kind of trouble? Did Shreddermauler press charges against me? Aren't G-men supposed to capture Nazis instead of defending them?

I want to get close, but I'm afraid the Feds will recognize me from when Nana sent them packing. For a second I consider borrowing Ronnie Samuel's Huck Finn hat as a disguise, but he seems to have a phobia about removing it, and I don't want his cooties anyway. As kids file out of the mess hall, I ask my friend Jonathan Rabinowitz to grab a mop, push it over to the corner, and eavesdrop where the G-men are speaking to my father. Mop duty is the worst, so Jonathan's favor will probably cost me the rest of my canteen money.

I take up a position at the other end of the hall so I can keep an eye on things while I scrape Chef Boyardee off the table. Jonathan gets close enough to mop Pater's shoes, but my dad's too preoccupied to notice. The agents are obviously getting under Pater's skin. Distracted, I slip on a patch of tomato sauce and drop a pile of plates onto the concrete floor.

Uh-Oh! SpaghettiOs.

The crash and clatter blow my cover. Both G-men look right at me. Friday glares like a hawk who just spotted a mouse. Good Cop Gannon half-smiles. My face turns meatball-red.

The horse-sized head of Big Ben, the cleft-lipped kitchen chef, appears and orders Jonathan to help me mop up after the disaster. Jonathan doesn't seem to mind as this puts him closer to the exit. He shoves the mop into my hands, wishes me good luck, and books off to the Friday night dance.

Two carefree weeks in paradise just burned up like a shooting star in the atmosphere. Two weeks of good friends, great times, and bad food. Goodbye to the dream world of beaches, folk songs, and campfires. Two weeks without Mumu Marie, Grumpy Chuck, and the Man Who Cuts Legs Off. Two weeks of feeling Jewish and proud of it. The real world has broken through the cracks. J-Camp is over.

The G-men leave without shooting the kitchen full of holes or arresting my father, who races off to chaperone the dance before I can interrogate him. I finish cleaning up my mess, but I now smell like a Shakey's pizza, so I'm less inspired than usual to stand around tapping my two left feet at the Friday night dance in the rec hall. But I've got nowhere else to go, and besides, where better to feel sorry for myself than in a room full of happy campers?

After extracting myself from a near death experience on my way to the rec hall, I manage to find a bench within earshot of the stomping feet, gyrating torsos, and clapping hands at the Friday night dance. The sound of a well-worn Beatles record drifts through the fragrant night air. I gaze up at the sky and wish that the Starship Enterprise would just beam me up without further humiliation.

Instead, Captain Kirk sends a perfect specimen down to torment me. Darlene Ginsburg, Miss Perfection, USA, comes out for a breath of fresh air. Her tanned forehead glistens in the

144

fractured glow of moonlight and mirror ball. "What's wrong, Max? Why aren't you dancing?"

"Not feeling so hot." The last thing I need is a pep talk from Supergirl, but Darlene is an ambassador for her species, and I must look like a potential convert.

"I'm way too hot. Mind if I sit down and catch my breath?"

"Free country." I really want to like Darlene. Worse, I want her to like me. I want her to be my friend, but I'm not going to worship her like everyone else does. She can outrun any boy, swim like a dolphin, and defy gravity, but I refuse to be impressed. On beach day, Darlene is the first in and the last out of the waves. She has a sunny disposition, adults love her, and boys go gaga because she's cute beyond anything five thousand years of Judaism has ever produced. To make things worse, she's smart, sweeter than saccharine, and her parents are rich. That's what makes her so annoying.

"Something bothering you, Maxie?"

"You are."

"Just trying to be neighborly." Darlene stands up.

Neighborly? She lives in a Palisades mansion and I live in a canyon A-frame. We're not even from neighboring planets.

"Looked like you needed a friend but it sounds like you just need a spanking."

"Sorry," I say, but then I giggle, which doesn't sound very apologetic. "Wait … speaking of spankings, I just kicked Freddy Lazar in the nards."

"What a burn!" Darlene seems genuinely impressed. "Did you knock the wind out of him?"

"He's probably still doubled over." I still feel like barfing, which is the last thing I want to do in in the presence of her most perfect highness, Miss J-Camp, USA. "I feel a bit dizzy."

"That's the thrill of victory," Darlene plops down on the bench and pats my back. "I get that sometimes after a race.

145

Sometimes before. Take a few deep breaths. Oxygen works wonders."

"Yeah, oxygen is A-OK... or, A-O_2. I mean, it's good stuff," I blather, my brain turning to lukewarm Ovaltine.

She laughs, so I laugh. I don't want her to stop patting my back, but I do feel better. If I found Darlene annoying, it was because I assumed anyone this perfect had to be a wall-to-wall phony. But she seems real enough tonight, and it's not her fault if she was born with super powers. Nana always says it's not what you have, it's how you use it. Maybe Darlene is okay.

"Did Freddy ask you to take a walk? That sex pervert! I hope you didn't go with him."

"You kidding? I was on the way over here and he shows up out of nowhere like he was waiting in the bushes or something. Invited me to climb up to Inspiration Point with him to see the ocean in the moonlight. I said, 'No way, Jose.' Then he started poking at me and saying F-word this and F-word that. He's asking me if I know how babies are made and do I know if any of the girls here are bleeding yet. Then he tries to shove me in the bushes so I kicked him in the nuts. "

"Chop on him."

"Yeah, but if the outlaw James Haggerty doesn't kill me, now Freddy will."

"Nah. That sissy will never bug you again. He's looking for easier prey."

"What's his trip, anyway?"

"Who knows?" Darlene laughs. "He's totally cracked. Hey, you want to hear something crazy?

I can't believe Darlene wants to hang around. Records are playing, and she still has a hundred hearts to break before the last dance. Not that I'm complaining. Talking with Darlene, just being next to her, is better than a triple scoop of Rocky Road ice cream. How did I misjudge her so badly?

"I shouldn't be telling you this, but last week, he took a few of us into the woods. Said he had something important to show us."

"You went?"

Darlene leans over to whisper in my ear. The feeling of her breath in my hair spreads goose bumps up and down my arms. "He takes us into the woods and then, I still can't believe this, says he knows how to get sperm!"

"What?" I turn my head so fast that we brush noses. "Get sperm?"

Darlene doesn't seem to have minded the accidental Eskimo kiss. "We should have run away and told your dad or a counselor but before anyone could think, Freddy drops his drawers and starts making sausage."

"Wait … what … sausage?" I'm confused. Darlene's hazel eyes are full of the most delightful mischief. I wonder if this is what being drunk feels like.

"Saddles up the baloney pony. Spanks the monkey. Whacks his pud. Slams the ham."

"Uh… you mean … *masturbating*?"

"Well, duh! If you must be so scientific about it. Anyway, there we were, face to face with his one-eyed worm. He's draining the dragon and we're all, like, totally frozen."

"Gross!" I blurt between gasps of laughter. I can't believe Darlene is talking so dirty.

"He's beating his meat. We start yelling like it's James Haggerty or something. Freddy freaks out and runs away with his pants down."

"Yikes! I hope he got poison oak on his … you know."

Darlene laughs. "You're okay, Maxie. A bit of a Poindexter, but cool in your own dorky way." She squeezes my shoulder and I try not to misinterpret it for affection. She's just being friendly. "Come on. Let's go back in and show those kids how to dance."

What the heck. I can't dance, but Darlene lives in a world where anything's possible and her enthusiasm is more contagious than the mumps. Besides, what do I have to lose? Camp's almost over. The lights are low, the music is loud and nobody really cares how stupid I look on the dance floor. If there's a time and a place for everything, this must be it.

I stumble around to Sly and the Family Stone, flailing on the dance floor until I find a pattern that matches the beat. Nana's right: there's more to music than meets the eye. Darlene drifts back just in time for a dreaded slow dance. My only goal is not to step on her feet so I keep her at arm's length. "Going to the banquet this year?" I ask, like an idiot. Of course she's going.

"You mean am I going with Aaron Wexler, third-fastest breast-stroker in the state? Hey! You just stepped on my foot."

"Sorry. With a little practice, I could definitely get the hang of this." It makes no sense why a goddess like Darlene would slow dance with an earthbound geek like me.

"Let's make Aaron jealous," Darlene whispers.

Now it all makes sense: I'm a pawn in her game. But this is fun, and I don't care. We sweep the floor to a Blood, Sweat & Tears tune and I wish J-camp could last forever. Away from the city, away from our parents — mostly away in my case — barely supervised by the hippie staff, how much better can it get?

To answer my question, the Kahuna announces the last dance will be the Hokey Pokey, a strategic dose of musical ice water. Some of us were getting a bit too hot, and that's not what it's all about.

"The Hokey Pokey's for squares. Let's get out of here," I say to Darlene, with sudden audacity.

"Yeah." Amazingly, she agrees. "If we start walking now, we can beat the bedtime rush to the sinks and toilets."

We sneak out of the rec hall and jog up the trail toward the cabins. Darlene is fast but merciful enough not to leave me in the dust. She's testing my stamina but as long as she doesn't start sprinting, I have no trouble keeping up. She may be a Palisades Princess, but I'm a half-Chumash canyon kid.

The trail is dark but the moon is bright so we don't need our flashlights. Still, I keep a tight grip on mine in case Freddy Lazar appears with James Haggerty and I have to brain them both. "I've been thinking, Darlene. When you're the first woman on the moon, I'll probably be the scientist who designs your rocket."

"The moon? Are you kidding?" She laughs, and I realize there's no need for the moon when you're from heaven. "I don't want to be an astronaut. I can barely stand riding the bus."

"Are you claustrophobic?"

"No, I just hate the smell and all the bouncing around. Besides, didn't a rocket blow up on the launch pad last year?"

"Yeah, okay, so how about this: When you're president, can I be in charge of NASA? I mean, we need some Jews to keep an eye on all those Nazi rocket scientists."

"What are you talking about? Do you think Nazis are still around?"

"You don't?" Darlene's sunny disposition isn't clouded by the long shadow. She's seen the documentaries but doesn't have the Shoah in her blood like I do. God, what luck. "Just promise me the NASA job so I have something to live for once we leave camp."

"But I don't want to be president. I don't want to be assassinated."

"Me neither. Guess we have a lot in common."

"That's what I've been thinking." Darlene takes my hand. Not handshake style. Full on "Here is the church, here is the steeple, open the door and here are the people" interlaced-finger style. She looks around to be sure no one's following. "Let's cut through the chapel."

~ ~ ~

It's cold when I wake up, so I snuggle way down into my sleeping bag and relive the best moment of my life so far. Holding hands with Darlene might have been the sweetest thing I'll ever know. I wiggle my toes into the bottom of my sack and fall back asleep for a few delicious minutes.

But daylight has different ideas. Darlene didn't even say hello at breakfast. What was I expecting, anyway? Nana says there's a lid for every pot, but I must be a frying pan. Too many songs have been written about Friday night dances, holding hands, and broken hearts, but I still feel as if one more is needed. No words or melody exist to describe how low I feel. The chapel in the woods may be the only place to feel God's presence and lock fingers during his off hours, but now that he's back on duty all sinners must pay. By fire. By water. By wild beast and James Haggerty.

Darlene didn't look at me during the Saturday service. She didn't wish me a Shabbat Shalom or sit at my lunch table. Didn't she and I share something magical last night? I thought we were best friends, but I'm afraid to ask in case I was dreaming. Seeing her at J-prom will be agony.

Last night I went to sleep with visions of sugar plums. Today I'm swimming in prune juice. I must have misunderstood the slow dancing, hand-holding and that quick peck on the cheek under the sycamores. I thought it meant we were best friends, but Darlene probably does it all the time. No reason for the Jewel of J-Camp to lose her luster on a dork like me.

150

I can't wait to get out of here. I miss my loft at the top of our A-frame in Laurel Canyon. I miss Nana. I miss my Joni Mitchell record and my transistor radio. I even miss my stupid brother who's about to have his butt schlepped off to jail or the Army or both. J-Camp is a fantasy, one big distraction. Time to stop dreaming.

See you in the funny papers, Darlene. I've got a mission to accomplish. I'm Max Strauss, Nazi Hunter. Once I bust Shreddermauler, I'll find the rest of them.

Instead of going to the pool and suffering the indignities of the locker room, I break the rules and wander off on my own. Why jump in a pool full of peeing rich kids when I can swim in my own self-pity? I make sure nobody is looking and then drop down into the arroyo that leads to the beach.

I hop from stone to stone as long as I can, careful to avoid the plant that smells like skunk butt. I pull a few seeds off the flower that smells like licorice and pop them in my mouth. I slosh through a little pool of green water to get past a clump of prickly pear cactus that has colonized the embankment and then creep through the culvert that runs under the Pacific Coast Highway. I emerge into a wall of ocean spray and sunshine. Once my eyes adjust, I gauge the tide and find a rock perch above the incoming surf.

I try not to think about Darlene, but I wish I'd never met her. Holding hands was her idea, not mine. I wish I'd known that the price for a moment of friendship would be a lifetime of pain. She found me tolerable in the darkness, but revolting in daylight. Maybe Darlene and the rest of the world would be better off if I throw myself into the waves. Nobody will ever notice I'm gone.

I look for a sign from the Great Spirit of the Chumash, but their God is as silent as mine. I glance uphill toward the big menorah where creepy Freddy Lazar wanted to make a human

151

sacrifice out of me. The bright sun makes the menorah glow like Hanukkah. I stand up on my boulder, not sure what to do next.

The Chumash had everything they needed right here. Why did we have to come along and wreck things? I notice a dolphin fin and then another beyond the waves. They have come for me. Time to join them and pass beyond the Western Gate.

"Max?"

Why does the Great Spirit of the Chumash sound like my dad? Just like him to spoil my plan to join the blue dolphins. "Pater? What are you doing here?"

"I followed you, silly." He climbs across the big rocks to join me. Spray rises from the incoming tide. "You know what happens to campers who break the rules and wander off?"

"James Haggerty kills them?" A dive bombing pelican hits the water so hard I wonder how it can survive the impact. A second after the splash collapses it pops up with a fish in its fleshy gullet. "What did the G-men want last night?

"The FBI? Those idiots?"

"Idiots with guns, a bad combination. What did they want?"

"They wanted to talk statistics." Pater looks at me for a moment, but knows he can't fool me. "I would have invited you over to chat but you seemed kind of busy smashing plates."

"Not my best moment."

"We're trying to teach campers valuable kitchen skills, but it might be cheaper to hire professionals to bus dishes." The sea breeze ripples through his brown hair. Another wave breaks nearby and splashes us.

"So, what statistics did the fuzz want to talk about?"

"Fuzz? Oh, yeah." Pater takes a deep breath and pretends to enjoy the fresh ocean air while he considers his answer. "The FBI finds it interesting that more of my male advisees go to college than boys from other high schools."

"But that's your job, right? Helping kids with college and trades."

"Yes and no. They say I'm 'helping' more than other advisors."

"How much more?"

"A lot more." Pater finally looks at me. He's smiling, but serious. "They claim that I'm gaming the college deferment rules to keep boys out of Vietnam."

"They came all the way to Malibu to say that?"

"Good excuse for a beach day." Pater sees I'm not buying it. "They claim I'm the ringleader of a gang of guidance counselors that helps boys evade the draft."

"Hope it works for Tommy." I say, but Pater winces, and now I feel worse than when this bad day started. "Sorry. I'm sure that things will work out. Even if those spooks are right, there's nothing illegal about sending boys to college."

"Nope. Perfectly legal. Even boys who flunk high school can wait out the war at a community college. Tommy included."

We sit and watch the green water boil and foam for a while. This is the most time we've spent together without Pater rambling about his movie since I can't remember when. "If it's legal to send boys off to die, it should be legal to send them off to learn. Sounds like you're just doing your job."

"Maybe too well. J. Edgar's boys also observed that the most active advisors in the district just happen to be Jewish. Many are members of our temple."

"A real Jewish conspiracy? Finally!"

"Right. We distracted people by controlling Hollywood and the banks in order to muscle in on the community college admission process. That's always been the real plan."

"I'm proud of you for helping those boys, Pater." Guess I won't be joining the blue dolphins today.

"Proud of you, too, Maxie."

153

Pater puts his arm around me and we sit for a few minutes watching the sea.

Tommy Invades Normandie

I'm the only J-camper left in the temple parking lot, and there's nothing worse than being last. I've said goodbye so many times that I deserve a lifelong exemption. I never want to say "have a bitchin' summer" again. I hugged everyone except best camper Darlene Ginsburg, who avoided me, and worst camper Freddy Lazar, whom I avoided.

Pater's still at camp, so I've been watching for Tommy's old white van. My brother Tommy didn't inherit the internal cuckoo clock that makes my grandmother three days early for everything. I'm beginning to worry that the van broke down. Maybe he got ambushed by the cops again.

I'm wondering if he ran off to San Francisco for good when the coughing Ford Econoline finally pulls into the empty parking lot. I need his help to lift my footlocker because I traveled with too much stuff. Last year all my underwear disappeared on laundry day, so this year I took no chances.

"Hey, kid." Tommy's hair has grown enough to turn his head into an unripe peach. He struggles with the footlocker. "Wow. This mother's heavy! Hope there's nothing illegal in here."

"Clothes weigh more when they're dirty."

"You can ride shotgun," he says, even though no one's competing for the passenger seat.

Tommy pulls out into Wilshire traffic, and I re-enter the so-called real world of stop lights, shop fronts, and billboards urging me to buy stuff I don't want or need. A gray dome of smog hovers over the City of Angels. I look around to see if old

Shreddermauler is waiting on every corner. For now the coast is clear, but you can never be too careful about angry ex-Nazis.

"So, *nu*? What's the verdict?" I ask, mainly to interrupt Tommy's drumming on the steering wheel. "Any news on the crime-and-punishment front?"

"Jesus got the judge to throw out most of the charges."

"Jesus saves," I say, noticing a guy with a sign that says so. He waves at me, so I flash a V for victory just in case he's right.

"Thirty days for all the unpaid tickets and warrants. Thirty days in the slammer. Thirty days in the big house. Thirty days and thirty nights."

"Huh? Why do you sound so happy?"

"Free meals. Interesting people."

"Like J-camp for criminals. Uh, hey, Doctor Tom-tom, aren't we going the wrong way?" I can see downtown L.A. shimmering in the haze. "I hope you're not taking me to another Doors concert."

"Quick detour," Tommy says. "I want to show you something."

"I've been to the Tar Pits. I've seen your ancestors. Let's just get home."

"Look!" Tommy takes a hand off the wheel and his eyes off the road. "There's the Ambassador Hotel. You know how many greats have played the Coconut Grove? Unreal."

"Isn't that where Bobby Kennedy was assassinated?" This is now the official worst J-camp re-entry ever. "Hope Springs was there the night he was shot."

"Yup." Tommy's so fascinated with the view that he nearly rear-ends a Lincoln Continental in front of us. "Bobby was killed in the kitchen."

"That's what you wanted to show me? The saddest place on earth?" The hotel looks like a big, faded pink dog house. Even the palm trees look hunched and depressed.

"That's the Brown Derby restaurant across the street," Tommy says as if some place that looks like a hat is the eighth wonder of the world.

"Derbies are square. I just want to go home."

We spend a few minutes stuck behind fancy cars and taxis before turning down a small street.

"See that hamburger stand?" Tommy points to a small burger joint that looks like a castle. "Nana used to bring dad here back when burgers cost a nickel."

"Wow. Five-cent burgers. Imagine that. Okay, tour over. Next stop: Laurel Canyon."

"Got a new band," he says.

"Didn't you need a bass player?"

"Think I found one," Tommy fiddles with the radio but can't land a signal. "Japanese chick I met at the library."

"Cool. A bass-playing bookworm." For the last year, Tommy has been working through the record collections in local libraries. A to Z, Animals to Zombies. He was born a preemie, but when it comes to the libraries, he's always overdue. Tommy makes withdrawals, Nana manages the returns. "Did you say she's from Japan?"

"Nah. Her parents, I think. They were interned at Manzanar during the war. Name's Midori, but we just call her Dori. She plays great and writes outtasight lyrics."

"Sounds like you've got a crush on her, Tommy-boy."

"Shaddup." The Tommy-mobile chugs north along Normandie Avenue, spelled the French way. It's an old street full of little Spanish-style apartments. There must have been a sale on red roof tiles and pink stucco when this part of town was built.

"Nana and Dad shared a small place with two other refugee families around here." There's no place to park, so Tommy just

157

stops the van in the street and throws the hazard lights on. "Jump out!"

There's no traffic on the small street, so I hop out.

"248 South Normandie Avenue," he says. "This is the place."

Three arches, four apartments, maybe two bedrooms each. Red-and-white-striped awnings hanging from the second-story windows. The building is set back from the street behind a brown summer lawn.

"They came here without a penny. Nana made rent working down the street at the Ambassador. Started off cleaning rooms and eventually got a job in the kitchen."

"The kitchen where Bobby Kennedy was killed? Weird."

"I once asked if she saw lots of famous people, but Nana said they couldn't have been so famous because she didn't know who they were."

"Sounds like something she'd say."

"Here's where they lived." Tommy points to the lower apartment on the left. "Mom's Aunt Sadie, the yenta who introduced them, lived next door. After they got married, Aunt Sadie tried to collect a matchmaker's fee."

"Strange. It's hard to believe that Nana survived Dachau, managed to find Pater in Israel, and then travelled all the way to Los Angeles only to clean up after mucky-mucks at the Ambassador."

"She paid some dues, all right."

A car honks, so we jump back into the van and pull away. Five minutes ago, this street had no significance. Now it will haunt me. I want to know more. Why didn't Nana stay in Israel with my father? Why did they come here of all places? Who helped her along the way, and how did such a long chain of coincidences lead to my being here right now?

"The Summer of '68 belongs to Garage Sale," Tommy says without making eye contact. Or sense, for that matter.

"You're having a garage sale? Can I buy your *Mad* magazine collection?"

"Garage Sale is the name of the band, idiot."

"I thought you were called Jail Bait, idiot."

"That's what you're called, shrimp skin." Tommy runs his fingers over his scalp as if checking to see if his hair has grown back in the last half-hour. Tommy had a crush on his hair and he's still not over it.

"Garage Sale, huh? Lots of free advertising, I guess. Better than Swap Meet."

"I wanna spell sale 'S-A-I-L.' Either way, we're gonna hit the big time."

Eighteen years to my twelve, Tommy is the Pepsi generation to my Uncola. I'm not sure where confidence ends and insanity begins, but Tommy's got both in spades. If he fell headfirst in the sewer he'd surface with a twenty-dollar bill in his teeth. Aside from the buzz cut, his recent trip to the clink doesn't seem to have changed him much.

"If Garage Sale's still around in October, you can play at my big B.M." I had been meaning to ask Tommy about organizing a jazz service for Friday night.

"We'll be so famous by October you'll need to move the party to the Hollywood Bowl."

"Don't you need a hit song to be famous?"

"Hit songs are history. We're an FM radio band. Dori wants to write a rock opera."

"So ... what? Madame Butterfly meets Mama Cass?"

"We've already started laying tracks. I traded a couple of sessions for studio time at Elektra."

As usual, Tommy has a plan. As usual, it's crazy. "Isn't Elektra a dump? I thought you said the studios at Capitol were better."

"Forgive them, Lord." Tommy makes the sign of the cross into the cracked windshield. "They know zilch of which they speak."

Tommy's been in and out of so many bands that I don't give Garage Sale much future. He's also been in and out of jail recently, which is a more immediate concern. "Listen: You've never been in trouble before. Why not get Rabbi Wolfson to write a letter or something? I'll bet you can get that sentence reduced to nearly nothing."

"Thirty days is the reduced sentence," Tommy zigzags over to Alexandria Avenue. "I have a prior arrest record, remember? It wasn't easy getting all those fake drug and 'corrupting a minor' charges dropped. Paying off the expired parking violations wiped out my session savings, and they found a million things wrong with the van that I'm still supposed to fix."

"You make thirty days in the pokey sound like a good deal."

We manage to catch a couple of green lights in a row which, in L.A., is reason to celebrate. Tommy turns onto Melrose and notices a kosher burrito stand. "Hey, you hungry? They make these beef tongue taquitos that will put you in a coma."

"Just lost my appetite. Possibly forever."

Mercifully, Tommy keeps driving.

"It was a good deal. Thirty days in the hole, or two years in Vietnam."

"Thirty days will sail by quick," I say, trying to sound like one of those radio announcers who can make a train wreck sound like good news. "I guess a bit of bread and water never hurt anyone. Right?"

The van inches toward a freeway onramp. The decrepit Hollywood sign floats like a ghost in the brown air.

160

"I've been thinking—"

"Danger, Will Robinson! The last time you tried to think, I almost ended up in a foster home. You have many talents, but thinking isn't one."

"Chuck you, Farley."

One second before the light changes, a chrome-toothed T-bird behind us starts honking. Unable to wait her turn, the ditzy driver whips around us and nearly triggers a head-on collision with a very surprised Helms Bakery truck.

"Her daddy should take that T-bird away."

"See you at the stop sign," I say. Another Nana-ism.

"It's just not fair."

"Yeah. That crazy chick should get a ticket, not you. The cops were quick to pull us over for nothing. Where are they now?

"Do you know who's fighting this war?"

"Huh?" I glance at my brother to make sure he's watching the road and not the girl in the miniskirt who just appeared on the sidewalk alongside us. Fortunately, Tommy doesn't notice her or the way her tank top shows off her bare brown shoulders. He's lost in thought, and if it lasts another minute, I'll have to go in after him.

"Spades and beaners, that's who."

"Huh?" He doesn't normally talk like this. Normally, he calls them spooks and cholos. "You trying to be funny? Think you're Don Rickles or something?"

"Cannon fodder, that's all they are. Poor kids who can't get student deferments. Maybe they don't know how."

"So, now you're an activist?" I wonder if he's been talking to Hope Springs. Maybe she's back from Prague or whatever South American revolution she ran off to start.

"Spades and beaners, black and brown people. That's who's dying. You know who isn't dying? Middle-class white boys. "

161

There's a deeper side to Tommy than he generally lets show, but right now I wish he'd keep it hidden. "Do you ever miss Mom?"

Silence. Tommy never talks about mom. Pater swallowed his heartbreak and rewrites his unfinished screenplay. Tommy pounds on drums and hides his feelings. Nana stays neutral and I try to remain half-Vulcan.

"I had a long chat with Hope Springs before she left for Prague. You know how many black men we have in the U.S. Senate? Exactly one. How many black people serve as big city mayors? One."

"Earth to Tommy: What are we talking about?"

"I'm going to enlist."

"You WHAT?" I take a deep breath and instantly regret it since Tommy's van produces half the smog in L.A. I need air, but there isn't any left in this town. God, I miss Malibu. I feel like puking until it occurs to me: I've been back barely twenty minutes and he's already messing with me. "Tell me you're kidding before I murder you."

"Bad idea to kill the driver."

"Thomas Q. Strauss!"

"Army. Maybe I'll join the Army."

"Sure. Makes sense. You like hitting stuff with sticks so why not hit people?"

Tommy pulls onto the 101. He hasn't had the alignment checked since forever, so the van shakes until we're north of forty. Someday this bucket will just rip itself to pieces and send Tommy hurtling forward like Wile E. Coyote, holding nothing but the steering wheel. "I might start boot camp in late October."

"Fantastic. *Mazel tov*. The Army needs more Jewish drummer boys."

"Infantry. I'm not looking for special treatment."

162

"You trying to get killed?"

"Nope. Just doing my part."

"Nana will disown you."

"She doesn't know yet."

I still don't know if he's joking, but I've had it with his charade. "Once Nana finds out, you won't have to go all the way to Vietnam to get killed."

Traffic on the freeway grinds to a halt within sight of the Capitol Records tower that looks like a stack of records with a giant phonograph needle on top. Tommy did a couple of sessions there and said everything inside the building is round including the people. He also told me that the tower is really a nuclear missile silo.

"Elvis. Jimi Hendrix," he says. "They served."

"I guess they call this a freeway because you're free to do anything but drive," I say. "You're also free to talk complete nonsense, and I'm free not to listen."

I want to ask Tommy how joining the Army will help one single ghetto kid when I notice that the same crazy T-bird gal who nearly took out the bakery van is now right next to us. She takes advantage of the stalled traffic to refresh her mascara with Vincent Van Gogh brush strokes. Her fake lashes are so long she could paint a house with them. Bleached and teased hair sticks out from under her scarf like a toilet brush. She inserts a Virginia Slim between her lacquered red lips, but I can't bear to watch her for fear she'll set her head on fire.

"Do you think it's fair?" Tommy asks.

"Fair? What's fair? And since when did you give a hoot about what I think? Enough of this crazy talk already."

"I'll get drafted either way. Why have jail on my permanent record?"

"Permanent record? Your permanent record? Death is pretty permanent, Tommy."

He answers with silence, his backup weapon when he runs out of sarcasm and doesn't have a drumstick to throw. I notice him glancing at the gas gauge which, if it's working, indicates that the tank's empty. I ask God to get traffic moving as a small sign of mercy for my brother, the Village Idiot of Los Angeles. "There's gotta be a way to undo this. What if we find a junior college somewhere that will take you as a late admission?"

"I hate school, Max. I'm not good at book learning like you are. I barely got out of high school alive."

"*Putz!* You don't need straight A's. Find a music program. Major in underwater basket weaving until the war ends."

"Nixon says he has a plan to end the war. With any luck, it'll be over by next Christmas."

"Are you on drugs? Nixon will never be president. Aren't you flat-footed or something? Maybe you can 4F out. What about going to Canada?"

"Canada? So, what, every generation our family changes countries? If it wasn't for the United States Army, we wouldn't even be here. We wouldn't be anywhere. Nana would have died in Dachau. Dad would have grown up orphaned on a kibbutz in the Sahara."

"You mean, the Negev, ding-a-ling."

"Shaddup."

I'll never know why the Ventura Freeway turned into a Sunday afternoon parking lot. Maybe Godzilla is throwing cars off the overpass a mile ahead. Maybe peaceniks are staging a die-in. Maybe some idiot ran out of gas like we're about to.

"Is your gas gauge accurate?"

"Don't worry. We'll be okay."

"You're not okay. You're throwing your life away, and I don't want to be an only child. Be honest: Are you just doing this to get back at Pater?"

164

"For what? Dropping me on my head as a baby? I've got no beef with the old man."

"Pater spends his life keeping boys out of body bags so you're going to poke him in the eye by coming home in one?"

"Maybe if I go, the FBI will leave him alone. Besides, I thought you of all people would be happy about this. I figured I was doing you a favor by clearing out."

"Like when you ran away to 'Frisco last summer? We were scared to death for you. You're not doing me a favor by getting your butt shot off. You're on the verge of making it as a musician—you're so amazing, Tommy—why run off to die in some jungle? Don't throw your life away."

"There's nothing wrong with serving the country that served us."

"Sounds like one of Grumpy Chuck's bumper stickers. What about your new band? Have you told what's-her-name—Dori?—about this yet?"

Some dipsy-doodle behind us notices that traffic has almost started moving again and begins honking in anticipation. I turn on the radio so I don't have to listen to any more of Tommy's depressing nonsense. I fiddle with the loose dial until I lock into a station playing "The Motorcycle Song." We're passing between the hills beyond the Hollywood Bowl, but Arlo Guthrie's nasal voice still manages to cut through the static. Seeing the Bowl reminds me of the night we got busted. If only Tommy had just taken me to temple. "The Motorcycle Song" reminds me that Tommy made us listen to Arlo Guthrie last Thanksgiving. We heard a long, funny story about getting arrested for littering at a place called Alice's Restaurant.

Then it hits me. "That's it!"

"Huh?"

"Alice's Restaurant is the answer!"

Tommy reaches over and touches my forehead. "Ouch! Hot. You're delirious."

"Alice's Restaurant!" I hit the dashboard. "That's the key. Do you remember how that story ends? The draft board's just about to sign him up when he admits that he's been convicted of a crime. He can't serve because he's been convicted."

"It's just a dumb song, Maxwell Not-so-smart."

"No. Don't you see, Tommy? That judge tricked you. If you'd just pleaded guilty and taken the thirty days, they wouldn't be able to draft you."

"What about my permanent record?"

"What is this, kindergarten? There is no permanent record. Nobody cares if you've done time for a traffic ticket. Maybe you can go back and plead guilty."

"Either way I still get drafted. Besides, prison isn't exactly the safest place on earth."

"It's a lot safer than the Ho Chi Minh trail. I'm sure Pater can help you. Just give it some thought, Tommy."

Seeing the Laurel Canyon exit makes me giddy. I feel like I've been away from home for a million years. I can't wait to see my trees and my arroyos, my house and my grandmother. Nana will be able to talk reason with Tommy. He'll listen to her, and if he doesn't, I will help her beat him to *schnitzel* with his own drumsticks.

I'm so happy to be home that I forget to worry about Mr. Shreidermayer, who is out front, working on his cactus garden. He looks up and glares directly at me as the van crawls by.

Phantom of the Library

Jail Bait is dead. Long live Garage Sale.

While I was away at J-camp, Tommy and Riff auditioned a boatload of bass players until they found one that was more than just a bottom-feeding guitarist. Small-but-mighty Midori Tanaka, Tommy's library friend, plays a three-quarter scale Fender P-bass with larger-than-life intensity.

Dori grew up a studio brat hanging around the mixing board, soaking in the big boss beat. Music runs deep in her veins. Her parents are busy studio musicians who met as kids at Manzanar. They've played on half of the hit parade, both solo and in horn sections.

Once the garage door opened, Tommy's phantom of the library quickly emerged as the heart, voice and soul of the band. I can't remember what the earlier versions of the group sounded like. The boys always had something to play. With Dori, they finally have something to say.

Dori speaks in mysteries, saying things like, "The bass player's job is to work the sub-groove." Tommy says having her in the band is like having a third foot on the bass drum pedal. She claims to be a Buddhist but often wears a Catholic school girl outfit because "nothing says forbidden fruit like pleats, plaid, and saddle shoes." Other days, she looks like a refugee from a Melrose Avenue thrift shop.

This afternoon the band is working through one of Dori's more lighthearted numbers, about a suicidal actress who is losing her mind.

Riff, still on guitar after surviving Jail Bait with his honor intact, picks fuzzy harmonics that Dori supports with a vague

167

bass drone. The guitar swirls, feeds back, and gradually reveals a sparse tom-tom pulse. Chaos swells until Tommy pops a sharp one-two and snaps the trio into an urgent and angry beat. My brother glances at Dori with love in his eyes. She sings like she just lost her best friend.

I got your letter.
Sad correspondence.
You said you were better but you sounded despondent.
Your words were nervous.
Your sentences terse.
Lost your direction. Succumbed to the curse.

I'm mesmerized by Dori. There's something magnetic about her rough, distant melancholy, something refreshing about her complete lack of sugar, spice, and everything nice. She's fierce and expressive. Smart, talented, and angry.

I still remember the night you called me long-distance.
Walking the edge, zero resistance.
Another rejection, another delay.
Shaky connection.
You're slipping away.

I don't know if the boys are paying any attention to Dori's lyrics. They seem adrift in the sonic hurricane, hanging on for dear life. Riff strums and flails, Tommy chugs forward like a train trying to outrun a twister. Dori looks ready to implode and take the garage down with her.

The band crescendos into a pleading chorus.

Amelia.
What did they do to ya?

Amelia.
If I'd only got through to ya.
They asked for an inch, why did you give 'em a mile?
You gave up your heart, they only needed a smile.

The tempo is urgent, the chords open, ringing and harsh. To my ears it is unlike anything that ever floated over the airwaves. In a world ruled by jingle-jangle guitars and sticky-sweet harmonies, Dori says music is her machete.

Trying to find balance.
Gambling on fame.
You got the talent, but can't take the pain
Little girl dreams.
Saturday matinee.
Your silver screen is fading to gray.

There's something exciting and scary about encountering a person with more talent than the planet is ready for. Talent so obvious and so overwhelming is almost a handicap. That's why geniuses can seem like space cadets.

Tommy shifts the beat, and the band locks in around him. There's ESP in the room, no eye contact needed. The music is alive and listening to itself. Sound strains like light trying to escape a black hole. A coda for the end of the world. This is one of those moments when God shimmers into existence just long enough to infuse the air with promise and mystery.

The song ends on an unresolved chord, leaving me to wonder if Amelia's star will ever shine or if it will just burn up in the atmosphere.

"Whadya think, Maxwell Smart?" Dori asks. It didn't take long for her to join the make-fun-of-my-name club.

"Cool." I try not to reveal how happy it makes me when she asks my opinion, or how relieved I am that Tommy hasn't called me retarded in the last two minutes. I think Dori knows that I'm the only person in the room with enough IQ to appreciate her lyrics. If she asks the boys, they'll just shrug their shoulders and grunt a one-syllable response. "I want to know what happens to Amelia."

"Trippy," Riff whispers into his mic.

"Outtasight," Tommy says from somewhere under a cymbal he's adjusting.

"Thanks, guys." Dori says. "I think."

"It's a boss song," I say.

"Huh?" Tommy crawls back onto his drum stool. "Do people still say *boss*?"

"I say scoop doop on the old blah blay and two blips on a blop." Riff saves me from disgrace by spouting a burst of nonsense with a big AM radio voice.

"Whatever," Dori says. She lets a rumbling sound rip from her P-bass. "Let's polish this turd."

"I kinda like it loose." Riff twangs a high string and turns the tuning peg to make a siren sound. "Loose as a long-neck goose."

"Keep your pud in your pants, white boy." Dori flashes me a conspiratorial raised eyebrow.

"What?" Riff feigns innocence and looks in my direction. "There are children in the room, you sicko. Go wash out your mouth with soap."

"Soap this!" Pretending to adjust my glasses, I flip him a bird that the others can't see. I like hitting Riff with things he doesn't expect from an almost thirteen-year-old. He's easy to shock but impossible to insult.

There's no way to hurt Riff's feelings because he doesn't have any. His feelings were lost in the rubble of his parents'

170

angry divorce. I understand how easy it is to bury the pain of losing a parent. The real Riff, if there is one, is locked behind a glacial wall. Unplugged, he's an emotional dial tone, but when the tubes glow and the speakers crackle, I hear the hurt that he can't put into words. He grew up in a domestic war zone and found refuge in a pawn shop Stratocaster and a Fender Twin Reverb. He learned to play by working through a stack of Coltrane records, the only legacy his dad left behind. Riff hides his feelings, but when his guitar cuts loose, it can sear the sky.

"I want to try a new number real quick." Dori sets up a funky bass pattern that the boys quickly lock into.

Like any kid with a new toy, Riff initially overdoes it on his Cry Baby, but his strum and pedal eventually agree on just the right amount of slinky wah-wah. Tommy plays it close and tight on the hi-hat.

When the cars were steel and the air was clean,
The land was rich and Elvis was king.
Daddy wore wing tips, Father knew best.
Mother had style and bullet-shaped breasts.
The world was a suburb of Disneyland,
Sweet paradise for the company man.
Is that the way it was?
Do you wanna' go back?
Everything seemed to be right on track.

Groove established, Dori lets her bass dangle, cups the microphone and preaches like a prophet standing before the flood.

There was another side to the American Dream.
Separate, not equal. Blind and mean.
Glowing crosses, flames at night.

171

Hooded shadows in cold fire light.
Color didn't mix in the public pool
Back when I was a kid in grammar school.
That's the way it was.
Do you wanna go back?
If you could, would you rather be white or black?

I wish Hope Springs could hear this. I'm sure she'd get the message. Hope's struggle might be the greater one—overthrowing the government seems like a bigger mission than overthrowing the Top Forty, but I think she would recognize Dori as a sister from a nearby foxhole.

Dori gestures for the band to drop a few decibels. Once all the electrons in the room settle into lower orbits, she whispers into the mic.

Letterman jackets. High school choirs.
Camouflage, boots, machine gun fire.
Stoke the forge with gasoline.
T-birds, war birds, M-16's.
The summer of love is dead and gone.
The jungle war is coming home.
That's the way it is.
Time to face the facts.
Before your brother comes home in a body bag.

The band pulses quietly as I choke back a sudden tear at the thought of Tommy coming home in a flag-draped coffin. If Riff ever gets drafted, bullets will bounce off him like rain off a duck. Terminally unlucky, Tommy will probably pee on a land mine.

Tommy is working the beat, cymbals glistening, drumsticks a blur. Dori flashes him a look of approval that borders on

172

affection. I try to picture the two of them falling in love after an accidental first kiss as they harmonize into a shared microphone. The way they met in the library would make for a good teen romance story if only they belonged to the same species.

Tommy was working alphabetically through record collections when he started noticing entire sections missing. Over the course of a few overdue notices, he saw the pattern and realized that he wasn't alone in exploring the musical alphabet. A sign of intelligent, or at least, compatible life in the universe.

Tommy checked out the entire M section and held vigil for a week. When Dori finally came looking, she found the section empty and Tommy waiting. This could have been the movie moment when their eyes met through a library shelf, when my brother's heart got tangled in the darkest hair this side of deep space. The right background music could provoke a few tears as the audience understands that only in America could a son of Germany and a daughter of Japan find common ground.

Instead, they began to argue so loudly that the old librarian threw them both out of the building. It wasn't love at first sight, but a common enemy was enough to unite them. In an act of egghead chivalry, Tommy risked his already shaky check-out status to let Dori walk away with the M collection on his library card. Being Tommy, he didn't even think to get her phone number. Fortunately, Dori returned a week later.

Tommy told me how they became friends and met every week so Dori could pass on her reviews and returned records. They traded insights and outrage. Why is Count Basie stashed on the C-shelf when Duke Ellington is with the E's? How can anyone think Buddy Rich, also found in the B-section, is the greatest living drummer when Gene Krupa is still playing? Speaking of the B's, how did The Beatles ever record *Sergeant*

Pepper's on a four-track tape machine? Dori insisted that if Les Paul hadn't invented overdubbing, George and Ringo would still be playing birthday parties in Liverpool.

Midway through the O section, Tommy said that Dori changed his life by sending him to the end of the alphabet and insisting he listen to Zappa before bothering with P and Q. I don't know if Tommy's eureka moment happened before the day we landed at Zappa's moon base, but Tommy before and after Dori are two different people.

Tommy and Dori took over the backbeat at Zappa's jam sessions and moved it downhill to our garage. Riff was happy to let Dori rattle the rafters with her tiny P-bass and big sub-woofer. After two sessions, she felt comfortable enough to bring in her first tune. On the seventh day she made the band in her image the way God made the lucky ones in his.

The Visit

Nana hates answering the door. It's one of her lingering phobias, like distrusting police and German Shepherds. When someone knocks, it's my job to look out the peephole, but today it's too hot to drag a chair over from the kitchen so I don't bother. The last three door knockers were the paper boy, the Mormons, and the March of Dimes lady. Today's visitor is probably just some poor *schmoe* selling encyclopedias.

I crack the door open enough to let a bit of light bend around the corner, but not enough to let possible brownshirts gain a toehold.

"*I beleaf you half sometink of mine.*" The dark, beady eyes of Klaus Shreidermayer, the Man Who Cuts Legs Off, stare down at me through the gap. Overhearing the deep voice and menacing tone, Nana approaches with a carving knife in hand.

"It's okay," I whisper to her, though it really isn't. I open the door. "It's just our neighbor, Mr. Shreidermayer."

Shredder looks at Nana and her big knife.

"I was just cooking something," she says, flustered.

"Please come in." I take the knife from her hand and lead both of them into the living room. I put the blade aside, but within reach just in case he noticed the *mezuzah*. "Have you ever met my grandmother, Hannah Straus?"

Shreidermayer shakes his head and extends his hand but Nana doesn't offer hers. They stare at each other like two solitary old cats.

"*Sind sie Deutsch?*" Shreidermayer asks. "Are you German?"

Nana says nothing.

175

"Well," I say. "This is nice. Why don't you both sit down?"

Nobody does.

"I believe your grandchild has something of mine." More tension. More thick accents.

I notice that the butcher knife is now closer to Shredder than it is to me. If he lunges for it, I'll jump from the couch and karate chop the back of his neck.

"Now why on Earth hasn't anyone ever thought to introduce you two," I say, but nobody's buying my sugar and spice and everything nice. "How long have we all been neighbors? Has it really been five years already?"

Nana regards me with a look that says: *Who is this old Nazi, and what's he doing in my living room?*

While it hasn't been an eternity since I broke into Shreddermauler's house, each passing day added hope that my theft had gone undetected. That hope just faded into the scowling faces of stiff, suspicious Krauts of a certain age.

The percolator burps in the kitchen.

"Nana just made coffee. Why don't we all sit down and enjoy a nice warm cup of Maxwell House?" I hear my words, but I have no idea where they are coming from. Maybe I'm quoting that perky TV commercial where a cup of coffee solves all problems. "How about a nice slice of *strudel?*"

I scoop up the big knife and rush off to the kitchen. Maybe I should kill myself before Nana does it for me.

"*Nu?*" She's right behind me with the universal word that can mean anything from "what's up," to "do you think I was born yesterday?"

"Put some cake on a tray. I'll be right back." I scamper up to my loft and return with Shreddermauler's drawing faster than Nana can find two cups. She's so startled by what I show her that coffee dances over the edge of the cups and onto the shaking tray. "I thought he was a Nazi," I whisper. "But now, I'm not so sure."

Nana puts the tray down and dabs dribbled coffee with a napkin. A stray sugar cube soaks up a few drops and I pop it in my mouth before she can react. "What do you know about this man?"

"I know that he's in our living room."

"Between you and Tommy…" she says, but doesn't finish the sentence that always ends with some variation on which one of us will give her the first heart attack.

Shreidermayer is looking at the menorah on our mantle. It's been there since December, because the last time Pater boxed it, he needed two Hanukkahs to find it again. Next to the menorah is a small frame, the kind that most people use to display a baby picture. Instead of a snapshot of Tommy in drumsticks and diapers, there's a yellow Star of David with the word "*Jude*," German for Jew, on it.

So, one cat's out of the bag.

"Coffee?" My hands are trembling but I manage to land the tray on our small table without a splash.

"*Juden?* You are Jewish?" Shredder says with the thick accent that turns every question into an accusation. He takes the picture frame from the mantle and inspects the frayed cloth behind the glass. "How did you escape?"

"Is this what you are looking for?" Nana hands him the sketch and relieves him of the star she was forced to wear on the streets of her old home town. The yellow patch identified her as someone to be shunned, a target for ridicule and abuse. Her family tree has five-hundred-year-old roots with this star on top.

"Funny." Shreidermayer helps himself to a cup of black coffee and indicates for Nana to do the same. "If it wouldn't be for your grandchild's little break-in, we maybe would never meet."

I nod toward Nana, suggesting with my best puppy eyes that she should calm down about the strange old Kraut in our living room. I sense her unease as the rise and fall of the Third Reich passes through her pounding heart. I feel terrible for putting my grandmother through this but we're safe in America and I really want a piece of her fresh *strudel*.

"So," I say, hoping to break the ice and stay out of jail for robbery. "What did you do during the war, Mr. Shreidermayer?"

~ ~ ~

"*Mein Gott*," is all Nana can say after Shreidermayer leaves. The two of them have been speaking German for the last hour, though I only understood a bit of it. "*Mein lieber Gott.*"

She sits on the couch without moving, barely even breathing. I've never seen her looking so exhausted. I know she wants to cry but has a thing about not showing weakness. My Vulcan blood must come from the German side of the family. I pour her a fresh cup of Maxwell House, but she waves it away with a shaky hand.

"Sorry for surprising you." I sit down next to her, close enough for her to put an arm around me, but not close enough for her to wring my neck. "Do you believe his story, Nana?"

"It was … most extraordinary …" A few minutes pass before she pulls herself together enough to tell me something more extraordinary still.

It turns out that Nana's gang, her Cantor's Deli *Kaffeeklatsch*, is a bit more than a bunch of little old ladies dunking rugelach in lukewarm coffee. Nana often has a surprise or two up her ruffled sleeve, but this one takes the cake. My grandmother is a

178

Nazi hunter. Her deli gang has been working with Jewish groups and authorities all over the world to track down hidden war criminals.

"Hundreds," Nana says when I ask how many ex-Nazis are still on the loose. "Thousands, maybe."

I feel a shiver run from the top of my head to the tips of my bare feet. Nazis on the loose? This is scarier than the H-bomb. "Does the government know?"

"Ha! The government brought them here." Nana considers how much information to share with me. I'm almost thirteen, but she thinks I still believe there's a real leprechaun in every box of Lucky Charms.

"We fought the Nazis. We beat them. Why would our government let them come here? Do you think LBJ knows?"

"It's an open secret." Nana clenches a fist in her lap. "Some lied about their past. Others were useful."

"For what?" Maybe life will make sense if I drink some coffee. I can't stand the stuff so I'll drop a couple of sugar cubes into the cup.

"Rocket scientists like Wernher von Braun," Nana says, but it's clear she doesn't want to talk about it. "America and the Russians scooped up lots of useful old fascists. Some more useful than others."

"This makes no sense. Is there something you're not telling me, Nana?"

"There's much I'm not telling you, *dah-link*. Much that you're better off not knowing."

"I'm almost thirteen, Nana." This line of reasoning hasn't worked in the past, but something about Shreidermayer's visit has her all shook up.

Mark the Mailman once commented on Nana's far-flung pen pals, but I never put the pieces together. It turns out that all those stiff, official-looking envelopes from faraway places were puzzle pieces in a much bigger picture.

"Right now we're looking for this one." Nana shows me a sheet of photos, side-by-side shots of a lean-faced Nazi officer and a pudgy man in his sixties. "I sang for him in Dachau. A survivor found him selling life insurance in Tarzana. Can you believe it? A Nazi selling life insurance? "

I don't know what life insurance is, but it doesn't sound good. Worse, Tarzana is just a few miles away. "Have you seen him? Does he still live there?

"Not any more, sweetheart."

"You got him?"

Nana's half-smile says she's told me all she intends to. "Things aren't always what they seem. People aren't always who they pretend to be."

Including her. There is far more to my grandmother than I ever imagined. For the first time she tells me that the story I've heard about American GIs liberating the camps, feeding the prisoners and setting them free is just that. A story.

"I was stuck at Dachau for almost a year after the war ended. The Allies let some of the Germans stay on to run the place. The gas chambers were turned off, but much remained the same. The Allies didn't want the Jews, and Europe was flooded with refugees whose homelands were gone."

As a German, Nana was classified as an enemy combatant along with German POWs. Some Germans lied about their Nazi service and got visas for America. Others were plucked from the camp mysteriously and given travelling papers to Italy. From there, they escaped to South Africa and Argentina.

"Jews and refugees rotted while the world hoped they would just go away. I had to use Nazi documents to prove that I was no enemy." She rolls up her sleeve and stares at the numbers for a moment. "As if I tattooed my own arm!"

180

I stare at the numbers she usually keeps hidden. They always make me feel like crying.

"The war against Hitler was over. The war against communism was starting. The enemy of my enemy is my friend, even if he's a Nazi." Nana's blue eyes droop and crinkle. She's sad but seems relieved to fill in some of the missing pieces of her complex story.

"Once freed, I tried to learn what happened to your grandpa, but found nothing. I sent out inquiries to find your father. He was your age when I sent him away to Palestine. It had been over five years. Five years without a word. I didn't know if he was alive or dead. If I found him, would he even recognize me? Would he understand why I had sent him away or would he hate me for it? What would I tell him about his father?"

I try but can't imagine being pulled away from Nana, Pater, and Tommy.

Eventually, Nana got help from a refugee agency that had kept track of all the children sent to Palestine. They got her a visa and helped arrange passage to Haifa, where she and Pater were reunited.

"We got out of there before the War of Independence," she says. "The birth of Israel was a great thing, but I had seen enough war for one lifetime."

Nana pours herself a cup of cold coffee, takes a sip, and puts it down and puts her arm around me. "So, *nu*? Here we are."

"A miracle." I snuggle in close to her.

"Yes."

We sit in silence for a moment and then Nana says, "So now I spend my time rounding up old Nazis instead of trying to forget them like a bad dream."

"What about Shreddermauler?"

"Who?"

"Shreidermayer. The guy who just ate half your strudel. Do you think his story's true? Is he lying about his past? How did he get into the country?"

"Hard to say ..." She mulls it over for a moment and asks me if I know what kind of work he did. "Scientist? Chemist? Spy?"

"Not sure. Everything seemed kind of normal inside his bunker."

"Bunker?" Nana laughs. A bit of color returns to her face. I didn't give her a heart attack, but the day is still young and she already looks ten years older than when it started.

"If Shreddermauler's a war criminal, why hasn't he been caught by now?"

"So many fish, so few hooks." Nana stands up and gathers the coffee cups and plates. "I'll send a few letters, make a few inquiries."

"Wait!" I surprise both of us. "He's my Nazi. I'm going to reel him in."

"In that case," Nana smiles. She seems both proud and shaken. "In that case, I need to teach you how to fish."

I wash the dishes. Nana brews fresh coffee and I brew an idea. I do my best to speak in my wise-beyond-my-years voice. "There's only one way to find out if Shredder's story's true."

"Ja? What do you suggest? Sneak back into his house? Torture him? Shoot his little Nazi dog?"

"Nope. We need to go to Germany." This is either the best or worst idea I've ever had, but I don't have time to wait for official letters and investigations. "The only way to verify his story is to return to the scene of the crime."

"Acch! I can't go back there. It's been twenty years. Why on Earth would I go back to that place?"

"Because I'm going, Nana. I'm going to Germany and I need your help."

Family Council

It's the dreaded "Family Council," the clan gathering where we are expected to talk through our conflicts, arrive at creative solutions and go forth with fresh love in our hearts. Go, Team Strauss!

Family Council is something Pater invokes when he gets sick of the tension in the house and forgets that meetings like this usually make things worse. He isn't big on feelings, but he hates disharmony. He says the world would be fine if everyone would just be reasonable.

I suppose tonight's assembly is my fault because I've been bugging Tommy nonstop. Maybe my only idea to keep him out of Vietnam is to make him so miserable that he runs off to Canada. I'm determined to get him across the northern border even if I have to pester him all the way there. Tijuana may be closer, but Tommy has a better chance of learning the language up North.

"Strauss Family Council is now in session." Pater bangs a plastic cup on the living room table.

Nana folds her arms across her chest and exhales. She doesn't understand Family Council but is careful not to give her son advice on child-rearing because she's pretty much raising us anyway. Back in her day adults didn't take kids' concerns seriously. A good kid got nothing, a bad kid got smacked.

Pater distributes half-sheets of paper and number two pencils that still have that chopped-down tree smell. "Instead of complaining about each other, tonight I want you to write five things you appreciate about the other members of this family."

"That's fifteen things!" I say. "Five more than Moses had to *schlep* down from Mount Sinai."

"I appreciate that Max can multiply," Tommy mutters. "One down, fourteen to go."

"Five total," Pater says to everyone's great relief.

Last month's exercise was to write the top three ways that we want to be treated by others, but I'm still required to take out the trash and none of my other wishes came true. I once heard Grumpy Chuck say you wish in one hand and shit in another and see which weighs more. Not quite a Nana-ism, but better than his usual backwoods wisdom. I'm still trying to figure out what it means.

Tommy drums on the table with two sharpened pencils. I stare at the knots in the worn pine floor that was once part of a tree. Each dark spot was once a branch reaching for the sun. Squirrels ran up these planks and jumped from tree to tree. Birds padded their nests with pine needles. How old was this tree when it was reduced to floor boards? Maybe it would have outlived us all, witness to mankind's backward evolution from Chumash to chumps.

"Let's take one more minute and then share what we've written," Pater says in his schoolteacher voice.

I can't find a positive way to say anything tonight. I'm full of frustration but I can't figure out what's bugging me so I write down that I appreciate how we inhale oxygen and exhale carbon dioxide.. I scribble a peace sign and the first few things that come to mind.

Tommy's in trouble.

The FBI thinks Pater is a radical.

I miss my mother.

Next fall in high school, vultures will tear me apart like a fish out of water.

Nana puts her pencil down first. I know she wrote one line about how she loves each of us, and two throw-away lines about how smart, talented, etcetera, we are. Tommy stops drumming long enough to jot something down.

"How 'bout we start with you, *Mutti*?" Pater points his pencil at his mother with an informality that would never be allowed in the old country.

"*Ja*," she says. "I wrote that I love my family."

"And?"

"I wrote it five times. Nothing else is so important."

Nana won the opening round, but she's cheating, so I refuse to feel guilty. Tommy whistles the opening bars of "What the World Needs Now is Love, Sweet Love."

"*Danke, Mutti*." Pater turns to Tommy, who never takes Family Council seriously. Last month, his only answer to the question of how he wanted to be treated by others was to get off of his cloud.

"Let's see," Tommy says. "I wrote that Max is very smart. Nana takes good care of us. Dad works hard. My band is outtasite."

Oy vey. Team Tommy pulls into the lead. What an apple polisher. Still, I need to revisit what I wrote. "How about you, Pater?" I stall for time. "Sure you wouldn't like to go next?"

"Fine." Pater unfolds his paper and puts the pencil behind his ear like a shopkeeper on "Father Knows Best." "I appreciate each of you for what makes you unique: Tommy for his music. Max, for your planet-sized intellect. Nana, *Mutti*, you keep this family together in so many ways, I don't know where to start."

"*Danke*," Nana says. She's glowing. She's radiant. She's going to have a heart attack if I read what I wrote.

"Maxie?"

"Uh, that was only three things, Dad."

"How 'bout you share three and then I'll read my last two?"

He's cheating, holding two in reserve that he probably hasn't even written yet. It's a good move, but not quite

185

checkmate. I can't read anything I've written so I just blurt out the first thing that pops into my head. "I appreciate the Federal Bureau of Investigation."

"The FBI?" Tommy says.

"That reminds me," Nana perks up. "I saw those two *nudniks* at the Canyon Store the other day. They were wearing flared pants and batik shirts."

"Batik?" Tommy says. "Where do they think we are, San Francisco?"

"Are they still packing heat?" I ask. "Are they still spying on us?"

"They aren't spying on anyone. They've just found a comfortable perch to sit out the turmoil down below," Pater says. "Laurel Canyon is a cushy spot to wait out the war."

"And ogle braless hippie chicks," I say.

"Max, can you be serious?"

"I am serious. The FBI is doing their job so well that Tommy's going to Vietnam."

"Huh?" Tommy stops drumming on the table though his bass drum foot is still wiggling. Maybe he hasn't discussed enlisting with anyone but me.

"Next item. I would like to express my appreciation for the Constitution of the United States of America."

"*Ja, dat's goot.*" Nana says, just like that.

"No, it isn't. We're supposed to be focused on family," Pater insists.

"Well… just like I appreciate that you're the founding father of this family, I want to recognize the founding fathers of our American family." Everyone stares at me for a different reason, so I seize the silence to drive home my next two articles of appreciation. With a handful of skill and a bit of luck I will shut down Family Council forever. "If it wasn't for the Constitution, there would be no America. If it wasn't for America, Hitler

186

would have won. If Hitler had won, we wouldn't be here having Family Council."

"C'mon Max…" Pater's not impressed.

I know there's a flaw in my logic somewhere. What would have happened if my father had not met my mother? What if he had stayed in Israel and married some tough *sabra*? Would I exist as someone else or would I not exist at all? Would the half of who I am that comes from my father have combined with half of someone else? Would my half be aware of the other half, or would I be an entirely different person?

"Max?" Pater interrupts my thoughts to bring me back to the task at hand. "Family Council is still in session. Play by the rules and stop your nonsense."

"Right… America… uh, just as the Constitution protects our liberties, it also protects your right to make a movie about nothing, Grumpy Chuck's right to beat his grandson, and Mumu Marie's right to say I killed Christ, and any maniac's right to pick up a gun and kill our heroes, and Tommy's right to get drafted, and Mom's—"

"—that's quite enough, Max." Pater's mad that my planet-sized intellect has knocked him out of orbit tonight. "Why don't you go to your loft and work on a list that doesn't completely miss the point of Family Council?"

"The point? You're the one missing the point. This family's falling apart. The country's falling apart. The whole stinkin' world is falling apart and you think writing a list is going to help?"

"Enough! You're upsetting your grandmother."

"No, I'm not." Nana didn't survive Dachau only to get upset by a twerp like me.

"Well, you're upsetting me."

187

"Good!" I storm up to my loft where I will proceed to feel sorry for myself. I'll steam and boil until Pater feels bad for yelling and tells me that it's okay to come down.

Except this time he lets me stew so long that I doze off in my clothes and almost sleep through my secret late-night TV session.

As Seen on TV

Once everyone's asleep, I sneak down into the living room to turn the dial on our big black-and-white Quasar. Nobody knows I do this, but bedtime doesn't mean much in summer, and I love the cool, still air, the feeling of having the house to myself, and the bone-crunching terror of an old monster flick.

The challenge on Monday is finding something worth watching. It's nearly midnight so the networks are running talk shows and the local stations are getting their test patterns ready for the nightly sign-off.

NBC, Channel 4, has the *Johnny Carson Show* from New York City, which is about five time zones and ten years east of here. KTLA, Channel 5, is gracing the airwaves with wrestling re-runs from the Olympic Auditorium. This so-called sport probably dates back to the ancient Romans. All we lack are the lions. Ancient Romans might question the Grecian Formula Hair advertisement on Channel 9. KCOP, Channel 13, has an old Bob Hope and Bing Crosby movie playing. Nana Hannah loves these guys, but I'm not sure why.

The vertical hold goes out of whack so I take a minute to stop the frames from flying by at twice the normal rate. Once stabilized, I click the dial back to KTTV, Channel 11, to see what trash they have to offer. I sit through the tail end of a Coppertone commercial just in case the little black doggie manages to tear the girl's bikini bottom this time, but no such luck. Next, a baldheaded dork in a baggy suit is selling used cars at what he insists are crazy low prices.

189

I'm so desperate I dial in the fuzzy UHF channel where some college professor is talking about race riots, ghetto schools, and the high percentage of black men dying in Vietnam. Ten percent of the population, fifty percent of the dead. I wish Tommy could hear this because the professor's solution isn't to send more white kids over there, it's to end the war.

Click. This is too close to home. Meanwhile, back on the road to Zanzibar, Hope and Crosby are practicing their ethnic jokes and golf swings, and I've struck out on finding anything worth wasting time on.

The only source of truth on the TV tonight is back at the Olympic Auditorium, where a paunchy Mexican wrestler named "El Chicano" is beating the tar out of a pale giant who calls himself "The Swede." I know how this story will end: El Chicano will get in enough licks to anger the diehards. The audience will howl for blood like ancient Romans. The true believers will scream and stomp and insult El Chicano to distraction, whereupon, the Swede will resurrect and clobber El Chicano with a folding chair. Justice will be served right before we break for another long harangue from the used car salesman.

It occurs to me that the only difference between heaven and hell is that hell might have more commercials. In heaven, characters from one channel will be able to cross the dial to other stations. El Chicano will climb out of the ring, cross the airwaves and hop up and down on Johnny Carson's couch. The radical professor will teach Bob Hope how to do the black power salute. The Swede will chase Bing Crosby around the ring with a bent golf club and the Marlboro Man will accidently set fire to his own moustache.

I'm halfway to the off switch when I hit pay dirt back on Channel 11. Godzilla! There is no mutant half as sad and tragic as Gojira, King of the Monsters. I turn up the volume until the sound effects make our speakers rattle like tinfoil in the wind, and then I turn it louder still. Godzilla's on a rampage, stomping and roaring through Tokyo. The Japanese military is a minor annoyance that feeds his anger. Nothing can stop this nuclear sea lizard.

Nothing except my grandmother.

"What's that noise?" Nana Hannah shuffles into the living room. Her bathrobe is wrapped tight but she still seems lost inside it. Her long hair is wild and unbraided. "Has the world ended?"

"Godzilla!" I say. "I wish we had a color TV. Can we get a color TV for Hanukkah?"

Nana pours herself a glass of milk and shuffles over to join me on the couch. "*Achh!*"

"Shhh! This is a good part."

Nana and I watch Godzilla destroy Tokyo until we're distracted by a sound at the front door that makes me tense up. Somebody or something is out there. What if a ten-foot-tall, radioactive lizard is prowling the canyon? "Probably just a raccoon," I say, mostly for my own benefit as Nana is already on her feet and squinting through the peep hole.

"A hundred times I asked Tommy to replace the porch light," she mutters. "*Achh,* that boy."

She turns the handle before I can warn her about mummies, creatures from black lagoons, and invisible men.

"Naomi?"

It's Cass Elliot, Laurel Canyon's earth goddess and Nana's voice student. My grandmother insists on calling Cass by her real name because she likes the idea of a Jewish rock star who, unlike Bob Dylan, can actually sing. "A little late for a singing lesson, no?"

A late-night visit from Cass Elliot is one of the few things worth interrupting Godzilla for. God, I love Laurel Canyon.

"I got lost," Cass says.

"You're found now, *liebchen*. Come in and have a nice glass of milk."

"I was driving around, trying to find my house when I recognized yours." Cass smiles as if it's just another normal night of being lost in Laurel Canyon. "Hi, sweetie."

"Maxie was just going to bed."

"Aw, come on, Nana. Godzilla and Mama Cass on the same night."

"Two of a kind," Cass says. She takes up half the couch and slaps the spot where she wants me to sit. Nana brings her a glass of milk, which Cass regards with suspicion and hands it to me. "Got anything stronger? You must keep a little *schnapps* around here."

"*Ja*, cookie." Nana smiles and shuffles off to the kitchen. Cass extends a big arm and wraps it around me like my mother might if she were still here. In Laurel Canyon, Mama Cass is everyone's mother. Tonight she's mine. "I don't think Godzilla is as bad as people think."

"No," I say. "He's misunderstood."

"Sad to be misunderstood."

"Are you okay, Cass?" Her eyes seem to be slow dancing in their sockets.

"Life's a trip, baby."

She sounds a bit sad. Hope and Crosby might be less disturbing than a monster flick, even though they're such squares. "Maybe Godzilla isn't the best thing to watch right now."

"Godzilla is just like me. Lonely. One of a kind." She sniffles like a schoolgirl. "Why does he have to die?"

"Music! How about some music?" I jump up and spin whatever record was left on the turntable. Fortunately, it's Bach, not Zappa. *Freak Out* might have pushed Cass off the deep end. I try to entertain her with my orchestra conductor

192

impersonation but her pupils are wide and her eyelids are heavy.

By the time Nana returns with a small bottle of *schnapps*, Mama Cass has stretched out on the couch and drifted off to dreamland. Nana shrugs and tosses a crochet blanket over our unexpected guest. "God keeps a big zoo."

"Can I try some *schnapps*?" I ask, knowing the answer full well. Nana kisses me on the head and sends me upstairs with a loving smack on the tush. "Go to sleep, little monster. No more TV."

~ ~ ~

I wake up early the next morning to find Dori Tanaka at the breakfast table and Cass Elliot gone. A deep indentation on the couch is the only evidence that I wasn't just California dreaming. The kitchen smells like prunes and nostalgia.

"Hi, Dori, did you and Tommy have a sleepover last night?"

"Huh? What? Are you cracked?"

"Too bad," I say. She and Tommy could make more than just music together. I know Tommy digs her, and I think she'd make a cool big sister. "Sleepovers are fun."

Dori's early for band practice and couldn't resist the gravitational pull of Nana's fruit-filled pancakes.

"Was Cass Elliot here last night?" At this point, I'm not sure if I just imagined our 3:00 a.m. chat about my crazy plan to go to Germany. I do remember flying around the canyon with a bunch of crows who were trying to outwit a coyote. "What happened to Cass, Nana?"

"Cass Elliot?" Dori can't tell if I'm joking. "Seriously? That would have been a fun pajama party."

193

"You must have been dreaming, cookie," Nana smiles and passes me a pancake as big as my face. I reach for the Aunt Jemima but she snatches it away. "You won't taste the fruit."

"Cooked fruit has no taste. Why do we have syrup in the house if we can't use it? Are we out of Cap'n Crunch?"

"*Achh!* I wish your father wouldn't buy such garbage."

I take a few bites while the fruit is still warm and bubbly. I sneak peeks at Dori, looking for any sign she might be sweet on my brother, but she just stuffs her face and reveals nothing. With a few bites in my belly, I remember last night more clearly. Cass was real. The coyote was a dream. "Cass liked my idea about us going to Germany together."

"I'm glad somebody likes it," Nana says. "But I'm not going back there."

Dori accepts another pancake. Which is unbelievable. How can someone as tiny as Dori eat so much, so fast? I poke at my now-cold pancake and wish we had a dog to feed the rest to. "Why don't we get a dog? We live in a canyon. Shouldn't we have a dog?"

"*Achh!* Not that again."

"Dori has a dog."

"No, I don't."

"She has a cat, too."

"Are you crazy?" Dori looks at me like I'm some kind of annoying three-year-old. "I live in an apartment."

"So, Dori," I say. "You and Nana should talk about concentration camps."

"What?" Nana asks, except that it sounds like "*Vhattt?*"

Dori stuffs another bite in her mouth. She can't possibly still be hungry.

"Dori's parents were sent to a camp during the war, Nana." I'm not sure how much Nana knows about the American concentration camps. I want her to see that the two of them have something in common. "They lost everything. Totally unfair."

Nana gives Dori a quizzical look.   "I would be very interested to hear about Dori's parents."

"Hey!" Dori changes the subject. "My parents are playing Vegas in Sammy Davis Jr.'s band this week."

"Sammy Junior Davis?" Nana likes Sammy but can't seem to get his name right. "He's such a *mensch*."

"He's Jewish, you know. It's true. I swear."

"*Achh!*"

"Did you know that Dori's parents have recorded with Frank Sinatra?" I want Nana to like Dori. She would be a way better girlfriend for Tommy than all the Paprikas in the canyon. "Did you know orange is Sinatra's favorite color?"

"Did not know that," Dori says. She's still trying to figure me out. "So, what are you, some kind of human encyclopedia of useless knowledge?"

"Sinatra?" Nana's impressed. Famous crooners is a better breakfast topic than concentration camps. "That man can really sing. Too bad he's Italian."

The phone rings, and Nana walks into the living room to answer it. Some people have phones in every room, but we've just got one. The cable is twisted in a knot and wouldn't stretch into the kitchen even if it were straight as wet spaghetti. I grab the syrup bottle and slather my pancake while Nana's distracted.

"It's for you." Nana sticks her head into the kitchen and frowns at seeing my pancake drowning in Aunt Jemima.

"Me? Who calls me?" This can't be good, and now my pancake will get soggy. I can't imagine any reason for somebody to be tracking me down this early in the morning.

"Maybe it's *Dialing for Dollars*," Dori says.

"Hi!" says a chirpy voice at the other end of the line. "This is Micky Dolenz."

"Funny." I shake my head, hang up the phone, and return to my flooded plate. "Probably some pervert from school," I tell Nana.

But the phone rings again and, this time, Nana indicates that I should answer it myself.

"Don't hang up!" the voice says. "It's Micky. You know, from the Monkees."

"Who is this really?" I ask. It does sound like the guy from the TV show, but his voice wouldn't be hard to impersonate. What if it's really him? "If you're a Monkee, then I'm your uncle."

"Good one! Never heard that before. Listen, kid: Cassie told me about your idea, and I want to help."

"Cass Elliot?" This guy just trapped himself. "When did you talk to her?"

"Around four o'clock this morning."

This would be too hard to make up. My heart skips a beat. I know my face is turning red. I'm talking to a Monkee! I put my hand over the mouthpiece and whisper to Dori that Micky Dolenz is on the line. She looks skeptical so I wave for her to come over and share the earpiece. It takes all my Vulcan power to not sound like a blithering teenybopper. "Well, any friend of Cass…"

"That's what I say. That's why I'm calling. I'm down with the cause and want to help out."

"The cause? Oh, yeah, hey, terrific." I flash Nana a quizzical look. She smiles as if she knows what this is all about. I can never be sure about her. "You mean the cause to keep my brother from getting drafted, or the one about deporting the Nazi down the street?"

"Yeah, that's the one. What if we have a benefit at my house?"

"Tell him we'll play," Dori whispers. "Get us a gig and I'll perform that song you wrote."

"What?" Micky says.

"How about if my brother's band plays a small concert in your yard? They're called Garage Sale."

"Groovy. Next Sunday afternoon? You know where my place is?"

"Of course." It's Laurel Canyon, after all. Everyone knows where everyone lives. "Next Sunday afternoon."

"Far out," Micky says.

Click. I feel dizzy. Dial tone. I need to sit down.

Dori's already pacing and waving her hands. "Oh. My. God. Next Sunday is too soon!"

"Can I play my song?"

"You can play all the songs."

"Cool! Really?"

"Really," Dori says. "You can play solo, 'cause I'm not doing that gig."

"Huh? It was your idea."

"Not all my ideas are good ones."

"But this is your big chance."

"Big chance to flop."

"Too late. We just promised. You've got a week to get your act together. Come on, Dori, where's your *chutzpah*?"

"In my throat." She looks very pale, considering. "I think I'm gonna barf."

I look over at my grandmother, who is scraping the crystallized syrup off my plate and trying to salvage my pancake. "Looks like we're going to Deutschland, Nana."

"*Oy vey,*" she says, but I'm not sure if that refers to me or the soggy pancake she's scraping into the garbage disposal. Nana's so distracted that she hands me the box of Cap'n Crunch.

Now my panic sets in. Nana didn't say no to the Germany trip. She didn't say yes, either, but I can tell she's beginning to think about it. Meeting the Monkees will be out of this world. Going to Germany? That's the other side of the world. I'm too excited to eat my favorite cereal. "After we come back from Germany can we get a dog?"

"A dog?"

Nana seems a bit frazzled. I've worn her out before her second cup of coffee. I know she hates dogs, but she hates Germany more and didn't say no to that. "How 'bout a beagle? They don't bark, they don't shed, and I promise I'll always take care of it."

"Beagle? You want a beagle? How 'bout I toast you one with cream cheese?"

Fringe Benefit

Most of the beautiful people in Micky's backyard don't know or care about the cause. They are happy to see, be seen, and pluck cold beer from a plastic kiddie pool full of ice. Money, music and marijuana are in the air.

Garage Sale came through on short notice, partly to help me raise funds, partly to raise their own profile. The benefit is mutual.

Pater insisted on chaperoning me at my own event. He says he wants to help the cause, but I think he's more worried about hippies than neighborhood Nazis. He also wants to pitch his screenplay to anyone who will listen, starting with our host. Turns out Micky Dolenz is a former student from Grant High School. Small world, smaller canyon.

Pater calls all the gorgeous people who have flooded the canyon AMW's, which stands for "Actor, Musician, Whatever." He says that waiters want to act. Actors want to write. Writers want to direct. Directors want to produce and producers want to discover rock bands. As a guidance counselor working on a screenplay, he's in a good position to understand why this town's so confused.

There's a rumor circulating that the tall gal with little Davy Jones will be this year's Miss October playmate. I heard that Hugh Hefner was here but I don't see anyone in a bathrobe.

Miss October may be a knockout, but no lady here can hold a candle to Joni. I thought I saw her earlier, sitting cross-legged at the foot of a big sycamore tree. Joni is lucky to have both talent and beauty, two gifts rarely doled out in equal measure.

Exhibit A: Mama Cass, proof of God's unbalanced generosity. Cass was blessed with raw talent and a gracious spirit, but came up short in the miniskirt department. Her inner beauty is deeper than her ample bosom, but for all her outer happiness, I know she feels sad inside. Pater says beauty is skin-deep, which is why there are so many sunburned people in Los Angeles. I still think that Cass Elliot is the one he should marry. Her beauty is the deepest, and I think she'd make a fine stepmom.

Assuming today's fundraiser doesn't end in a drug bust or armed robbery, I will raise enough money for my big *mitzvah*. This means I'm going to Germany with my grandmother. If she were here, Nana would remind me to stay anchored, because I feel as if my feet have wings. Too much happiness makes Jews nervous.

The cream cheese icing on my cake is that Micky Dolenz says he digs the song I wrote with Dori. He heard it during the sound check and likes it well enough to use it in the third season of *The Monkees* TV show. I don't want to rain on his parade, but he seems like the last to know the show's been cancelled. He'll find out soon enough, and, besides, I think his group is working on a movie that should be even bigger than their TV show.

At least Dori now takes me a bit more seriously. Before this week, it would have been easier to convince her to dance the Watusi than to listen to my song ideas. Maybe the initial version did sound a bit like a cartoon theme song, but the band needed material to fill the set, and my happy little earworm helped balance Dori's dark lyrics and quirky instrumentals.

So, yeah, big ups for me.

The idea for "Transistor Radio" came to me in a late-night flash long after I was supposed to be sleeping. My battery was dead again, and I tried to imagine life in a small Podunk town without a radio. No KHJ. No crosstown bus rides. No J-camp. No Dori, Joni, or Cassie. No Laurel Canyon.

After finally agreeing to give it a go, Dori came up with a perky opening figure that Riff plays on the seventh fret while she harmonizes on bass. Once the groove takes hold, Dori tells the story.

Across the lake near the field where the old man's buried,
there's a cedar shake church where my sister got married.
When sister left home she knew I would miss her,
so she gave me her phone and her cheap transistor.
Transistor radio. Oh, oh.
Transistor radio. Woah, oh, oh, oh.
I can still hear the static and the Wolfman howlin' on my transistor radio.

Dori's first reaction was that the song was too happy. I argued that there's nothing wrong with happiness. The U.S. Constitution guarantees us the right to pursue happiness, but Dori said happiness is overrated and the constitution didn't keep her parents out of Manzanar.

Dori also hated the simplicity of the chorus, but I said if you can't get your point across with a few nonsense syllables, maybe you don't really have a point at all.

Shoo bop da doo run
Pumpin' from a station down in T-T-Tijuana
Church bells rang but they never sounded sweet
as the guitar twang and the big boss beat.
Transistor radio …

Dori's initial idea for a bridge was to play a medley of cartoon show theme songs. The boys saw this as a chance for a great artistic statement and threw their weight behind a

Flintstones-Jetsons-Looney Tunes medley. Fortunately, they got too distracted to make it happen.

> Sellin' voodoo lotion from south of the border
> Back beat commotion and a hint of disorder
> Songs about cars, school, music and girls
> Songs about freedom and a brave new world
> Transistor radio. Oh, oh.
> Transistor radio. Woah, oh, oh, oh.
> I can still hear the static and the Wolfman howlin' on my transistor radio.

Dori, dressed like a nun, begins a run up the fret board. Riff tilts and slashes at his guitar. Droplets of sweat fly from the crewcut skull where shocks of Tommy's hair used to swirl in all directions. He pounds out the final chaos of the 1812 Overture mixed with the Who's "My Generation." The song ends with Dori shouting the closing lyrics over the rising noise.

> I was a little girl listenin' to a nine-volt box
> Trying to get the message as the signals crossed
> Pulling in the airwaves from across the nation
> Listenin' to the music from a rebel station
> I'm back in daddy's attic and the night is fallin'
> I can still hear the static and the Wolfman callin'
> I can still hear the static and the Wolfman callin'
> On my transistor radio.

Dori howls and the band crash lands in a false ending. Tommy shouts a fresh count. Riff toggles over to the bridge pickup and turns the volume knob to the ear-shatter position, and grinds his fingertips down to near-bloody nubs with a deafening solo.

202

Dori hoists her bass guitar overhead in a thunderous offering to the burning sky. The subwoofer she insisted on bringing rumbles as if a volcano is erupting beneath us.

Tommy twirls his sticks, throws one in the air and catches it on the downbeat. I wish I had a Polaroid to take a picture of my crazed brother pounding like a buffalo stampede. I can just picture his lost ribbons of waving blond hair. Seeing Tommy so completely in his element fills me with pride. He's turning out okay. I wish our mom could be here.

I peek at the kids' pool to see if the ice water has boiled away. People seem ready to evacuate when Dori howls a few more times and the band ends clean on an upbeat because ending on an upbeat is against the rules.

I'm happy to see that "Transistor Radio" got the guests to turn away from the shrimp platter long enough to stare dumbstruck at the band. Some of the musicians in the crowd look amused, though more than a few groupie girlfriends are too confused to bat a false eyelash. Pater seizes the frozen moment to circulate the collection basket.

"Happy Fourth of July!" Riff shouts, even though it's August. "Hope you enjoyed the fireworks."

Had I really grown up in the boondocks, a transistor radio would have been my only lifeline to a world beyond dirt roads, pickup trucks, and drive-through churches. I'm sure that the townies would have distrusted my Kraut grandmother, beaten up my long-haired brother and found it mighty strange that my dad still lives with his mama.

Los Angeles is a big enough swamp for a fish out of water to hide in. I can't be wise beyond my years because I haven't got many, but I do understand that the world beyond my little corner of California is a pretty grim place. Laurel Canyon is the only place on Earth where nuts roll uphill. Though some of the people at this party seem convinced that God worships them, I feel blessed to be here with Miss October and the lost angels of La La land.

I'm relieved that when the time comes for my speech, Micky the Monkee preempts me by jumping on stage and thanking everyone for supporting "The Cause" that "our dear friend Cassie" feels so strongly about. This triggers a round of applause, a gracious nod from our big mama, and a healthy swarm of deposits into the basket my father is passing around.

The hot sun feels as if it's hovering ten feet overhead. I bring Pater a cold bottle of Coke and take over the pass-the-basket duties. I've never seen so much money. A tall guy sporting a red velvet cape and a bushy, caramel-colored mustache makes a beeline toward me. A hippie chick in a belly-dance outfit hanging on his arm jingle-jangles along like a happy wind chime. He mumbles encouragement through the round cheeks that glow like Christmas ornaments and tosses a couple of hundred-dollar bills onto my collection plate.

I've never seen a hundred-dollar bill, and now I have two.

"Thanks, Caped Crusader!" I've seen this character racing through the hills on a big motorcycle. I remember worrying that his long scarf might get caught in the rear wheel and strangle him. I worry too much to ever be a hippie.

I'm sure we've raised enough money to fly me and Nana to Germany. One week from now we'll be up, up, and away with TWA. Nana never intended to return there. For the first time ever, she's more nervous than I am.

Cass Elliot's manager gave me his card and offered to help me set up a "charitable foundation," whatever that is, to provide "tax-deductible status" for any money we don't spend. As best I can tell, it's a scheme to reward rich people for waging the war on poverty.

The band is about to pack up their gear when people call for them to play another number. Dori hadn't planned on surviving the showcase, much less playing an encore. Her newest tune, "Restless Daughter," is a risky choice to close the show, but Garage Sale plays as if they have nothing to lose. Riff sets up a soft treble waterfall that tumbles into a warm pool of A-minor. As the chord fades, he offers a wiggle of the whammy bar.

Dori steps up to the mic and sings in a whispered hush.

Soft winter light fading gracefully.
Hot February night falling weightlessly.
Sweet jasmine wind rising through the sage.
The sun slips silently beyond the western gate.
Restless daughter of the sea.
Nightfall sets you free.

The eerie tune sweeps like coastal fog over Micky's backyard. People look up from their pipes, drinks and conversation as the music drifts in on the breeze.

On these rolling hills, scattered round the bay.
They lived peacefully in the land of hawk and snake.
The water gave them life and shelters her today.
Driven from this world by wingless birds of prey.
Restless daughter of the sea.
Nightfall sets you free.

At this point, the band adds a bridge that I never heard in practice.

On the surface of the water.
In between the day and night.
Dance the souls of restless daughters,
Dancing on the rising tide.

At first blush, "Restless Daughter" seems like a song about the Chumash, but the more I listen, the more I wonder if it's about Dori.

> Dusk on the wing, shadows float like birds.
> Rust moon following a trail of broken words.
> In exile she remains, the spirit of the land.
> Suspended in the waves like golden grains of sand.
> Restless daughter of the sea.
> Nightfall sets you free.

The music fades in a vibrato hush of suspended chords and velvety harmonics. The band stands still, awash in waves of dying sound. People are silent as sunset and then applaud quietly so as not to break the spell that will carry me across the ocean, back to the haunted land of my lost ancestors.

History Repeats Again

LAX to JFK. New York to old Düsseldorf. We finally make it to Germany after a long boring trip. Blurry with jetlag, I'm lost in the fatherland.

This all started innocently enough—a little breaking and entering, a theft so small it seemed like borrowing. I should have known that my quest for the truth about Mr. Shreddermauler would take a wrong turn. Now I'm on a questionable detour to the house he once lived in. Was he a Nazi? I'll soon find out.

Nana had some business to attend to and said I could trust the men she left me with today. Maybe my brain is playing tricks on me, but I'm starting to worry that Germany may still get the last word. I'm surprised Nana would have any faith in uniformed Germans.

One has a square head that makes him seem top-heavy, like Herman Munster without the neck bolts. Herman the German. German Munster. His companion is bald, bird-nosed, and beady-eyed. A Colonel Klink lookalike, minus the monocle. Munster and Klink may look like TV characters, but this isn't "Hogan's Heroes," and neither of them are acting. Their lack of guns suggests power far worse than bullets.

What if they kidnap me? What if they're Shreddermauler's old Nazi cronies? I've lived for nothing and might soon die for less. Nana always said that if reality didn't kill me, my imagination would. Now it's finally happening. *My Life, Part One* might be cancelled after the first season.

I keep mum, hoping my stern hosts will reveal something. Best not to let on that I understand a bit of German. I hear one man mention my neighbor Klaus Shreidermayer's name and can't resist a shudder. What if his story was a lie? I wish Nana had stayed with me today. Nana's *Deutsch* is old, full of wisdom mixed with a healthy dose of Yiddish. The German I'm hearing today is exact, harsh, and hard to understand.

My grandmother says if you anticipate the worst, life will exceed your expectations. So far, so bad. I'm not even sure which side of the Berlin Wall we're on. If we're east of Checkpoint Charlie, I may never return home.

Home. What I wouldn't give to be snug in my loft at the top of our A-frame. God, if you're out there, this would be a good time for a miracle.

If tortured, I vow to reveal nothing but my name, rank, and the serial number of my transistor radio. I will grit my teeth and lock my orthodontia to keep my tongue from flapping. My curtain call will be brief as I have only twelve quick years to relive before the lights go out. I wonder: does life pass before your eyes from start to finish or do you relive it backwards in black and white like a TV show in reverse?

Where will I go after I die? Heaven seems unlikely. Hell seems like overkill. My dad always tells me not to worry about what's next. He says heaven and hell are here on Earth, so we should bloom where we stand. Too bad I barely had time to sprout.

Nana always said the Nazis would be back. Maybe it's finally happened. History repeats, again. I guess some Germans can't accept that we drained the swamp. While the world sleeps, the fourth and final Reich oozes forward.

I am hustled into a black Mercedes and taken on a high speed drive toward I don't know where. Nazi Headquarters?

An East German prison? Perhaps we'll make a quick stop to lay flowers at Hitler's bunker. Maybe he's not really dead.

The speedometer is nearly pegged as we race down the autobahn. My restless stomach is squashed against my lower spine. I feel like an Apollo astronaut in a launch trainer. This reminds me that we'll put a man on the moon by the end of the decade and I won't live to see it.

Thanks for nothing, Wernher von Braun.

We pull off the highway and weave through a misty landscape purged of all color. We enter a small town clogged with mopeds and lined with drab shop fronts. Chubby, gray-faced people shuffle about. I consider shouting and kicking out the window, but these good citizens know better than to question authority.

Good citizens do as they are told.

I look for droop-shouldered children wearing yellow *Jude* stars like the one Nana keeps on our mantle, but there are no Jews left in Germany. A pig's head grins at me from a butcher shop window. Definitely not Kosher. We turn into a quiet residential neighborhood, one of the few that wasn't reduced to ash during the war and rebuilt in steel and cinder block. Timid bits of color peek through the cracks in the gray day.

The Mercedes stops in front of a three-story, turn-of-the-century house that almost looks edible. The house at 120 Bismarkstrasse is nicely landscaped with a gentle walkway leading to an inviting front door. A gingerbread roof curves under at the eaves. Pruned azaleas look like cotton candy, and the beveled glass windows cast syrupy rainbows to lure unsuspecting little Hansels and Gretels into the kitchen.

The place looks enchanted, but I'm not fooled by this dose of Disney Deutschland. There's no doubt in my bones about what's waiting inside. Basement cells with thousand-watt spotlights and shackled skeletons.

209

We've arrived at Klaus Shreidermayer's old house.

"*Wir sind hier,*" German Munster says.

"*Stimmt,*" Klink mutters. Unlike the TV character who, oddly enough, is played by a Jewish actor, this no-nonsense chrome dome tends to swallow his words and digest them twice. He pulls two shovels from the trunk of the car.

Shovels? Shovels are for digging. Digging holes. Holes to plant trees. Or people. Shreidermayer said he buried something in his backyard and supposedly we're here to find it. But what if that was a lie? What if they force me to dig my own grave, like those documentaries we watched at Hebrew school?

A frumpy old *hausfrau* peeks through the dark curtains of the home next door. Go ahead, madam. Pretend it's just another normal day. Look away like you did when the brownshirts broke down my grandfather's door on *Kristallnacht.* You survived. He didn't.

The commander grips my arm. I consider resisting by going limp like a Berkeley student protester, but I don't want to get beaten like one. Nana says that panic is the only true enemy, but Nazis seem like a bigger threat. I look for an escape route that doesn't run into a brick wall or the backend of a shovel. *Think, Max. Think! Supposedly, that's what you're good at.*

A man in a white lab coat answers the door. His blue marble eyes and slick golden hair are master-race perfect. His tight smile runs no deeper than his thin lips. The fascists exchange quick pleasantries with formal conjugations.

"Is everything ready?"

"*Ja! Natürlich.*"

The first floor of the house is disguised as a dentist's office. This explains our host's starched lab coat. Who better to administer torture than someone with a college degree in pain? We step into a dimly lit waiting room. I look for evidence of a Hitler Youth scholarship or a commendation from the Kaiser, but all I see is the current edition of *Der Spiegel* sitting on a glass table. There's a tank rolling across the blood-red cover. A bold black headline says something about a tragedy.

My heart jumps when a nurse enters the room. She looks like an East German javelin thrower.

"*Guten morgen,*" she says in a voice lower and more menacing than those of any of the men here. Her tone makes it clear she doesn't serve the *schnitzel* at Oktoberfest. This battle-hardened Broomhilda would give the Brothers Grimm nightmares. Ten feet tall and half as wide, she eyes me like a bridge troll might a tethered goat.

Cooperate with the Gestapo and maybe we spare you the pain of having Broomhilda extract your teeth one by one. Novocaine? Sorry, nationwide shortage. Laughing gas? No, we'll be the only ones laughing.

I stumble out the back door where German Munster is waiting with the shovels. Perfect hedges and clusters of gladiolas border the backyard. A granite boulder seems to have fallen from the sky amid a patch of obedient geraniums. Even in August, the ground here is wet.

The moment of truth is upon, or more accurately, under us.

I notice a pine tree in the corner of the yard, waiting to cast a shadow should the sun ever shine again. The lowest branch may be within my reach. It will take time to dig a deep enough hole in which to find Shreidermayer's treasure, or dump my bruised and bullet-riddled corpse. If needed, I can scramble up the tree and get over the fence.

O Tannenbaum, O Tannenbaum. Please help me dodge the bullets.

As long as Eva Braun's Rottweiler isn't on the other side of the fence, I can run to the nearest train track and jump on a freighter bound for... where? Poland? I don't know east from west and there is no star to guide me. I'm behind enemy lines without a compass or cyanide tablet. I might aim for Paris and land in Stalingrad.

"Under the rock," Klink says. There is a sick trace of satisfaction in his voice. He and Munster roll the boulder out of the way, being careful not to damage the geraniums.

Kill the Jew child, but don't hurt the flowers. Mustn't hurt the flowers.

Unless I make my move soon, this rock will sit *shiva* on my soul. If I could only remember the words to the *Kaddish* I would chant last rites for myself. I wish Nana were here to — what? — die alongside me? It might be better that she misses today's tragedy.

The stiff-jawed dentist drifts back inside the house as the thugs begin digging. I can hear Broomhilda smashing around in the surgery, preparing some unimaginable concoction. After they stuff me into the hole, will she pour scalding acid over my head? What's left of my eyes will be eaten by ravens.

I try to get my imagination under control, but a burst of wind rustling the pine tree reminds me that escape is still possible. What I wouldn't give to be back in the garage listening to my brother pounding on his drum set. I hope he becomes famous and dedicates a song to my memory.

One guy digging, two watching. These Germans aren't all that different from a California highway crew. They dig mechanically until Munster's shovel hits an object about two feet below the surface. From the dull thud I'd say he's found something made of wood.

The commander nods as if this is all part of the plan. "Careful not to break it," he says.

Munster uses his hands to clear dirt from around the obstruction. He rocks the long object, trying to wriggle it free. I edge closer and see the wooden box. A small, moldy coffin buried vertically.

212

Maybe I'm not the first one to die and be buried here. The box appears to be about one foot square across the top. Too small for me to squeeze into unless they chop me to bits. That must be the plan. I can hear Broomhilda rooting around in the kitchen, probably sharpening a meat cleaver.

Disregarding the geraniums, German Munster is now splayed out on the ground trying to pull the box from its burial place. He manages to pry the coffin away from the earth's silent grip with a few choice grunts.

Colonel Klink raises an eyebrow, the closest he gets to looking excited. He scrapes mud off the sides of the rotted coffin. It's about three feet long, barely big enough to contain a baby.

God, if you're out there, I'd do anything to be home in Laurel Canyon right now.

My heart is pounding, knees too soft to run. I try to calm the big butterflies in my little stomach. Each chamber of my heart pounds out a different rhythm. If life is going to pass before my eyes, it better get moving. There's not much time left.

I listen for the sound of angels, but all I hear is a telephone ringing.

Klink produces a crow bar, but instead of bashing my head in, he cracks open the box. I've watched enough late night TV to know that opening this coffin might release evil spirits that will never rest. I hold my breath, waiting for a hiss or a screech, but the air is dead silent. Trembling, I look into the rotting box and see that Mr. Shreidermayer wasn't lying.

The commander pulls out something older than a corpse, wise and ancient, more powerful than a restless ghost.

Sadness in the Soil

The week flew by. I've barely adjusted to the time zone, and it's now our last morning in Krefeld, Germany. This afternoon we will fly home from Düsseldorf with the treasure I recovered from oblivion's backyard. The box we found in Mr. Shreidermayer's old garden doesn't prove his innocence, but it tips the balance.

Even Nana is starting to trust our mysterious neighbor. A back channel request to the Israeli embassy returned clean. She's still waiting for a response from the Jewish Documentation Center in Vienna, but so far, so good for the former Man Who Cuts Legs Off.

My grandmother has been in demand here in Germany thanks to our hosts, Pastor Schmidt and his wife, Hilde. Hilde knew Nana as a girl and was eager to host us when my grandmother made contact after so many years.

Pastor Schmidt saw Nana's return as something bigger than a reunion between childhood friends. After he convinced Nana to say a few words at his church, a high school teacher asked her to speak to his class. As much as Nana wanted to remain anonymous, one encounter led to another. A reporter heard about her and wrote an article in the daily paper that translated into more requests from schools and churches. She was interviewed on the radio and was even asked to visit the capital in Bonn the day I dug for treasure in Mr. Shreidermayer's old backyard.

Younger Germans seem hungry to hear her story. Nana's generation, not so much. For them, the past is better left behind.

Few Jews return to Germany. Fewer have the *chutzpah* to suggest that schoolkids ask their grandparents about the war. "It will be uncomfortable," Nana says, gathering strength with each word and appearance. "My generation may refuse to speak of those terrible times; they may feign ignorance. But if you neglect to ask, you will always regret not having done so. You will always wonder. You will always feel tainted by your inheritance."

In one crowded classroom, Nana unrolled her left sleeve so that every student could see the numbers tattooed on her forearm. "You, the grandchildren of the Third Reich, did not put these numbers on my arm, but now that you see them, silence is no longer an option. These numbers can never be erased, but they can be cleansed. Whatever your grandparents did or, more likely, did not do, their guilt is not yours unless you hide in their shadow. You cannot change the past, but I ask you to not let it repeat through silence. By daring to remember, by looking directly into the face of history while it still lives, you may prevent such a tragedy from ever happening again."

Nana did not want to come back to Germany. She had no desire to return to the scene of the crimes, but I needed a chaperone and she let me persuade her. I've never doubted my grandmother's strength, but until this trip, I never knew just how brave she is.

So here we are, sitting in Hilde Schmidt's quiet solarium on our last morning in Krefeld. There are no more schools to visit or holes to dig. In a couple of hours, Pastor Schmidt will drive us to the station, and we'll catch a train to the airport. Soon, only vapor trails will remain of this strange week in the fatherland.

Sun streams through the glass doors that open to the garden. A tiny bird is flitting around a bright red feeder. Nana stares into her coffee cup, looking happy and sad at the same time. I'm

215

finishing a second helping of Bundt cake that's so light it defies gravity.

I'm about to sneak another slice when Frau Schmidt appears with an apologetic look and a woman who showed up uninvited at the front door. The woman introduces herself as Ulrike Linden and says she's from a nearby town. She looks to be about Nana's age. Formal and serious, stiff in her dark blue linen. She clutches a small hat in one hand, the kind old ladies wear in temple. Not waiting for an invitation to join us, she sits down on the chair that the pastor's wife had been using and begins speaking in German.

"You might wonder why I insisted on seeing you. I'm sure you look at me, guess my age, and wonder what I did during the war."

"The thought never crossed my mind." Nana says with cold diplomacy. In spite of the rare sunshine, there is no warmth in the solarium.

"I was a nurse," Frau Linden says. "I worked in a children's hospital."

"How nice," I say, in German. I want her to know I'm listening. I look her in the eyes but can't lock down a first impression.

"I chose to work with children because I had none of my own. You see, my husband died of influenza shortly after we were wed."

"We have some packing to do and a train to catch, Frau Linden." Nana's thin lips are drawn tight. The crow's feet around her eyes are looking for an excuse to fly away. Nana enjoyed interacting with students and young adults this week, but I can tell she still finds it difficult to speak with Germans of her own age. She's showing Frau Linden roughly the same warmth that she showed the FBI when they came to our door last month.

216

"What is it you seek here, Frau Linden?" I ask.

"Ah!" This time it registers that I understand German. She seems happy to address me instead of my impenetrable grandmother. "You are the grandchild?"

I nod and she begins to speak without pause or punctuation.

"When the troubles began I kept my head down and continued my nursing work. I thought Hitler was a passing fad until *Kristallnacht*. That was the point of no return."

I shiver at the mention of this terrible night, the night of shattering glass, the dress rehearsal for the Holocaust. The terror haunts my grandmother like a shadow she can reach out and touch thirty years later.

"Jewish children were no longer being admitted to the hospital. Medicine and beds were in short supply. We were told the nation was ill-served by wasting time and resources on enemies of the fatherland."

Frau Linden has yet to take a breath. I'm holding mine. What if my father had fallen ill during the time she describes. Would German doctors have let him die? Would they have ignored him like the lifeguard who let him struggle and almost drown because of the yellow star on his swimsuit?

Frau Linden speaks faster. "As the war heated up, the best doctors were sent to the front lines and military hospitals. I could have smuggled medicine and supplies to my Jewish neighbors but I was scared. I did not want to be arrested for defying the Nazis. I did not want to be shot and left for dead in an alley. I was just another good German."

"We all live with regrets, Frau Linden." My grandmother wants to be rid of this nervous woman who seems lost in her own guilt. "We really must be going."

Frau Linden just talks faster. "People, good people, were disappearing. To where? I didn't know. As the war went on, food became scarce. In spite of the propaganda, I knew we were losing. Soldiers did not return home. Children were malnourished. Despair was everywhere, and destruction soon followed. When, thank God, Hitler was defeated, I learned just how stupid, I had been. How stupid we all had been. Medical personnel were in short supply so I volunteered to serve as a nurse with the Allied forces. I was assigned to Bergen-Belsen shortly after it was liberated by the British."

"You volunteered?" I tap Nana's arm and edge toward the front of my chair.

"I know that you were interned at Dachau, Frau Strauss. So you are well aware, painfully aware of the sort of conditions I encountered. Perhaps you also know that many so-called liberated prisoners were not just sent on their merry way when the war ended."

"I was stuck at Dachau for almost a year after the so-called liberation," Nana says. The memory hangs like a ghost in the air. "Nobody knew what to do with us."

"I was shocked at how slow the Allies were to process and free the prisoners. Shocked that so many of the Nazi guards and administrators kept their jobs. Some were allowed to slip away into the night. Life changed slowly for the prisoners. Some survived the war only to die waiting to be set free."

This matches the story Nana recently shared with me, the story not told in our history books. She says history is rarely written by the people who lived it.

"Displaced Persons. DPs, they called us," Nana says from a faraway place. This has been a tiring week, and I can see the exhaustion on her face. I can tell she'd rather not relive this chapter of her life. "Prisoners from every corner of the continent. Many had no country to return to."

"As you can imagine, many of the prisoners were disoriented. Some had been in that living hell so long they couldn't remember where they came from." Frau Linden seems desperate to tell us something, though slow to arrive at her destination. "If it weren't for the Nazis' obsessive record keeping, we might not have known where people came from or where they belonged. Some were lucky enough to find surviving family through the refugee agencies. A few refugees were granted transit papers to faraway places."

"I know all of this, Frau Linden." Nana seems to be at her limit. "What is it you seek from me?"

"There were over fifty thousand prisoners at Belsen when it was liberated. Over ten thousand corpses." Frau Linden chokes on her words. Tears well in her eyes. "Typhus was a constant danger. Survivors were starving."

"Frau Linden, I'm afraid I must ask you to leave." Nana stands up. Her pale blue eyes are now icy. "We have a train to catch, and there's nothing I can do for you."

Frau Linden stares off into the garden, pulls herself together and resumes talking. "Conditions were terrible, and many died for lack of food and medicine. The defeated Nazis destroyed much of the documentation. It took us over a year to process all of the prisoners, to locate distant relatives and arrange for visas and transit papers. In the end, there were only a few cases left."

It suddenly occurs to me that Frau Linden has not come seeking forgiveness. I grab my grandmother's hand and prevent her from leaving. "*Setz du dich*. Sit down, Nana. I think we need to hear how this story ends."

"I'll be brief," Frau Linden insists, though nothing so far indicates a knack for brevity. "In the end, a hundred or so prisoners were impossible to identify or trace. Their files said things like 'unknown provenance' or 'unverifiable identity.' One man in particular had a very deep and genuine amnesia. He simply did not remember who he was."

"Who was this man?" I ask, more for Nana's benefit than mine. A coffee feeling burns in my stomach.

219

Trembling, Frau Linden produces a black-and-white picture, ragged at the edges and hands it to my grandmother.

"*Mein Gott im himmel!*" Nana gasps. Had she not been seated, she might have fallen. She wipes her eyes and looks again. "God above."

"Is that my grandfather?" I look over Nana's shoulder at the scrawny man in gray hospital scrubs.

"But… this is impossible." Nana's voice crackles as I reach around her to grab the trembling photo she's about to drop.

"Is that *Opa*?"

The moment waits in silence so thick I can barely breathe. Jews sit *shiva* for seven days. Nana's has lasted thirty years. Equal parts hope and despair have kept her stuck in one place, unwilling or unable to let go of her missing husband, my missing grandfather, Otto Strauss.

"Here he is a few years later." Frau Linden hands over another picture, still black and white, but less upsetting. My smiling grandfather is now wearing a black hat and gray suit.

"Where is he?" Nana asks. A tear hangs like a glass bead against her pale skin. "I must see him."

Frau Linden's sigh contains the answer. "I have a car outside, Frau Strauss. I can tell you the rest of the story as we drive to the cemetery."

Our unexpected visitor offers to drive us directly to the airport in order to buy us enough time to visit my grandfather's grave. Fortunately, Nana, being Nana, we were packed and ready last night. Pastor Schmidt helps load our luggage and my precious cargo into Frau Linden's Volkswagen. Hilde Schmidt gives us big hugs and insists we return to visit her.

In the car, Frau Linden explains that when the camp was being decommissioned, a man known only as Otto had nowhere to go. "He remembered nothing, and nothing was known about him beyond the obvious fact that he was a German Jew. His lack

220

of recall for anything but his first name suggested that he had been deeply traumatized. The British doctors believed that his amnesia would fade and his memory would return over time. His picture was circulated with the Jewish refugee agencies and the U.N. High Commission, but no one could place him."

"I saw many such photos," Nana says. "But never his."

One stray photo, snapped and forgotten in an instant, could have made thirty years' worth of difference. I reach forward from the cramped back seat to squeeze her shoulder.

"It was thought that time would heal his wounds and that the best therapy was to return him to as normal a life as possible," Frau Linden says. "I agreed to take him back to Köln, to nurse him like a wounded bird until he was able to fly."

"If only…" Nana lets the thought fade, but I know how her mind works. Somehow, she's found a way to blame herself.

"It's a miracle he survived, Nana," I whisper.

"The entire country had amnesia, so he fit right in," Frau Linden says as we take an exit at the edge of a large city. "This country was such a wasteland after the war. We barely had food, let alone psychiatrists. The idea that someone could forget his past was not so rare in a country where everyone was trying to forget it. For many years I had to research this on my own. It's how I became one of Germany's first psychiatric nurses."

"Did he forget everything?" I ask. "Could he read and write? Add numbers?"

"Those things are like walking or riding a bicycle. He even remembered how to hem a pant leg, but never knew why."

"What about his childhood?" Nana asks. "Or his wife and son? Did he remember us?"

"Toward the very end of his life, he remembered just enough for me to make the connection when I read about you in the newspaper this week. I'm so sorry, so very sorry that nothing he said could have led me to you sooner."

"Presumed dead," Nana says. "The refugee agencies gave up. The German government had no records. For lack of a memory, my Otto was forgotten all these years?"

The small car turns into the overgrown entrance to an old Jewish cemetery. The gate is locked with a rusted chain. A sign says that it's forbidden to enter, but Frau Linden leads us through a narrow gap in the fence. Tall pines bear silent witness to skewed and broken tombstones with names like Herrmann, Oppenheim, Schwartz, Mayer, Berger, and Kahn. Some of the graves are hundreds of years old, none appear more recent than 1939. Many were vandalized, and none have been repaired. There is too much sadness in the soil for Jews to ever rest in peace here.

"It took about ten years before I could get a doctor interested in your husband's case. By that time, 1955 or so, he had developed a new identity and life. He was Otto Linden—"

"You were married?" I ask, mostly so Nana doesn't have to.

"No," Frau Linden laughs. "Once was enough. Otto needed a last name, and mine was as good as any. I found him piecework in a tailor's shop, and he eventually got good enough to open his own business. Was he a tailor by any chance, Frau Strauss?"

"Silk merchant," Nana says, embellishing a bit. She always told me he was a *schmata* salesman. "His father was a tailor, so I'm not surprised."

Frau Linden leads us to the only new grave in the cemetery. The tombstone is marked with a Jewish star. The birth year is blank. The man known as Otto Linden died in 1966.

"In the end, Otto slipped into a sort of second childhood. His doctor said it was dementia, but his life was built on a foundation of sand and I think it just crumbled."

"What did he say?" Nana dabs her eyes with her handkerchief. She walks around the grave as if measuring it,

222

doing her best not to fall apart on the spot. "Did he have any final words or memories?"

"Three images kept returning. He remembered Russian soldiers on a bridge."

"He served in World War One," I say. Nana told me about this. "Awarded the Iron Cross for bravery."

"He also remembered soldiers coming to his house and taking him away."

"*Kristallnacht*." Nana's voice cracks.

"More than once he said, 'Is this the thanks I get for serving the fatherland?'"

As Frau Linden says these words I feel as if a lock just opened. Whatever doubts I might have harbored about Frau Linden have now evaporated. My grandfather said these exact words as he waved his World War I medal, his iron cross at the Nazis.

"You said he repeated three things." Nana looks up into the pines as if expecting to see God sitting on a limb. "What was the third?"

"Your name. Hannah."

I hold Nana's elbow as she drops slowly to her knees. I can only imagine what she is feeling because I feel like sobbing. A second later all three of us are kneeling at the graveside, watering the grass with our quiet tears. I put an arm around my grandmother to comfort her, but we're both trembling.

I feel my grandfather's presence. This is our family reunion.

"He was born in 1890," Nana runs her hand over the Star of David on the tombstone. "Both of our families were from Frankfurt." She falls silent for a second and then laughs. "When we were courting, we would go to the train station and pretend to kiss goodbye. That was a long, long time ago."

"I would be happy to have the tombstone changed to your name," Frau Linden says. "We can add any detail you like."

Nana thinks about this for a moment and then surprises me.

"I would be honored for Otto to keep your name, Frau Linden. You saved him. You took care of him. You brought him back from the dead." Nana puts her arm around Frau Linden and draws her close. "You are a person who brings light unto the world."

Frau Linden returns the embrace and the two share a silent moment. A pine breeze washes over us. There's a slight, hopeful smell of late summer in the air.

"I will always remember this." I say, helping both women to their feet. "I will return here and place flowers on my grandfather's grave."

"*Danke*, Maxie." Nana says. "I'm so glad the two of you have finally met."

"Should we say *Kaddish*, Nana?" I ask and she nods. I know the first couple of words, which are enough to start her chanting our prayer of mourning. I join in on the phrases I know and hum along with the rest.

"Blessed be His name, whose glorious kingdom is forever," Frau Linden says in German once we have completed the Hebrew. "We had a visiting rabbi conduct the funeral. I remember these words very clearly."

"My family will forever remember your goodness, Frau Linden."

"Perhaps you will return someday as my guest, Frau Strauss. I should very much like for us to be friends."

"*Natürlich*," Nana looks back at the grave. "We have much in common."

Nana never wanted to return to Germany. There were too many memories here, old scars that didn't need scratching. Now she feels as if she waited too long.

The Whole World's Watching

Frau Linden drove us all the way to the Düsseldorf airport, where Nana and I now wait for our boarding call. It's the last leg of the marathon and the beginning of the long ride home.

I'm the only kid in a sea of charcoal suits, thin ties, knee-length skirts and stiff blouses. I'm glad to be leaving Germany, though I sense there is hope here. I felt it in the air and witnessed it firsthand in how young people welcomed my grandmother. My generation might restore some color to this gray land.

The floor rumbles as a plane takes off and disappears into low-hanging clouds. The windows continue to rattle long after the jet is airborne. Pilots, like Jews, must believe in the sun even when it isn't shining.

I notice an old black-and-white Telefunken TV flickering in the corner of the waiting room. People gather before the antique screen like cavemen around a fire.

I wander over to see what's on TV. It's Saturday morning. Maybe they'll show some cartoons.

No such luck. People are watching a military documentary. The sound is barely audible above the flight announcements and jet engines. I look for the tallest man in the crowd and ask him to turn it louder. Amused by my accent, he lips his cigarette, and scowls as if it's my fault when the volume knob twists off in his hand.

"*Sheisse!*" Someone mutters a curse word that I'm not supposed to know.

I edge closer and see Soviet markings on the tanks. A war movie? They appear to have crossed into Czechoslovakia. This doesn't look like World War II. A bad reenactment perhaps. A reporter is talking about an invasion, but this isn't footage from the last war. This military operation is happening now, a few hundred miles south of here. Unless I'm losing something in translation, the Russkies just planted an army boot into what Hope Springs called socialism's human face. With the exception of my all-knowing grandmother, nobody expected Warsaw Pact troops to invade one of their own. This wasn't supposed to happen. The Soviets have occupied the countryside and are mopping up the capital.

Is Hope Springs still in Prague?

The man with the volume knob says that the end of the world has begun. He throws his cigarette butt to the floor and doesn't bother to step on it. Thin smoke rises from the scuffed linoleum. A woman in gray linen asks him if the Russians will stop at the border, or if they intend to invade Germany. He silences her with a hand gesture as if waving away a mosquito.

Her question seems reasonable to me. Why would the end of the world stop at the German border? If history is any guide, World War III will start here.

The woman frets that this is the beginning of an all-out assault on the west. There's a hint of hysteria in her voice. With a little help from their friends in East Germany, the Russians could pincer Germany and *blitzkrieg* their way to Paris before LBJ can finish his morning coffee. Brezhnev could have the keys to the Eiffel Tower before Charles de Gaulle finishes lunch. Someone says the Allies should have never trusted the Russians to end the last war. It was a deal with the devil.

My grandfather fought the Russians in the First World War. He was awarded the Iron Cross for valor. A few years later, his fatherland turned against him. What's with this screwed-up

226

continent? We've barely put the ghost of Otto Strauss to rest and they're starting all over again. Maybe Nana and I can get on our plane and disappear into the clouds before all hell breaks loose down here.

If not, it's a good thing I had that drop-drill training in elementary school. I look around for a table to hide under when the H-bomb hits. I don't have to worry about my permanent record anymore, but I still feel like crying. I'll never see Tommy, Pater, or Mama Cass again. I don't know whether to race back and tell Nana the news or try to protect her from it. The world's about to end, and I'm stuck in the Düsseldorf airport watching the grand finale in black and white.

"LBJ probably asked the Russians to invade," someone mutters, but it takes me a minute to untangle the logic. If the Russians storm across Europe, we may not have an election in November. LBJ, president because of one tragedy, will become a dictator because of another.

Dominoes can fall in both directions.

The screen goes dark for a few seconds and then lights up with a different news reel. We're seeing the invasion from street level now. It appears that not all Czechs have welcomed their Soviet brothers. Young people are fighting back against the onslaught. Soldiers in gas masks chase protesters through the streets of Prague. Bystanders' faces are covered with blood and bandanas. The camera follows the steaming arc of a tear gas canister fired into the crowd. A hooded student picks up the hot projectile and hurls it back at the line of advancing warriors.

The camera zooms in on a soldier beating an unarmed woman. Furious protesters try to free her, but more soldiers rush in to join the fray. The cameraman loses his balance. As he tumbles I see a familiar black face in a crowd of fist-waving students.

Hope is not lost. She's in Prague, going down with the ship. What was it Hope Springs said about Czechoslovakia being the place that people would finally get it right? They're getting it, all right.

Stunned travelers stare at the TV screen. Ash grows at the ends of cigarettes dangling from lips and fingers. A thin cloud of tobacco smoke hangs above us. One fellow loosens his tie as if he, too, has just been tear-gassed.

Police beat long-haired protesters on TV. One person holds a sign that says "Welcome to Prague" as if dreams were made to be trampled.

Hope Springs is gone from view. I clench my teeth and will the camera to find her again. I need to know that she isn't lying beaten and bleeding on some smoke-filled street full of cops and soldiers.

"The people united," protesters shout, "will never be defeated!"

"America and Russia," says a man behind me. His German is simple enough, though I don't understand the comparison. "Same thing."

Arrival and departure updates click into place on the big mechanical flap display. My plane has been delayed slightly, maybe because of the invasion. I hope we escape the red tide before the commies arrive with statues of Marx and Lenin.

"The whole world's watching!" protesters shout with one voice. "The whole world's watching!"

I recognize an American reporter on the screen. His mic sports the NBC peacock. I can't quite hear what he's saying, but I get the odd feeling he's not in Prague when a distinctly American-looking cop comes up from behind and knocks the microphone away with a billy club.

I gasp for breath as if the club hit me too. This dispatch isn't coming from Czechoslovakia. Russian soldiers aren't stomping

228

on these protesters. This report comes from the USA, where corn-fed cops are stomping on students. Hope Springs isn't in Prague. She's in Chicago.

"Hey, hey! LBJ! How many kids did you kill today?"

The Soviets are invading Czechoslovakia at the same time cops are invading the Democratic National Convention in Chicago. I don't have the heart to tell Nana that the world's gone crazy.

Rites of Passage

My big day finally arrived and got off to a bad start.

The police eventually issue an all-clear and I return to the *bimah,* the orange-carpeted stage at the front of our brand new sanctuary. I'm not sure who called in the bomb threat, but I suspect it was Sammy Jacoby's older sister Debbie, who isn't much of a morning person. She probably thought a bomb scare was a good way to catch a few extra winks after a night of painting the town the same color as her bloodshot eyes.

Now she's nodding off in temple like one of the old funny-hat ladies.

In addition to making us late, the bomb prank could cost us Game Three of the 1968 World Series. Fortunately, Pepe Mitnik, one of Sammy's friends and the world's only Jewish lowrider, has a small transistor radio. He's with the other hoodlums in the back row monitoring the battle between Detroit and Saint Louis.

"Detroit's up by two runs," Sammy whispers during a prayer neither one of us is following. Sammy, the scourge of Hebrew school, also claims to have taken LSD an hour ago. "Detroit's up by three."

"Try to stay focused," I whisper.

"Focus pocus," Sammy whispers back.

It's hard to believe that this ceremony will render us adults in the eyes of the congregation. If we were really adults, girls our age wouldn't feel the need to chase after derelict high school boys, and boys our age wouldn't act five years younger than they really are. Maybe thirteen-year-olds were more mature back when Moses took that wrong turn in the desert. Back then, a boy of fifteen was old enough to be his own father. In this modern desert we're not old enough to do anything. We can't drive, smoke, or vote. We can't drink except on Passover. Thank God that boys are too young to be shipped off to Vietnam. For now, that is.

Maybe when I'm a real adult I'll be able to get through the never-ending Hebrew of our Saturday morning service without falling asleep. The only thing that keeps me from nodding off today is fear. I'm terrified that I'll forget my speech or just babble the lyrics to a Monkees song. If a sacred Torah falls on the ground, tradition says it must be buried. I'm scared to death that when it's my turn to lift the Torah it will leap from my hands.

Please God, give me strength and bless the Detroit Tigers while you're at it. I've got five bucks riding on this game.

It's the bottom of the third inning when I'm finally called to the scrolls. I scale the booster step but can hardly see the congregation beyond the lectern that's big enough to skate on. I look off to the side and exchange a smile with Nana and Pater. Tommy squints and scratches his nose with an extended middle finger.

I'm distracted by the stained-glass windows, one for each tribe. I wonder if the tribes ever agreed on anything. Twelve tribes. Not ten, not twenty. Tribes like the Chumash and the Cherokee? The trippy stained-glass windows were probably designed by hippies. Pater says the hippies are the lost tribe of Israel. Nana agrees that the hippies are lost but isn't ready to give them tribal status.

Shafts of sunlight, God's long fingers, reach down through the high windows. I try to soak in the moment, but I'm too nervous to enjoy it.

I approach the sacred Torah, the history of our people from Moses to the Marx Brothers. I kiss the parchment with my prayer shawl and stumble through the tropes, relying more on memory than the mysterious text. Every Torah is handmade, the words copied by scribes just like in ancient times. If the scribe makes one mistake, he has to start all over. If I screw up my Torah reading, I can't blame the scribe.

Old Maier Lipinski, the temple sexton, stands beside me and sings off-key prompts in my ear. Oddly enough, Nana doesn't like Lipinski because he is Polish, a Yiddish speaker, a ghetto Jew. Turns out that even in Auschwitz there was a pecking order. Go figure. Lipinski calls the tattoo on his left forearm his lucky number. It meant he was strong enough to work. The Nazis didn't waste ink on the weak.

I chant and follow the silver pointer as Lipinski moves it from right to left across the scroll. For a second, I can see myself as if looking from above. I'm in God's house, standing in front of this vast pulpit, reading from the holy book, hoping my aching bladder doesn't burst on His eternal orange carpet.

I'm doing reasonably well until Sammy Jacoby whispers, "Al Kaline scores for Detroit!"

Half the boys in the back row throw their yarmulkes into the air. The others slump in their pew. Since the Civil War ended, nothing divides our nation like an election-year World Series. Or religion. Pater said that Jews may have been criticized when Sandy Koufax refused to play on Yom Kippur, but that season left every Jewish kid dreaming to become a ball player, a catcher in the rye bread. Koufax would have ruined it for all of us had he listened to his mother and become a doctor.

The good news about Kaline's home run is that Pepe Mitnik may have just lost our bet. Peeling five bucks off Pepe is sweet because he's a rich kid who hates to lose. Pepe's real name is Shlomo. His parents are tough-as-nails refugees who grew up in Israel. Pepe may not realize that the Tigers are winning because he's currently making out in the back row with his Mexican girlfriend, Graciella. A borrowed blue yarmulke balances on top of Pepe's big Elvis pompadour. Grace's doo is teased high over a red comb that any rooster would kill for. It's a photo finish to declare whose hair is bigger; God alone can see the top of their heads.

Sammy's crowd is rich, mine not so much. My family is hosting cookies, coffee, and gefilte fish in the temple auditorium after today's service. Sammy's parents will be serving Beef Wellington at the Sportsmen's Lodge. With luck, I might gross six hundred dollars in B.M. *gelt*. One hundred has been committed for my new Schwinn Varsity tenspeed. One hundred went to help Carly and Danny get away from Grumpy Chuck. The rest must go toward college as ordered by God on Mount Sinai in the secret Eleventh Commandment.

I survive my Torah portion better than the Detroit Tigers do the next inning. Maybe God is punishing them for having played on Yom Kippur, but I don't think God pays attention to baseball. If God were really in such a hurry to finish the world in six days, there's no way he'd have patience for baseball.

After trudging through the tropes, I return to my big seat and notice that many of the old folks—the *alter kockers*—are smiling. I know they are glad to see the child of a Holocaust refugee, someone who by all odds might never have been born, step up to join the community of adults. Some of these elders survived the Holocaust; all of them saw the tribe come close to annihilation. To them, this ceremony is a milestone in the Jewish marathon for survival.

After what seems like hours of Hebrew, it's finally time for our speeches. Sammy is called to the podium and announces the final score. The rich kids in the back row make a "T for Tigers" sign by extending their arms like airplane wings and hop up and down like prairie dogs. Pepe Mitnik owes me five big ones.

Sammy was too lazy to compose a speech, so I offered to write one for five bucks. This wasn't my first sale as a ghostwriter, but it paid better than the book reports I sold for comic book loot back at Sherman Oaks Elementary School. It's still too early to know if there will be a market for my discreet homework services at Ulysses S. Grant High School.

My speech for Sammy is a sarcastic masterpiece aimed directly at our youth rabbi who says going to Hebrew school is how we refute Hitler. Refuting Hitler is why we spend six hours a week in afternoon classes and three hours of kiddie temple on Saturdays? Hitler's dead. He'll never get the message. Wouldn't my time have been better spent learning to play guitar or swing a baseball bat? I think Sandy Koufax and Bob Dylan refute Hitler better than a room full of bored Hebrew students. Pepe Mitnik, Jewish Lowrider, is a bigger poke in Hitler's eye than I am.

My family's very existence refutes Hitler. I hear about him daily. In our house, "letting Hitler win" is a big concern. If I don't go to Hebrew school, I'm letting Hitler win. Goofing off with my cousin Eddie during the Passover Seder is letting Hitler win.

Speaking of Nazis, the Man Who Cuts Legs Off just walked into the synagogue.

I scrunch down into my chair and pray that Sammy creates a distraction with my disaster of a speech that starts off with a few thanks and a mild joke about what it means to be an adult when your big sister still calls you a shrimp. I'm hoping the bland preamble will lull the congregation into a false confidence that another fine young specimen has stepped up to refute Hitler.

It was a safe bet that Sammy would not have practiced or even read the text in advance. The speech I wrote goes something like this:

"Does God exist? If so, I could have used his help with the Hebrew in my Torah portion today. Where was he then? (PAUSE IN CASE OF LAUGHTER.) God is present every day in the Five Books of Moses. God spoke directly to our patriarchs and prophets. He intervened in their daily lives. He sent down rewards and punishments, omens and miracles. He hid in a burning bush, and even gave us a homeland to fight over. His presence is everywhere in the Bible, but where has he been since then? Why did God's magic just stop? Why did God let his so-called chosen people drift and suffer across the centuries? If God was ever here at all, he has long since left us to fend for ourselves. Otherwise, why would he have allowed the Holocaust? The answer is that God gave us free will and free rein to use it. Just this year, we have seen assassins misuse their gift of free will to kill Martin Luther King and Robert Kennedy. Was giving man free will a mistake? No, because God is perfect and doesn't make mistakes. If God is all-knowing, then he knows what will happen. God has a plan, right? But free will implies there is no plan. We can't have it both ways. Either God has a plan or he doesn't. There is only one logical conclusion: Free will is a powerful and terrible gift. I promise to use mine wisely. Thank you. *Shabbat Shalom*."

I sold the speech to Sammy last June as revenge for all the torment at Hebrew school and J-camp. This speech seemed like pretty good payback until the cold dead panic that just hit me. Sammy can barely conjugate the present tense. Nobody who knows Sammy, including everyone here today, will believe this speech came from anyone but me.

Handing Sammy a ticking time bomb seemed like a good idea, but so did trying to become Fiona Westmont's best friend. I'm still mad about Fiona, but I'm not mad at our youth rabbi anymore. I'm not as frustrated with my father, either. He's doing the best he can, and at the moment, he's radiating the kind of happiness that does not deserve Sammy's impending H-bomb.

There's a time and a place for everything, and this is neither. Sammy's speech will be the second-biggest mistake of my life, and that's only because I'm reserving first place for a future screwup. Please God, deliver me from this and I will never question your existence again. If you ask me to bind and sacrifice my firstborn, I will do so as soon as I have one.

Sammy fixates on the arched, abstract gilded menorah that looks like an inverted octopus even to people who aren't on acid. The eternal flame over the arc flickers in and out of existence. I hope Sammy doesn't get hypnotized by the flames or, worse, freak out and start screaming.

But Sammy appears serene, calm as the Buddha, bobble-heading above the sea of suits and skullcaps with a Talmudic grin. Even Debbie, Sammy's restless big sister who single-handedly launched the sexual revolution, is smiling with something resembling innocence.

To my utter horror, Sammy pulls my speech out of a pocket, and then, to my complete delight, Sammy tears the page in half and smiles back at me.

God comes through in the pinch.

"Wow!" Sammy says into the microphone and then pauses to ponder the big moment. "Detroit's in the World Series, but does God care? Why would the God of Abraham, Isaac, and Jacob waste a second on our great American pastime? Why? Because a second in the mind of God is like a million years to us. Just imagine that. In the time it takes for a baseball to cross home plate, God created the whole universe. The very same universe that we enjoy today. Does God care who wins the World Series? Ladies and gentlemen, friends and family, God is the World Series. Thank you and *Shabbat Shalom*."

My heart pounds as I step up to my own World Series.

236

My Big Moment

I swallow hard and step up to the lectern to address the congregation. It's time for the big moment when I become a link in the ancient, unbroken chain of Jewish history from Moses to Mama Cass.

"Good morning, I mean good afternoon." The congregation smiles but it's too soon to joke about this morning's bomb threat. "If you'll permit me in advance to exceed my allotted three minutes, I'd like to share with you a personal story of sin, fear, and accidental redemption. Not to give away the ending, but I am the sinner in the story. You know that commandment about not bearing false witness against your neighbor? Well, I broke it."

I thought that breaking a commandment would have more shock value, but this is a tough crowd.

"Growing up in the long shadow of the Holocaust, I felt that my answer to Hitler had to be more than just going to Hebrew school and planting a few trees in Israel. I wanted to capture a Nazi and bring him to justice."

A slight murmur runs through the crowd. This is not business as usual. Mr. Shreidermayer shifts in his pew. He still makes me nervous, so I avoid eye contact.

"Once this idea took root, I began to look for Nazis everywhere. Older people riding the public bus became suspects. Those kids on the school yard with German last names — where were their parents during the war? Anyone driving a VW without a peace sign was questionable. I was

237

about to give up the search when I noticed some suspicious activity on my own street, Wonderland Avenue, up in Laurel Canyon. Now we all know that Laurel Canyon is full of weirdos—'God keeps a big zoo' as my grandmother says—but what I noticed was odd even by canyon standards. A few doors down I found an ex-Nazi, hiding in plain view!"

I pause for a second to let the congregation and my own heart simmer down. Some people seem disturbed by what I'm saying, but a few survivors I recognize are leaning forward in their seats.

"A Nazi in my own neighborhood? I began to gather evidence. I enlisted the neighborhood kids to keep my suspect under surveillance. I befriended the mailman and learned of official letters from Germany. But after weeks of surveillance my case was circumstantial at best, and this important day was fast approaching. Drastic measures were needed, and, in my mind, justified. I believed my story so much that our laws became a mere formality. I needed proof, so I broke into his house. The police need a warrant to enter your home; I had no such justification. Kids who ransack houses, even Nazi houses, are breaking the law. Even if they find evidence. Which I did."

I take a moment to enjoy the full attention of the audience. From the *alter kockers* to Sammy's spoiled friends, everyone is looking at me.

Including Jesus, who just walked in with my mother. This throws me for a loop. Mother, yes, but Jesus? What's he doing in temple? I feel my stomach rumble, so I take a deep Vulcan breath and call on my inner Spock.

"I did not find any photos or commendations from Hitler. No iron crosses or stolen loot. There was no smoking gun. All I found was a sketch of German soldiers dragging a family from their home. The evidence was not incriminating. In fact, it wasn't evidence at all.

238

"By now it should be clear that I don't lack for imagination. I convinced myself that the sketch was proof of a guilty mind, the tip of some dark iceberg. But the more I looked at the drawing, the more I wondered what it meant. It wasn't drawn from a soldier's point of view, but neither was it drawn by a victim. The observer wasn't neutral, but it wasn't clear where he stood, even when he came to my front door to confront me.

"There is an important Bible verse that we sing in summer camp to a simple melody: Justice, justice shalt thou pursue! The God who my grandmother speaks with daily, the God who appeared before Moses, the God I was trying to impress, our God, is known as the God of Justice. Had I done an injustice with my hasty conclusions and lawless behavior?"

Justice indeed. My mother saved Jesus Gomez y Perez from deportation, but she fell in love with him during the process. She may have saved his life but she kind of wrecked mine. Someday I may see this as a fair exchange, but for now, it's hard to be Vulcan about it. Still, Mom and Jesus were pretty helpful when I had questions about springing Tommy from the clink.

I glance down at my notes and then look across the crowd. Tommy flashes me a peace sign. Nana is smiling. Others seem restless, but most are still paying attention. I gather the courage to smile at my mother and Jesus. He winks and Mom waves from what seems like less distance than I was feeling a moment earlier.

"We have just exited the High Holy Days where justice is a central theme. During the time between Rosh Hashanah and Yom Kippur, we believe that God opens his Book of Judgment. During those Days of Awe, God decides who will live and who will die. Who by fire. Who by water. Who by wild beast, the one I always worry about up in Laurel Canyon. Jews believe that the only way to be forgiven is to seek forgiveness directly from those we've wronged. We cannot ask for mercy from God for our sins against man. We can't say a few Hail Marys and toss some coins in a collection basket. With this in mind, I'd like to ask my neighbor, the man I thought was a Nazi, to join me here on the *bimah*."

Mr. Shreidermayer rises and shuffles forward. I step down to escort him up the carpeted stairs to the pulpit. I can't tell if he is trembling or if the shaking I feel is my own heart beating in the place where my tonsils used to hang. Climbing the last stair is harder than ascending Mt. Sinai.

I wait for the murmuring to die down and then turn to face the Man Who Cuts Legs Off. The crowd seems to have vanished. At this moment, it's just him and me. "Mr. Shreidermayer, the High Holy days have passed. God has sealed his Book of Judgment. I have committed an injustice against you, and it is now too late for me to reverse whatever decree God has made."

My voice is quivering. I feel a tear about to fall.

"God's book is closed, but I hope that in your book there is still time for me to ask forgiveness. I am sorry for having misjudged you, for having convicted you in my mind, for having entered your home and stolen your drawing."

Shreidermayer nods. He's lived like a hermit for so long that this can't possibly be a comfortable moment for him. He smiles when I take his hand and look into his sad eyes.

"If any good has come out of my transgressions, it is that you have agreed to share the truth with us today." I turn to the congregation who, miraculously, have reappeared. "Friends, I would like to ask your indulgence for a few more minutes while Mr. Shreidermayer shares his story."

The Man Who Doesn't Cut Legs Off steps over to the microphone and clears his throat. He is completely out of his element, more nervous than I am. He spent the last thirty years living with ghosts. Now he's facing a crowd with ghosts of their own. I worry that he will just start sobbing and leave everyone wondering what the heck just happened.

"Hello," he taps the microphone. "My name is Klaus Shreidermayer. I am not Jewish. I am a German."

The house of worship is silent. Jewish radar is on full alert, everyone thinking the same thing: Was he one of them?

"I was too young to serve the fatherland in World War One. I was too old to carry a gun when the next war came, but not too old to watch Hitler come to power. Like many, I was raised Christian. Like most, I did not put Christ's teachings into practice. When the Nazi darkness fell, I did nothing. I was what you disdainfully call a good German."

An uncomfortable silence falls as if the enemy has wandered into our sanctuary. Not the reaction I was hoping for.

"I wish I could say that I opposed Hitler from the very start. I wish I had been a hero but to be honest, Hitler didn't threaten me personally. In fact, my small metal shop benefited financially from his military buildup. This is no excuse, but I considered his rants against the Jews, the communists and Gypsies to be nothing more than bluster. I was married, had kids, and was too busy making ends meet to worry about politics. Besides, the pendulum swings back and forth. Give it time, I thought. This, too, will pass."

A few old folks are shifting in their seats. One man glares as if I've defiled the temple, but Shreidermayer seems to have found his voice and enough of an audience to continue.

"I kept trying to convince myself that the glass was half-full until it smashed to pieces. I know that for many of you the night of November 9, 1938, *Kristallnacht,* is forever etched upon your soul. You have taught your children and grandchildren like my young neighbor here about this terrible dress rehearsal for the Holocaust. November 9, 1938, was the night that Nazis kicked down Jewish doors, burned synagogues, destroyed storefronts, and dragged Jewish fathers away from their families."

I hear a sob erupt in middle of the room. "What is the meaning of this?" someone asks in a loud whisper.

"The meaning is clear," Shreidermayer continues. "*Kristallnacht*, the Night of Shattering Glass, confirmed to Hitler that we good Germans would neither question nor oppose him. That night, we good Germans gave Hitler and his henchmen permission to pursue the Final Solution.

"I know that many are wondering what I did. Did I oppose the brown shirts? Did I join the underground? The truth is that until *Kristallnacht*, I did nothing. Worse, I had a Jewish employee that I had been told to fire a week earlier. I would like to say that I resisted the pressure, but I did not. I was a coward, and I obeyed. Werner Steinberg was more than an employee, he was a friend. But when push came to shove, I dropped him like a hot coal. Why? Because I thought I had too much to lose if I didn't obey. Besides, Werner was a clever man. He would land on his feet once the troubles blew over.

"I was no different and certainly no better than many Germans asked to make similar choices. Like them, I took the easy way. Now, the question none of you will ever have to ask is this: If you had not been born a Jew, what would you have done? I don't say this to make myself feel better for my mistakes or to paint you with my guilt. I will forever be tormented by my inaction. I merely point out that we'd like to imagine ourselves as heroes, but until the moment arrives, we don't really know."

The silence hanging over the room makes me question my judgment. I don't know if any Jew has asked himself the simple question Mr. Shreidermayer just posed. The synagogue is stiff with discomfort at having the tables turned. It's one thing to be the victim, but if the shoe was on the other foot, would I fight or would I run?

242

"My home town of Krefeld had a beautiful old synagogue. Something inside me snapped the night I saw it burning. Laughing Nazis threw rocks through the beautiful stained-glass windows and marched through the streets. When I heard doors of Jewish houses being kicked open and neighbors dragged away, I could no longer pretend that this, too, would pass.

"That night I ran ahead of the brownshirts, sneaking through the alleys to Werner Steinberg's home. I told him that the temple was burning. He could hear the shattering glass. He could hear the shouting. I pleaded with Werner to come and hide in my home, at least for the night. He refused. I begged him to let me keep his children safe from harm. Maybe he was too proud. Perhaps he no longer trusted me.

"'I served in the Kaiser's army,' Werner said. 'I am more German than you are.'

"He was wrong. Jews were no longer Germans. It was a fatal mistake to refuse my help. A mistake for which I hold myself responsible. Had I not fired him when ordered, had I been more convincing that night, had I just overpowered him and taken his children away, they might have survived.

"The next day his house was in ruins. It took years to learn the fate of Werner Steinberg, his loving wife, Greta, and his adorable children, Siegfried and Hilde. I'm sure you know how their story ends."

Everyone in the room knows someone whose story ended in the same way. Even in Los Angeles, the Holocaust eclipses the sun.

"Tears fell as I stood in front of the ruined house of my former friend and employee. I should have been crying for them, but in truth, I was crying for myself. I was afraid. Afraid, because I knew that I had to do whatever I could to stop Hitler's mad plan. I was just one person, but if one person named Hitler could make a difference, then why not one person like me?

The Dutch border was controlled, but still porous. As a small metal merchant, I had permission to drive my truck back and forth between Germany and Holland. After *Kristallnacht*, I started transporting a new kind of cargo: Jews. At first, I smuggled one or two people a week, delivering them to resistance contacts in Holland. The border guards knew me by sight and just waved me past the control post, so I grew bolder. I was just one link in a chain, but I was able to move over one hundred Jews west before I was discovered.

"One day, the soldiers were tipped off. They insisted on searching my truck. They removed the scrap metal and pulled up the floor boards to find a terrified family of four hiding in a false compartment.

"I don't know what fate befell this family, but the odds were stacked high against them. As for me, I was arrested and taken for interrogation. I lasted longer than I would have imagined, revealing only small insignificant bits of information and only after making the Nazis work for it. Oddly, the more I was tortured, the more I grew numb. I revealed nothing. After a few days, they brought a lock of my wife's hair into the room. Then they brought her wedding ring, still on her finger. At that point, there was nothing more they could do to me. The worst that could happen already had. My family paid the ultimate price for my actions."

I don't know where Mr. Shreidermayer is finding the strength to tell this story, but he manages to overcome cloudy eyes and a cracking voice to continue.

"The Nazis understood that the ultimate torture was to let me live. They assigned me to a labor camp where I worked like a slave alongside many other so-called enemies of the fatherland. Hoping to die, I threw myself into the backbreaking work. I often gave away my ration of weak soup and stale bread

244

to keep the weak from getting weaker. I had no expectations of heaven, but hell could be no worse than Germany.

"Most of us did nothing to stop Hitler. I make no excuses for our choices. I am not asking you to understand or forgive anyone. I will forever regret having done too little, too late. Had I acted sooner…"

The room is silent enough to hear Mr. Shreidermayer choke on his words. I reach over, take his hand and continue his story. "There is one more thing we'd like to share with you today," I say. "When Mr. Shreidermayer saw the synagogue on fire, he did something very courageous. Once the Nazis had moved on to their next target, he ran inside the burning structure. He ran through the smoke and burning pews and tore the flaming curtains from the ark. One of the two sacred Torahs had yet to catch fire, so he wrapped it in his coat and took it away."

I squeeze Mr. Shreidermayer's hand, and he picks up the story.

"I sealed the Torah into a wooden shipping crate and buried it under a large rock in my backyard. That was thirty years ago next month. Then, one day this past July, I found this impulsive young girl in my kitchen with a cockamamie excuse for having broken into my home. The picture she took from me — a memory of *Kristallnacht* — reminded me that I had an open wound and some unfinished business. When I confronted Maxine about the theft, she asked me a very simple question."

"Mr. Shreidermayer," I ask for all to hear, "what did you do during the war?"

"The question hit me like a mortar shell! Was I a Nazi? There was no simple answer."

"Mr. Shreidermayer," I say, "The answer is no. You chose to act when confronted with evil. You saved lives and paid a terrible price. You are not a Nazi. You are a friend of the Jewish people."

The congregation exhales, murmurs, and begins to applaud, slowly at first but with increasing confidence.

Mr. Shreidermayer waits for a moment and then continues, "This summer with the money that this audacious young girl and her rock star friends helped raise, she and her brave grandmother travelled back to my former home and got permission to dig in the backyard of a very surprised young dentist. The box I buried there had decomposed and the Torah was in bad shape, but they were able to rescue it and bring it here to share with you on this most important day."

The rear curtains open to reveal the scroll stretched out across a long table that normally would have been laden with coffee urns, sweets, and after-Shabbat snacks. Today, the pickled herring and rugalach can wait.

Sensing that services have ended, Rabbi Wolfson jumps up to shake Mr. Shreidermayer's hand and offer his blessing to Sammy and me. "Maxine Strauss. Samantha Jacoby. On behalf of myself, your families, friends, and the entire congregation, I congratulate you both on becoming Bat Mitzvah. We all look forward to a fine future for you two bright young women. "

That's it. Yesterday I was a girl, now I'm a young woman. *Oy vey.*

I feel like collapsing, but I find the strength to escort Mr. Shreidermayer down from the *bimah*. Pater shakes his hand and gives me a big kiss. Tommy pinches my cheek. My mother is glowing. I hug Nana and feel like maybe, just maybe, I've accomplished something worthy of her suffering.

Schlepilogue

I'm strumming the guitar that Joni Mitchell gave me, wondering if I should become a singer-songwriter. Bob Dylan may be the greatest Jew since Sandy Koufax, but I'm sure his mother's still hoping he grows up to be a doctor. Becoming a songwriter might disappoint a Jewish mother, but my Jewish mother disappointed me, so I'm tempted to break with tradition.

It was weird to see my wayward mom and her refugee boyfriend at my big event. Jesus saves, but when he couldn't save himself, my Mom married him. Nana says that when you save a life, you save the universe. But what if saving the universe puts your kids into orbit? A fair exchange, perhaps, but I got the raw end of the deal when Mom dropped out of our lives. Call me selfish, but it still seems crazy for an immigration lawyer to save her client by marrying him.

Still, it was good to see my parents talking again. Mom said she wants to reconnect with us, but I'm not going to overdose on hope just yet. I'm glad she came, but it's not like one appearance changes anything. To every comedian who makes jokes about overbearing Jewish mothers: I wish I had one.

Hope Springs seems to have gone underground after skipping bail for trying to start the next American Revolution at the Democratic Party Convention in Chicago. Tired of waiting for her to reappear and worried that our local G-men might show up with a search warrant, I opened the envelope she entrusted to me the week that Bobby Kennedy was shot.

Man, that seems like a long time ago.

I didn't know what to expect. A last will and testament? A family tree dating back to slavery times? The combination to a storage locker full of cash and dynamite? No such luck. All

247

Hope left me was a tiny three-by-five index card with this quote from a guy named Mario Savio:

"There's a time when the operation of the machine becomes so odious — makes you so sick at heart — that you can't take part. You can't even passively take part. And you've got to put your bodies upon the gears and upon the wheels, upon the levers, upon all the apparatus, and you've got to make it stop. And you've got to indicate to the people who run it, to the people who own it that unless you're free, the machine will be prevented from working at all."

I guess Hope has joined those trying to jam the gears. I wish her luck, and hope that the next time I see her won't be on the mugshot wall at the post office. Pater and I will miss her on our morning commute.

With Hope gone, Pater and I have even less to talk about. These days, I play radio roulette while he rambles about new ideas for "Tentatively Untitled." I'm probably the only person in L.A. not working on a screenplay, but I'm barely thirteen, so there's still time. Maybe someday I'll write a story about how my father and a few other guidance counselors ran an underground railroad to keep boys out of Vietnam. I hope Pater and his co-conspirators can keep their operation going now that the FBI has unearthed it. I hope they save lots more boys from coming home in pine boxes.

Nana managed to get Tommy cleared for a German passport when she went off to Bonn on the day I helped dig up the Krefeld Torah. Weird that Germany could save Tommy after nearly exterminating the possibility of his existence. I guess a lot can happen in a generation.

The garage went silent after Dori got accepted into UC Berkeley and then surprised everyone by leaving to join a commune up in Mendocino. The commune sounds like a militant version of the Renaissance Pleasure Faire. Within a month Dori will be running the place or expelled for being too cynical. Like Hope Springs, I suppose Dori is looking for solutions, but I'm not sure how overthrowing the government or retreating to a time before flushing toilets solves anything. Dori said Nixon's election means American society is doomed and we need to experiment with new ways of living. Pater says American society has always been doomed and that's what propels us forward. Nana says she's seen doom and it has no fixed address.

I saw Nana Hannah chatting with Mr. Shreidermayer the other day. She was out front trimming the ivy when he walked by our place with his little Nazi dog. He didn't used to walk his dog much, so at least one creature benefited from the trouble I put the old man through. It's good to see old Mr. Shreidermayer getting a bit more sunlight these days. Nice to see that Nana has a new friend, too. Maybe someday he'll take her for a ride in his VW. Maybe she'll enlist him in her *kaffeeklatsch* of blue-haired Nazi hunters.

Meanwhile, the Torah we rescued is on a West Coast temple tour. Mr. Shreidermayer and I accompanied it to a couple of local *shuls* and gave a condensed version of my Bat Mitzvah presentation. People are very moved by the story and fascinated by the scrolls. Someone even told me it would make a good movie.

I'm forever grateful to Cass Elliot and Mikey Dolenz for helping to fund my trip and rescue my big B.M. from pointlessness. I think both of their groups are on tour since I haven't seen either of them around recently. Maybe they'll start a new band called The Mamas & the Monkees.

I haven't seen Joni Mitchell for a long time. Rumor has it she's working on a new record and a new boyfriend. I'm head over heels in love with the Martin D-28 she sent to replace the

249

old Mexican guitar whose string she broke. I call the new guitar Martine, though I'm not worthy of her affection. Not yet. The steel strings still feel like razor wire. I'm thinking of performing in coffee houses as soon as I can play barre chords without lacerating my fingertips.

Nana Hannah tells me that if I keep practicing, I'll develop callouses that will protect my tender parts. Is this what happens as you grow up? Do you stop feeling the pain, or do your senses dull just enough to find the melodies hidden behind life's sharp edges?

Speaking of senses, I kissed my first boy at Sammy's party. We were playing "Spin the Bottle," and I got lucky when mine pointed to Pepe Mitnik. Lucky that his girlfriend Graciella wasn't there to kill me with the switchblade I heard she hides in her hairdo. The kissing closet smelled of mothballs, which wasn't terribly romantic, but then again, I'm not exactly Miss October. I offered Pepe five bucks to just pretend the deed was done, but he wanted ten, which was more than it was worth. The thought of his fat, flicking lizard tongue still grosses me out. If this is how they kiss in France, I will never visit Paris.

How many girls can claim their first kiss came from the world's only Jewish lowrider? Half the girls at Walter Reed Junior High School, that's how many. Now it's half plus one. I skipped junior high school, so I'll never know the joys of seventh, eighth and ninth grade. I went directly to high school, where I'll never know any joy in tenth through twelfth grades, either. The classes aren't bad, but the teachers treat me like a space alien.

God's big zoo, indeed. I'm still not sure which exhibit I belong in.

Tommy warned me that the high school scene would be awkward because I'm a dumb twerp and everyone else is cool. Then he almost joined the Army, which is the least cool thing I can imagine. It turns out that my lack of cool pretty much renders me invisible. Until someone decides it's cool to talk with a twerp, I'll eat my lunch alone and try not to get towel-snapped by the mean girls in hot pants and tube tops. Undoing the daily locker room trauma will take years of psychotherapy.

Tommy had second thoughts about the Army after Jesus managed to get all the Sunset Boulevard arrest charges thrown out. After my big B.M., Tommy packed his gear in the van and headed up to San Francisco. He plans to enroll in a music program, get a student deferment, and start a new band. I hope he can lure Dori away from her commune. It's clear those two are made for each other, even if I'm the only one who sees it. I still have no clue what Tommy was thinking when he almost joined the Army. I'm not sure he did, either. He thought I'd be happy as an only child, but the truth is I already miss him. I say a prayer for Tommy every night before going to sleep in my loft at the top of our Wonderland Avenue A-frame.

Does God hear my prayer? Nana says he does as long as my heart stays open. I still wonder if God exists. Nana says that as long as I wonder, it's proof that he does. She's been right about everything else, so I'll try to keep the faith.

Glossary

Aliyah: Immigration to Israel

Alter kocker: Old fart

Ashkenazim: European Jews

Bar or Bat Mitzvah: A 13- year- old boy's or girl's rite of passage into a Jewish congregation

Bimah: The raised platform or stage in a temple

Gelt: Money

Goy: Gentile, non-Jew

Hausfrau: Housewife

Hamentaschen: triangular pastry with fruit filling

Kaddish: The Jewish prayer of mourning

Kaffeeklatsch: A coffee group or circle of friends

Kristallnacht: Crystal Night. The night of breaking glass. November 8, 1938

Liebchen: Sweetie

Mach schnell! Go fast!

Mazel tov: Congratulations

Mein Gott im himmel: Oh my God. God in Heaven

Mensch: A real character, a genuine human being

Mezuzah: a small case containing a prayer written on parchment typically placed on the doorpost of a Jewish home

Mitzvah: Good deed

Mutti: Mother, mommy

Natürlich: Naturally

Nu?: So? And? What?

Nudnik: An annoying person

Opa: Grandfather

Oy vey: Woe is me

Putz: Dick, fool

Sabra: A native Israeli

Schlep: To drag, move with great effort

Schmoe: A stupid or obnoxious person

Schmaltz: Rendered chicken fat, sickeningly sentimental

Schmuck: Jerk

Schnapps: Strong liquor

Schul: Temple

Shabbat: Sabbath

Shalom: Peace, hello, goodbye

Sheisse: Shit

Shiksa: Gentile female

Shiva: The seven-day Jewish period of mourning

Shmata: Rag, clothes

Shtick: Act, comic theme

Stimmt: Correct, of course

Torah: The five books of Moses in the form of a scroll.

Tuchus: Butt

The Last Word

My grandparents got out of Nazi Germany in April, 1939, not long after Kristallnacht. They were lucky to have had a distant relative in America to sponsor them. Most of their extended family was not as fortunate.

Fast forwarding thirty years, I grew up close to Laurel Canyon, between the bright lights of the sixties and the long shadow of the holocaust. My father's surviving family was scattered far and wide, but I met them all. Aunt Ilse and Uncle Otto survived concentration camps. Uncle Werner fled The Netherlands and snuck across occupied France. My Aunt Helene was sent to Palestine as a young girl, never to see her parents again. Aunt Alma, a Christian, hid her husband Max in the attic until the war ended. My German family had been to hell and back yet were some of the most cheerful and optimistic folks I've ever met.

I began "Life's Big Zoo" in 2015 as a memoir of being a precocious Jewish kid coming of age in Los Angeles during the era of Vietnam and flower power. Like most memoirs, it quickly turned fictional.

I hope you enjoyed the ride. If so, please be kind enough to find me online and post a review in the usual places.

R.S. Gompertz
Seattle, March 2017
www.rsgompertz.com